THE
MISSING
PIECE

Also by Sharon Sala

DARK WATER RISING
IN SHADOWS
LIFE OF LIES
RACE AGAINST TIME
FAMILY SINS

Secrets and Lies

DARK HEARTS
COLD HEARTS
WILD HEARTS

Forces of Nature

GOING GONE
GOING TWICE
GOING ONCE

The Rebel Ridge novels

'TIL DEATH
DON'T CRY FOR ME
NEXT OF KIN

The Searchers

BLOOD TRAILS
BLOOD STAINS
BLOOD TIES

The Storm Front trilogy

SWEPT ASIDE
TORN APART
BLOWN AWAY

THE WARRIOR
BAD PENNY
THE HEALER
CUT THROAT
NINE LIVES
THE CHOSEN
MISSING
WHIPPOORWILL
ON THE EDGE
"Capsized"
DARK WATER
OUT OF THE DARK
SNOWFALL
BUTTERFLY
REMEMBER ME
REUNION
SWEET BABY

**Originally published
as Dinah McCall**

THE RETURN

Look for Sharon Sala's next novel,
available soon from MIRA Books.

PAPL
DISCARDED

SHARON SALA

THE MISSING PIECE

mira

mira

Recycling programs
for this product may
not exist in your area.

ISBN-13: 978-0-7783-0828-7

The Missing Piece

Copyright © 2019 by Sharon Sala

All rights reserved. Except for use in any review, the reproduction or utilization of this work
in whole or in part in any form by any electronic, mechanical or other means, now known or
hereafter invented, including xerography, photocopying and recording, or in any information
storage or retrieval system, is forbidden without the written permission of the publisher,
MIRA Books, 22 Adelaide St. West, 40th Floor, Toronto, Ontario M5H 4E3, Canada.

This is a work of fiction. Names, characters, places and incidents are either the product of the
author's imagination or are used fictitiously, and any resemblance to actual persons, living or dead,
business establishments, events or locales is entirely coincidental.

® and TM are trademarks of Harlequin Enterprises Limited or its corporate affiliates.
Trademarks indicated with ® are registered in the United States Patent and Trademark Office,
the Canadian Intellectual Property Office and in other countries.

For questions and comments about the quality of this book, please contact us at
CustomerService@Harlequin.com.

BookClubbish.com

Printed in U.S.A.

This book is dedicated to people who don't quit on life.

To Kathy, for your indomitable will to survive.
I model every strong heroine I've ever written after you.

To Iris, who held out for ninety-eight years, the last fourteen with dementia.
Her spirit never quit. But her body finally did.

To my Bobby. He left this earth, but he never left me.

THE
MISSING
PIECE

CHAPTER ONE

Driving behind a semi on the Dallas beltway during morning rush hour wasn't for the faint of heart. Doing it in the rain was like driving blind. The windshield wipers on Charlie Dodge's Jeep weren't making any headway with the spray coming off the truck tires in front of him. Although he'd been in this situation countless times, that didn't make it any easier.

The knot in his gut had nothing to do with the weather, and everything to do with going to see his wife in the Alzheimer's facility. His frustration was that he had to stop by his office beforehand because Wyrick demanded it.

He still wasn't sure how he'd let a woman that bossy and eccentric become his office manager, but she was now entrenched. She was a shade over six feet tall, thin as a rail and usually dressed like a cat burglar. Sometime in her past, before he knew her, she had survived a bout with cancer. She'd kicked the cancer, but it had left behind a calling card.

She was, to her disgust, forever bald. Plus, no eyelashes, no eyebrows and no boobs—the last due to refusing breast reconstruction, solely her choice, in an act of defiance at the fact that she could no longer grow her hair. If she had to look weird, she was doing it on her own terms.

Being ex-military, Charlie was shockproof, so he didn't give a rat's ass what she looked like. She was a tech genius, a member of Mensa, better at karate than he was, had a pilot's license and drove a Mercedes.

He had yet to find something she couldn't do—and do well. But it was her unwavering honesty, her dedication to making his company successful, and knowing she always had his back that made him tolerate her constant and brutal assessment of what he was doing wrong.

When he finally saw the I-35 exit that would take him to downtown Dallas, he accelerated into the curve. As he was turning, his phone rang. Assuming it was Wyrick calling to ask him where the hell he was at, he answered with an edge in his voice.

"What?"

"Is this Charlie Dodge?"

He frowned. It wasn't Wyrick.

"Yes, who is this, and how did you get my number?"

"This is Jason Dunleavy of the Denver Dunleavys. I want to hire you."

The tone of Charlie's voice reflected his disbelief as he was trying to remember why that name was familiar. "How did you get my number?" he asked again.

"Ted Dunleavy gave it to me."

"Dr. Dunleavy gave out my personal number?"

"Not exactly. I might have gotten it off his phone without his permission, but he did recommend you, and this is a matter of great—"

Charlie disconnected and focused on the drive.

Getting to the high-rise where his office was located was second nature, and driving into the attached parking garage eased some of his tension. He turned off the windshield wipers and drove up to the sixth floor, then to his assigned parking space and got out.

He paused, giving his stiff knee a few minutes to adjust, then started walking. The sound of the rain drowned out the normal echo of his footsteps, which made him jumpy. If he couldn't hear himself, he wouldn't be able to hear anyone else. He glanced over his shoulder more than once as he continued toward the entrance that would take him into the adjacent building, and breathed easier once he swiped his key card and went inside.

He was wondering what was so important that Wyrick needed signed, and made quick work of getting to the office.

The moment he walked in, he smelled the sandalwood candle Wyrick burned discreetly in the break room—and then did his best not to react to what she was wearing when he saw her coming out on her way to her desk.

Skintight black pants tucked inside knee boots, a black turtleneck, a black bomber jacket. Her only concession to femininity was the black eyeliner and the purple eye shadow. She looked far taller than her six feet, and when she glared, she was almost scary.

"Good morning," Wyrick said.

"That's debatable," Charlie muttered. "What is it you want me to sign?"

She opened a file, feathered a half-dozen pages with tabs marked for signature in front of him and handed him a pen.

He was just about to scan the text when the office door opened. The secretary from the insurance agency across the hall walked in carrying a notary stamp, followed by two of the agents who worked there.

"What are they doing here?" Charlie asked.

She pointed at the papers. "If these are agreeable, we need them notarized."

He looked back at the papers. "Exactly what am I reading here?" he asked.

"The papers you asked to be drawn up regarding Annie's care should anything happen to you."

"Oh."

He scanned the pages all the way to the last one and then stopped.

"Why isn't my cousin Laura's name on these papers like I asked?"

"Because when I ran a background check on her, I discovered she's in rehab, for the third time I might add, and for a gambling addiction. I assumed you wouldn't want her in control of the money for Annie's care."

Charlie blinked. "Straitlaced Laura gambles?"

Wyrick pointed to another file on her desk. "The facts are all there."

He waved that aside.

"Then there's nothing to sign until—"

"Read page three, paying closer attention to section A, subsection 1, this time," Wyrick insisted.

He fumbled through the pages, read the text, then suddenly stopped and looked up. "You?"

"Until you find someone else, I'm the logical substitute. I don't need money, and I honor your devotion to your wife. When you find another more agreeable family member, we can change it. This just protects her until you do."

Charlie stared. First at the purple eye shadow, and then at the nearly black lipstick she was wearing—and realized he trusted Wyrick with his life every day. He could trust her with Annie's, as well.

"Thank you," he said gruffly. He signed the papers and handed them to the notary, who instructed the witnesses where to sign. She stamped and signed them before handing the papers to Wyrick as they left the office.

Charlie was still speechless about the fact that his cousin was in rehab when Wyrick got up to make copies. She gave him the original, filed the second one and laid the last one on her desk.

"I'll mail this one to your lawyer to have on file."

He nodded. "So, am I done here?"

"Yes, unless you want to—"

"Whatever you were going to say, the answer is no. I'm going to see Annie. Don't bother me with phone calls. Whatever happens, take messages."

Charlie paused, waiting for her to acknowledge she'd understood. His eyes narrowed.

"Damn it, Wyrick, did you hear me?"

She was addressing an envelope to his lawyer and didn't bother even looking up.

"Of course I heard you. I may not have boobs, but there's nothing wrong with my ears. Stop being pissy and go see your wife."

"Who's the boss in this office?" Charlie snapped.

Now she did look up, pinning him in place with that black, bottomless stare she'd perfected, and said nothing.

He stared back at her, willing himself not to be the first to look away, and focused instead on the tic beside her left eye.

"Fine," he muttered, and had started to walk off when he heard the sound of running footsteps and a man burst into the room, slamming the door behind him.

He was middle-aged but fit, and his Gucci suit attested to either a big spending habit or big money. He took a handkerchief from his pocket and began mopping his brow, then straightening his tie, as he fixed Charlie with a frantic look.

"Are you Charlie Dodge?"

Charlie thought he resembled an older version of the actor Robert Downey, Jr, right down to the dapper black mustache.

"Yes," Charlie said. "Who are you?"

"Anson Stiller. I need your help. Someone is trying to kill me."

Before Charlie could respond, they all heard another set of footsteps out in the hall. The stride was long and the steps were heavy. He glanced at Stiller. The man looked like he was going to faint, and then the door flew inward and Stiller screamed.

"That's him! That's the man who's trying to kill me!"

The man saw Stiller, doubled his fists and headed toward him, roaring with rage.

Charlie was braced to stop him when Wyrick stood up from her desk and shot him with a Taser. The man dropped like a felled ox, jerking and seizing.

Stiller spun, looking at the six-foot Amazon in disbelief.

Charlie glared. "Damn it, Wyrick, I had it covered."

"The last time you had a fight in here, you broke my desk," she said.

"Fine." Charlie stared at the man still in the throes of the electrical charge. "Call the cops. I'll handcuff him."

He yanked the Taser prongs out of the big man's chest and rolled and handcuffed him before he could come to his senses.

Stiller's mouth was agape.

Charlie pointed. "You said this is the man who's trying to kill you?"

Stiller nodded.

"So I believe your problem's been solved. I have a minimum charge of five thousand dollars for a simple service. I take check or credit card. Wyrick will write you a receipt."

Stiller frowned as he reached for his wallet.

"Out of curiosity, why was he trying to kill you?" Charlie asked.

Stiller shrugged as he pulled out a gold credit card and handed it over.

"I was having an affair."

"What does he have to do with it?"

"He's the one I was having the affair with," Stiller said. "I broke it off this morning. He didn't take the news very well."

Charlie could hear sirens, which was good. A few minutes later the sound of more footsteps could be heard. He went to the door, and then waved at the trio of police officers coming down the hall.

"In here," he said.

The trio from Dallas PD entered the room.

"Hey, Dodge, what's going on here?" one of them asked.

Charlie pointed at Stiller.

"He'll tell you all about it. Right now, all you need to know is the dude in handcuffs was supposedly trying to kill the dude in the Gucci suit. I'm late for an appointment. If you need anything else, ask Wyrick. She's the one who took him down."

The officers knew all about Dodge's assistant. He realized she made them nervous, but a witness was a witness. They walked toward her desk as Charlie went out the door. By the time he got to the parking garage, he was already thinking of Annie.

It would be twenty-three years this May since they'd married, and going on three years since her early-onset Alzheimer's diagnosis. She'd lost cognizance so fast that he'd been forced to place her in Morning Light for her own safety. It was a memory care center, twenty minutes from his Dallas town house, and the fact that they were now in charge of her care and he was just the visitor in her life grated on every nerve he had.

He drove out of the parking garage and back into the rain with all the intensity of going to war. He hadn't seen her in a week. She didn't miss him, but he missed her, to the point of physical pain.

He wondered if the cops had left his office yet, but wasn't worried. Wyrick could handle herself. And most times she handled him, too, even though she was supposed to answer to him. He was, after all, the damn boss.

Memo to self: but he *did* answer to her. She ran his private investigation business like a Fortune 500 company, while treating him like the janitor who never swept the corners. And he tolerated it.

He braked for a red light and as he did, saw the car in front of him shoot through the intersection and get T-boned by the driver of a delivery van. Both drivers got out in the rain. One was yelling. The other was waving his arms. One swung, one ducked, and the fight was on.

As soon as the light turned green, Charlie drove out around them and moved down the street. A couple of blocks later, he was turning the corner toward the care center when a cop car came toward him from the other direction, running hot. The cop's lights and siren probably had more to do with the fight than the accident.

When he drove into the parking lot at Morning Light and saw emergency vehicles in front of the building, he frowned. Surely if this had anything to do with Annie they would have notified him. He checked his cell phone to make sure he hadn't missed a call, and then breathed a little easier when it was clear.

He parked as close to the entrance as he could, then ran into the building, dripping water as he went. And as always, the moment he crossed the threshold he felt off balance—like the residents who lived here.

The receptionist, a middle-aged woman who went by the name of Pinky, saw him coming. He could tell she was trying to gauge his mood. However, their relationship was barely cordial, so she quickly looked away. She'd pissed him off once and clearly didn't want a repeat of that day.

No smile.

Steely eyes.

Square jaw.

He knew he scared the shit out of her.

"Good morning, Mr. Dodge."

"Who's the ambulance for?"

"It's not for your wife. She's in the solarium," Pinky added.

Charlie signed in, then strode past the desk, still dripping water, and stopped at the door, waiting to be buzzed in. As soon as he heard the click, he went inside, moving past the patients wandering the halls without making eye contact, ignoring the ones slumped over in wheelchairs and cursing beneath his breath as he passed the woman crying in the hall.

Once, he'd asked what was wrong with her, and they'd told him when she wasn't sleeping, she just cried because it was all she remembered how to do. He couldn't imagine Annie ever being in that condition, and yet he knew it was only a matter of time.

The solarium wasn't as bright as usual because of the rain. The dark red blooms on the crape myrtle, visible from the windows, drooped heavily on the limbs from the added weight. Today the heavens cried for Annie and others like her, and tomorrow the ground beneath those same bushes would be red with blossoms—a little bloodshed in the residents' names.

An old man sidled up to him, staring intently into his face.

"Are you Marty?" he asked.

"No, I'm not Marty," Charlie said.

"Are you Marty?" he repeated.

Before Charlie could answer, an aide came after the old man and walked him away.

Charlie swallowed past the knot in his throat. He hated this part of coming here. His heart was pounding now as he scanned the room until he saw her sitting at one of the long tables with pieces of a jigsaw puzzle scattered before her.

He approached her with a calm he didn't feel, thinking as he came closer that she still had the same pretty curve to the back of her neck. Same ash-blond hair as the day he'd met her, and she was wearing blue, her favorite color.

He had a dream of her that recurred often.

The one where she turned in her chair and smiled at him.

The one where she laughed and wrapped her arms around his neck.

That dream.

His gaze slid from her to the table.

Annie loved jigsaw puzzles—at least she had in the time before. Today she was picking up pieces, then putting them down in another spot on the table or in her lap and repeating the process over and over—picking them up, putting them down, unable to remember what to do with them next.

As he slid into the seat beside her, he wanted to lean over and kiss the spot behind her ear that used to make her sigh. Instead, he began picking out the pieces that made up the border and putting them together.

"Do I know you?" Annie asked.

She always asked him the same thing, and it was a blood-less gutting every time he heard it.

"You used to," he said.

She picked up a piece of the puzzle from the pile in her lap and handed it to him without making eye contact.

He took it without comment and laid it aside as he contin-ued to search for pieces of the border. The more pieces he fit in, the more she gave him, until she'd handed him the one that finished the border.

She leaned forward, staring intently at the puzzle and all the empty space yet to fill in, then looked at him and smiled.

"It fits," she said.

He watched her eyes, trying desperately to hold on to that brief moment of cognizance, but it was already gone. She'd forgotten the puzzle, like she'd forgotten him, and was look-ing through the windows into the garden.

His cell phone rang. He glanced down and saw his office number on the caller ID. Damn it! He'd told Wyrick not to call him. He ignored it.

A moment later he got a text.

Answer your fucking phone. We have an issue.

He sent back a text.

I'm with Annie.

There's a gas leak at our building because the one across the street is on fire. What do you want saved most—your computers or your hard copies?

"Shit," he muttered and sent back a text.

Computers and I'm on the way.

Annie was still staring out the window when he got up and paused long enough to whisper in her ear, "I remember us."

He walked away, trying not to focus on how much it hurt to breathe.

Pinky looked up as he strode past the front desk.

"You didn't sign out," she called.

He kept walking. By the time he got to the car, he was running. Despite the rain, he could already see a black cloud of smoke billowing above the Dallas skyline as he headed for the office.

Wyrick was in recovery mode and making what was probably her third or fourth trip, carrying computer equipment to her Mercedes, when Charlie pulled into the parking garage, parking in the slot beside her.

Not for the first time did Charlie wonder how she could afford a Mercedes like that. They started at 115 thousand dollars, went from zero to sixty miles per hour in 5.3 seconds, had a 536-horsepower engine and 560 pounds of torque. He knew because he'd Googled it in a moment of curiosity. It had more gadgets inside it than something out of a James Bond movie.

He drove a Jeep.

"I have one more trip to make for the computer stuff," she yelled as he got out. "The hard-copy files are boxed. You get them." She ran back into the building.

The urgency in her voice shot through him, and he lengthened his stride as he ran inside behind her.

"I thought we were leaving the hard copies," he said.

"I wanted both."

"Where is everyone?" Charlie asked, staring at the office doors all standing ajar.

"They began evacuation soon after you left," Wyrick said.

He frowned as he stacked two boxes of files. "Then what the hell are you still doing in here?"

"Same thing you are," she snapped. "Hurry up. We can finish this in two trips now that you're here."

He ran without thought, dumped the boxes in the backseat of his Jeep and was on his way back to the office as a work crew from the gas company pulled up inside the parking garage. They followed Charlie and Wyrick inside, shouting as they went. "You're not supposed to be here!"

Charlie came back out carrying another stack of boxes.

"Tell her," he yelled and kept running.

He heard the sharp tone of Wyrick's voice, but not what she said to them. When he turned around, the men were gone and she had the last box of files. He took them from her, tossed them into the Jeep and pointed at the Mercedes.

"Get your ass into that fancy ride and get out of here."

"Where do you want me to take these?" she asked.

"I'll call you," he said. "Just get the hell out."

They drove out of the parking garage in haste and quickly steered into the flow of moving traffic. As soon as he could get his wits about him, he called her.

"Head for my town house. We'll figure something out there."

He was ten minutes from home when he heard an explosion. It was so powerful that it rocked his Jeep and the street on which he was driving. He saw the fireball in his rearview mirror, followed by another huge cloud of black smoke. The office was officially closed.

Then his cell phone rang. It was Wyrick.

"Yeah?"

"The building and the block are gone."

"How do you know that?" Charlie asked.

"I have connections," she said and hung up.

He dropped the phone back in its console and thought about the people who'd had the coffee shop next door to the office building, and the bakery down the street, and wondered how long it would take to clean up something like that, and how many of the displaced owners would start over somewhere else.

His phone rang. Had to be Wyrick again. His tone was clipped. "Yeah, what now?"

"Mr. Dodge! It's Jason Dunleavy from Colorado again. I called you this morning. Please don't hang up. I apologize for intruding on your personal space, but my family needs your help, and money is no object."

Charlie frowned. The Dunleavy guy was persistent and he'd said the magic word. He decided to give him a break.

"Look, I'm in the middle of a situation. Call this number tonight and we'll talk," Charlie said.

"Thank you! Thank you so much!" he said and disconnected.

Charlie dropped the phone in his pocket as he drove into the parking garage attached to his building. He was home.

Wyrick followed him in, parked in the guest slot beside him and got out of her car talking.

"I'll set the computer stuff up on your dining room table for the time being, and we can just leave the files boxed up. If I need something, I'll dig it out."

"Who are the Dunleavys of Denver, Colorado?" he asked as he grabbed a stack of boxes.

Her eyes widened. "Seriously? Carter Dunleavy… Dun-Tech Industries. PolarDun snowmobiles. DunStar Studios? Need I go on?"

"Oh, that Dunleavy," he muttered.

"You have no idea who he is, do you?"

"I guess my next question is, why do you?"

And with that, she clammed up and picked up a PC monitor.

"Let's get this stuff unloaded," she said, and while she was waiting for him to grab some more boxes, she added, "You do know Carter Dunleavy is missing? Some people are already presuming he's dead since no one received a ransom call. I have to believe you watch national news now and then."

He ignored her snide tone.

"If you'll remember, I was down in Houston's Chinatown on a stakeout last week. National news was not my top priority," he said, but now he was intrigued.

"Presumed dead" was not the same thing as "we have a body." He wondered how many heirs the man had, and who inherited what.

Charlie made for the elevator with Wyrick behind him.

"How did he go missing?" Charlie asked as he pressed the button to take them up to his apartment.

"He left his office for a meeting and never showed. They haven't found his car or received a call for ransom. Why do you ask?"

"Because someone named Jason Dunleavy wants to hire me."

"What for?"

"I don't know. I hung up on him the first time, and relented when he called back a little while ago and said money was no object."

She made no attempt to hide her shock.

"You need a keeper."

"I have one," he muttered and left the elevator with her on his heels.

Charlie was stressed to the max by the time Wyrick went home, but the dining room table was now a fairly decent replica of their desks in the office, and the file boxes stacked along three sides of the dining room wall would have looked like Christmas was in the works, except the boxes weren't wrapped, and there was no tree, and it was only August.

Charlie made himself a roast beef sandwich smothered with horseradish sauce, added lettuce and garlic dill pickles, and for good measure dropped a mound of potato chips onto the side of the plate. He took a dark lager from the fridge as he headed for the living room, intending to watch television as he ate.

As fate would have it, he caught the tail end of an update on the missing Dunleavy, and a fifteen-second clip of Jason Dunleavy offering a fifty-thousand-dollar reward to anyone with information leading to the recovery of his uncle.

"Judging from the phone call to me, the family already has him dead. All they want is a body to bury, which is where I would come in," Charlie said, frowning.

He was developing a habit of talking to himself.

He washed down the last bite of the sandwich with a swig of the lager, then carried his plate back to the kitchen. He was banging cabinet doors, hunting for one of the Snickers candy bars he routinely hid from himself, when his cell phone rang. He glanced at the clock. Almost 8:00 p.m.

"Right on time," he said, then glared at his reflection in the hall mirror as he went to get the phone. "And stop talking to yourself, damn it. You're turning into an old maid."

He grabbed the phone. "This is Dodge."

"Mr. Dodge, this is Jason Dunleavy."

"Okay, I'm listening."

"My uncle Carter Dunleavy is missing and we're on the verge of presuming he could be dead. There's been no ransom call, no contact from him, and it's now going on two weeks. He has literally disappeared without a trace. Uncle Carter has no wife, no children. Only an elderly brother who went blind a few years ago, a brother in Dallas, who's your wife's doctor, and a sister, who is my mother. I kept the family last name because I'm this generation's only heir. He had a meeting on the other side of Denver but never arrived. There were no emergency calls. No sign he was in any kind of trouble. His cell phone is off, and no calls made on it since before he disappeared. The authorities have him on traffic cameras on his way to the meeting. The last sight we have of him was going through a traffic light—and then nothing. Of course we're all devastated. But there is also a bigger issue than our personal grief. He has many holdings, and the livelihoods of thousands of people are hanging in the balance. We need to find him, or we need a body to move forward legally to protect the family holdings. The police are still running leads but so far, nothing."

"Let me get this straight. You want me to go look for a man the entire Denver Police Department couldn't find?"

"Please, Mr. Dodge. Uncle Ted, the doctor, assured me you're the best in the business."

Charlie sighed. He heard the nudge of guilt in Dunleavy's

voice. It was the mention of Annie that swayed the deal, but he wasn't going to tell him that.

"It's going to cost you. I'll require the daily rental of a car, and any other vehicles I might need. Five thousand dollars a day, and I want a flat twenty-five-thousand-dollar deposit before I start searching. Also, if I find him, it's an extra hundred thousand for the recovery. If I don't find him, the aforementioned fees will suffice."

"Done."

"Okay…so my first question is, does he have any enemies? Who in the family is on the outs with him?"

"Most everyone who did business with him could be considered an enemy," Jason said. "He's ruthless when it comes to business."

"What about your family? Who hated his guts?" Charlie asked.

Jason hesitated. "No one hated Uncle Carter. He wasn't mean. Just hard, which was what made him a good businessman."

"Who among you benefits in his will?"

This time, Charlie heard an edge in Jason's voice. "All of us…equally, and I would become CEO, which he's been grooming me to be since I was twenty-one. Look, Mr. Dodge. I asked you to find my uncle, not turn this into a game of Clue, where everyone in the house is a suspect."

"Well, technically, all of you are, and believe me, the Denver PD are working that angle, too. If you don't like my methods, call someone else," Charlie snapped.

"No, no, you took me by surprise, that's all," Jason said.

"I'll need access to his personal computer," Charlie said.

"You can have anything you need. Just find him."

"Where's his office? That's where I'll begin."

"Here in Denver. I'll text you the address and a person to contact."

"I'll be in touch," Charlie said and disconnected.

★ ★ ★

Wyrick was sore all over as she drove home. She needed to work out more, focusing on her upper body strength. It was a shame about the explosion. God only knew how big a hole that blew in the downtown area. It would take months to clean up.

She was thinking about the Dunleavy family as she turned off the street into her garage and drove up to the fifth level.

She pocketed her Glock and keys, then got out, slid her phone into the back pocket of her leather pants and headed for the elevator.

Her stride was long and the heels of her boots made a clacking sound that echoed inside the garage, giving her the false impression that she was being followed. Even though she was used to that misconception, she didn't like it. But the walk from the garage to the elevator was short and the ride up to her apartment even shorter.

There was a note on her door from LaRue, the woman who lived across the hall.

A package was delivered to you today. I signed for it. Knock and you shall receive.

Wyrick almost smiled. LaRue was a character.

She knocked on the door and waited.

The door opened. LaRue squinted at Wyrick, then handed her a padded manila envelope.

"I love what you've done with your hair," she said.

Wyrick rubbed her bald head as LaRue closed the door in her face. Wyrick liked the old woman because she didn't ignore the obvious.

She entered her apartment, tossed her keys and the envelope on the kitchen counter and began the usual routine of checking every room and window until she was certain no one had been inside. Then she went back to the kitchen, curious about the delivery.

There was no return address and no postal markings, which indicated messenger service. She turned it over three times before she decided it was safe to open, then ran a knife beneath the flap and turned the envelope upside down.

The contents slid out.

She saw the old photo first. It was of a little girl in a white ruffled dress. The man holding the child was named Cyrus Parks. The child was her. Cyrus Parks was the head of Universal Theorem, where she used to work, and he called himself her father. But she knew better now. He'd only donated sperm to fertilize the eggs donated by Janet Birch, the woman who'd raised her. Her heart was pounding as she opened the letter that came with it.

Found this picture of us in a drawer in your old desk. Thought you would want it back. Call when you're ready to come back to work. We're so thrilled you conquered cancer. We're working on one of your old theories. Thought you might like to get in on it.

This was so much bullshit. That man was no father to her. The company had dumped her when she'd gotten sick, with no excuse except to say they were sorry that she wasn't what they'd expected her to be. And she'd fooled them all. She was far more than they'd imagined, and now they wanted her back. They could kiss her ass.

As for the job offer and the tease of coming back to work on her own projects, they were going to be pissed as all get-out if they ever figured any of it out and went to file a patent. She'd already changed the processes, completed everything she'd left behind and held the patents on all of it.

But this envelope meant they'd been in her building. Someone from the company, or hired by the company, had stood in the hall outside her door and talked to LaRue. They'd ruined the place for her now.

"Bastards," she muttered, then turned on her heel and marched to the bedroom.

She hauled two suitcases from the back of the walk-in closet and started packing. This would be her third move in the city in the past two years. It was a damn shame because she liked this apartment, but in reality, it was just a roof and four walls. She pulled her lockbox out of the closet and dropped it in a duffel bag, stripped the sheets off her bed and piled them in the duffel, then proceeded to fill both suitcases with her clothing.

Within the hour she had everything she intended to take with her and was only slightly pissed that she was leaving a week's worth of groceries behind.

The apartment was a sublet of a sublet, and she was sending a text to the owner as she ran to the kitchen to get the envelope. She stuffed the picture and the note back inside, slipped it in a pocket of the duffel bag and dragged her luggage into the hall. Then she knocked on her neighbor's door again.

The door opened. LaRue saw the suitcases and arched a brow.

"Was it something I said?"

Wyrick dropped the key to her apartment in the old woman's hand. "Someone will be by to get this tomorrow," she said.

"So I'm your secretary now?"

Wyrick grabbed her suitcases and started pulling them toward the elevator.

"Hasta la vista, baby," LaRue said, waving the key.

Wyrick pressed the down arrow on the elevator and while she was waiting she heard her neighbor's door close.

Hasta la vista, LaRue.

A few minutes later, she left the parking garage, heading to an address on the far side of the city.

CHAPTER TWO

Wyrick took the Mercedes down the Woodall Rodgers Freeway like a jet through a mummers parade, weaving in and out among the strutters, drummers and trombone players.

After the day she and Charlie had been through, this wasn't how she'd planned to spend the evening. It wasn't like she was in hiding. She was just trying to live life on her own terms, and staying in one place too long made that difficult.

As she drove she kept looking in the rearview mirror, aware that she was probably being followed. She frowned at the funky headlights that had been behind her for at least three miles. Not slowing down or changing lanes or speeding up. Just there, stuck to her like she was some homing beacon.

Bastards.

She stomped the accelerator and darted across four lanes of traffic in a "forty-five-degree slingshot" move that took her to an off-ramp. Satisfied that she was on her own again, she made a loop back onto the same freeway she'd exited, and kept driving until she segued onto I-35 and took an exit into Old East Dallas.

She used to come here when she first moved to Dallas, but

they'd found out about the place, so she'd quit doing that. But she was confident enough of her welcome at her current destination to show up unannounced.

It was almost nine fifteen when she turned off the street and headed up the driveway to the elegant if somewhat crumbling estate. The security lights surrounding the property taunted the night-fliers. Moths swarmed beneath the cool white aura, and when she started toward the three-story mansion, motion-sensor lights came on, making the place glow like a church at Christmas. She pulled up in front and killed the engine. She put on her game face as she got out and rang the bell.

The door opened, and the old man looked a bit taken aback and then squinted at her as if trying to find a person within the oddity she'd become.

Wyrick sighed.

"It's me, Merlin."

His rheumy eyes widened in obvious shock. "Wyrick?"

"Yes."

He gasped. "Dear Lord! I say! What a wonderful surprise. You disappeared so suddenly that we were worried. Come in, come in!"

"Thank you, but no. I didn't come to visit. I need you to answer a question," she said.

"Ask."

"Is the apartment in your basement still available?"

"Why, yes... You need a place to stay?"

"I do."

He smiled, revealing a perfect set of obviously false teeth. "Then it's yours!"

It wasn't until he said "yes" that she realized she'd been holding her breath.

"What's the rent per month?" she asked.

"Last time it was rented, I got eight hundred a month, but—"

She took out her wallet, peeled off eight big ones and handed them to him.

"Thank you very much," she said.

He pocketed the money with a satisfied nod.

"Give me a moment. I'll go get the key."

She stood beneath the floodlights, struggling with the impulse to unscrew them.

A minute or so later, the old man returned.

"Here's the key. I don't know what shape the apartment's in. Might be a little dusty."

"Doesn't matter," Wyrick said. "I appreciate it. And I'll be quiet."

He paused, studying all the physical changes in her appearance until he was impelled to ask, "Are you okay?"

"Yes. I'm fine."

"We still meet every other Saturday night," he said.

She shook her head. "Thank you, Merlin, but that's no longer a good idea."

"I understand. At any rate, I'm happy you're here."

She returned to the car, followed the drive to the back of the house and unlocked the private entrance leading to the basement.

Thirty minutes later, she was unpacked and prowling through the place, looking for all the ways an intruder could get in. There were two windows with black shades, both facing the street in front. There was one door in and out of the basement, and a locked door leading upstairs. It would suffice. She'd buy groceries on the way home from work tomorrow.

She'd forgotten to ask Merlin if she could use his Wi-Fi and then decided that if he asked, she'd tell him. If he didn't, he wouldn't check to see what she was doing. Merlin might look like a doddering old man, but his IQ was Mensa level, which explained the group she'd belonged to that met here, before UT found her again. Coming back might have been a mistake, but with Wyrick, nothing was ever written in stone.

Charlie was almost packed when Wyrick showed up at his apartment for work the next morning. He was carrying a stack of underwear when he opened the door, then waved toward the dining room and their temporary office.

"I checked email. Nothing pressing," he said, and walked out of the room with the underwear to add to the suitcase, raising his voice to be heard. "I took the Dunleavy case. I'm heading to the airport to catch a plane to Denver. I left you a list of the information I need on them. I'll be in touch. Is there anything I should know before I leave?"

"I moved."

Charlie stopped and walked back into the living room. "Again?"

"Roaches," Wyrick said.

Her eyes narrowed, daring him to comment.

He glared, disliking the secrecy of her life.

"Whatever. The extra key to my apartment is by your computer. I'll worry about a new office when this case is over."

She added the key to her key ring, and when he left the room, she grabbed his phone. In less than thirty seconds she uploaded a little app she'd been working on and then hid the icon. The last time they lost contact was when he was out on a job. It took her two days of searching by air to find him, then a wild boat ride with a rescue team to get him out of the Everglades. When she finally got him back to civilization, he had a raging fever and a dislocated shoulder.

That shit wasn't happening again.

Cyrus Parks arrived at work late because he was waiting for a phone call—one he didn't want to take at the office. But since he was the boss, and the last word in decisions at Universal Theorem, he could be late whenever he wanted. He was refilling his coffee cup when his cell phone finally rang.

"Hello."

"This is Mack Doolin, Mr. Parks. Packet delivered as requested. I stayed around after she came home like you instructed, and she did move out. I followed her as far as I could on the freeway, but lost her in the evening traffic. And she drives like a bat out of hell, so there's that. What do you want me to do?"

"Do like before. Follow her home from work until you find her new location!" Cyrus snapped.

"Well, I can't do that, sir, because the building the office was in, plus a whole city block, blew up yesterday. Right now, I don't have any idea where they're doing business, or even if they *are* doing business," Mack said.

"Ah…pity. However, stay on the job, and when you find her, put a tracker on her car, and there'll be no need to have this discussion again."

"Yes, sir," Mack said and disconnected.

Thanks to the files Wyrick had put on his iPad, by the time Charlie's plane landed in Denver he knew more about Carter Dunleavy than he knew about his own mother, God rest her soul. He picked up his rental car, a Chevrolet Equinox in an unsettling shade of red, and drove to his hotel. Once he'd registered and was in his room, he pocketed the half-dozen flash drives Wyrick had sent with him, then texted Jason Dunleavy that he was on his way to the headquarters of the Dunleavy Corporation. It was nearing 11:00 a.m.

Jason Dunleavy was on the phone with Miranda Deutsch, his on-again, off-again girlfriend, who'd been calling him every day since his uncle's disappearance was made public.

She was in Europe when Carter disappeared and offered to rush home to be with Jason, but he'd promptly turned her down. It hadn't stopped her from calling him daily, and today she was calling from Rome.

"Jason, darling, is there any news?"

"No. I would've let you know if something had changed," Jason said.

"I'm so sorry, and I miss you like crazy. I've told you how much I love it when you make me come."

Despite the fact that he didn't love her, she was so damn good in bed he hadn't been fed up enough yet to break it off.

"Yes, and I like even better what you do for me," he said. "Have fun spending your daddy's money. I'll see you when you return."

Miranda giggled. "Oh, you know me so well. Kiss, kiss, my love. I miss you madly and can't wait until we're officially husband and wife."

She hung up before Jason could disagree, and the thought of actually marrying her, which was never going to happen, sent him reaching into his little drawer of goodies and doing a line of coke.

It was up his nose and rocking his world when his phone signaled a text. He closed his eyes as the drug shot through his system hard and fast, just like he had sex. He rode it out until the hair was standing on the back of his neck before he opened his eyes and wiped his nose.

"That's some good shit," he muttered and wiped the white residue off the black Carrara marble, then checked his message. So, Charlie Dodge was already in Denver and on the way to his office. The man came highly recommended. He hoped Dodge lived up to the reputation that preceded him.

It was just after 7:00 p.m. in Rome when Miranda called Jason. The eight-hour difference had confused her at first, but she soon caught on to the best times to reach him in the office. She always got hot talking to him, and as soon as they were off the phone, she grabbed her favorite dildo—an eight-inch, fully erect penis she called Rubber Dicky—and went at it, pretending it was Jason.

Rubber Dicky had caused something of an uproar at the security checkpoint in Atlanta, before she'd boarded her non-stop flight to Paris. Miranda, being Miranda, had not been embarrassed by Rubber Dicky's discovery at all, but reveled instead in the laughs and comments as it was repacked among her things.

Moaning and shuddering as the second climax rolled through her, she collapsed backward onto the bed with Rubber Dicky still inside her. After she'd calmed down from her adrenaline-laced high, she was so relaxed that she decided to order room service instead of going out to dinner. After she put in the order, she called her father, Johannes Deutsch.

Her mother, Vivian, had died when Miranda was eleven, so the bond she had with her father was stronger than might have been typical for an unmarried woman nearing thirty. As soon as she heard his voice, she smiled at his silly question. Even though he had caller ID, it was always the same.

"Hello. Miranda, is this you?"

She giggled. "Yes, Father, it's me. I'm in Rome now, and I just wanted to tell you I'm having a wonderful time. I'm finding the most beautiful clothing for my trousseau, and as soon as I get to Milan, I'll begin shopping for my wedding dress."

"I am so happy you are finding things that please you. You know how I love to see you smile. Making you happy is my joy. You make your father proud."

She giggled. "Thank you. You are the best father ever! So what have you been doing since I left? I hope you're behaving yourself, and that widow who sits behind us in church isn't flinging herself at you again. She doesn't like me, you know."

Johannes laughed. "I have no time for such things."

"So you say," Miranda said. There was a knock at her door. "Oh, I have to go. Room service is here. Love you. We'll talk again soon."

"Yes, yes, goodbye," Johannes said.

Miranda tossed her phone aside and went to the door.

While Miranda was taste testing her food in Rome, Jason was primed and waiting for the private investigator to be shown into his office.

A few minutes later, Charlie Dodge walked into the room, nothing like the man Jason had pictured.

Dodge was tall, and his body looked as hard as the glint in his eyes. He wasn't even close to rumpled and shuffling as Jason had imagined, and he wasn't the least bit soft or over-weight.

Now Jason had to adjust to the fact that Charlie Dodge was intimidating. Maybe that would work to their benefit. The Dunleavy Corporation needed to know where it stood business-wise. The sooner the answers about his uncle's status were revealed, the better for the family *and* the company.

Eyeing Dodge's dark hair and the olive cast to his skin, Jason rued his red hair and pale skin even more than usual, then shook off what could only be termed *jealousy*, and walked toward Charlie with his hand extended.

"Mr. Dodge, it's a pleasure to meet you."

Charlie was shaking the man's hand when he saw a streak of white on Jason's navy blue tie and filed away the fact that the man snorted coke.

"You missed some," he said, pointing to the smear.

Jason looked down, saw the cocaine on his tie and dropped Charlie's hand. Instead of acting embarrassed, he shrugged.

"Pity," he said and brushed it from his tie. "Have a seat."

After the flight from Dallas to Denver with his long legs cramped into a too-small space, Charlie took advantage of the big roomy chair as he studied the acting head of the Dunleavy Corporation. So far, he found him sadly lacking. He snorted coke and shook hands like a girl.

Wyrick's face slid through his mind and she was frowning, which made him edit his own damn thoughts. *So "like a girl" was too broad a statement. Excuse the hell out of me.* He groaned inwardly. Not only was he talking to himself, but his thoughts were turning into conversations, as well. Ridiculous. Fucking ridiculous.

Jason waited, assuming Charlie would begin talking, but was mistaken. "So, what can I do to assist you in starting the investigation?" he asked.

"Send the retainer to my office and give me full access to Carter Dunleavy's office and computers."

Jason took a slow breath, reminding himself to tread lightly with this man. So what if he didn't like Charlie Dodge? If he could find Uncle Carter, he'd pay him twice what he asked.

Jason buzzed his secretary.

"Please see that Mr. Dodge is escorted to Uncle Carter's office. He has full approval to see anything he wants and has permission to access whatever he needs."

Charlie heard the catch in the secretary's voice as she answered. "Yes, sir."

Jason stood up and walked Charlie to the door.

"If you need any other information, you have my number. I'm happy to help in any way I can. We need to find Uncle Carter. He means a lot to the company, but he means more to the family."

"There's one other thing. What's the name of the lead detective handling this case?" Charlie asked.

"Detective Cristobal. He's with the Denver Police Department. Our family home is actually in an area called Greenwood Village, but since Carter's disappearance is so high profile, Denver PD is handling the case. I'll give him a call and let him know we've hired you. They have some interesting footage you need to see about Uncle Carter's car disappearing on traffic cam."

Charlie mentally filed away that information and followed the secretary out and then down to the end of the hall without comment.

CHAPTER THREE

Carter's office was the entire southwest corner of the tenth floor, with two walls of floor-to-ceiling windows. The ornately carved rosewood desk was at least sixteen feet in length. A single computer screen sat on one corner, and what appeared to be an antique Tiffany lamp was on the other. The room was picture-perfect, almost staged in appearance.

Charlie turned to the secretary.

"Is this room always this sterile?"

She nodded. "Mr. Dunleavy didn't like anything out of place."

"And his desk was like this when he left to go to his meeting?"

"Yes, sir. Except for a detective from the police department, no one's been in here since Mr. Dunleavy's disappearance."

"Did he always keep his desk this clean?"

She looked a little startled and then shook her head. "Well, he usually had his daily planner on the desk, and a handful of pens beside his cup of coffee."

Charlie glanced at the carpet, noticing a slight variation in the pile that ran from his desk to the wet bar on the other side of the room and wondered if the man was a drinker, then let it go. He'd find out the details soon enough. Instead, he pointed at the desk.

"Is this his only computer?"

She hesitated. "Uh, no."

"Then where are the others?" Charlie asked.

She hesitated again.

"Look," Charlie said. "I have Jason's permission to see it all. I can't find this man if I don't know what was going on in his life."

"Yes, of course. Follow me."

As the secretary reached beneath the wet bar, Charlie heard a click, and then watched a small door opening in the paneled walls, revealing a concealed room. From where he was standing, he could see five computers. He walked past the secretary into the room. All the computers were on and running programs. Two printers were churning out hard copies, and at first glance it appeared that one computer was dedicated to constant updates from the New York Stock Exchange.

"Did the Denver police see this room?" Charlie asked.

The secretary looked anxious. "No, sir, but they didn't ask."

"Where would Carter Dunleavy keep his schedule of daily appointments?"

"Uh, even though he had his own planner, I gave him a daily agenda with updated schedules."

He handed her a card. "Please send the last six months of those agendas to that email. Also, did he use a car service?"

"Yes, the one that belongs to the company, except the day he went missing. That day he drove himself."

"Why?" Charlie asked.

"I don't know. He just did."

"Was that normal?"

"No, sir. It was a variation from his usual routine."

"I'll need the make, model and tag on the car he was driving, and while you're at it, please send a list of company-owned vehicles to that email address, as well."

"Yes, sir."

Charlie glanced back into the secret room. "I need the passwords to these computers."

"I don't know if—"

"I'll remind you again. I find people. One of yours is missing. I need to know if he was being threatened or blackmailed. I need to know if he had a girlfriend or a dirty little secret that sent him running. If any of those things are true, I will find info about them on his computers. I also want the password to the computer on his desk. That's all I need from you right now. If there's anything else, how do I contact you?"

She pointed to the phone on Carter's desk. "Pick up the phone and press Seven. That rings my desk. I'll get the passwords for you. It won't take long."

Charlie nodded, waited until she was gone and then called Wyrick. She answered on the second ring.

"Dodge Security and Investigations."

"It's me. I'm in Dunleavy's office, standing in a hidden room behind the wet bar. There are five computers here, a couple of printers shooting out hard copies faster than flying buckshot at a turkey shoot, one of them running updates from the New York Stock Exchange. There's another computer on his desk. I have the flash drives you sent and I'll have the passwords to these computers shortly."

"Call me back when you get them. I'll walk you through the rest of it."

The line went dead in his ear.

"Goodbye to you, too," he muttered, then went to Carter's desk and began going through the drawers. Even though he didn't expect to find anything in a room this sanitized, it was routine to check everything. He was still looking when the secretary returned. She handed him a list designating which password went with which computer and left him alone.

Seconds later, Charlie was back on the phone with Wyrick. Within fifteen minutes she had accessed everything.

"How long will this take?" he asked.

"You can leave now."

Charlie still hesitated. "What about the data on the flash drives?"

"Take them with you. I'm already in."

"Call me if you find anything wonky," Charlie said.

"Of course."

He tried to disconnect first, but she was already gone.

Damn it.

He pocketed the flash drives, then shut the hidden door and left the office. Next stop—Denver PD. When he got back to his car, he called Detective Cristobal's number, which Jason had given him. The phone rang twice.

"Missing Persons, Detective Cristobal speaking."

"Detective, my name is Charlie Dodge, I'm a private investigator out of Dallas. The Dunleavy family hired me to assist in finding Carter Dunleavy, and I wonder if I might stop by and talk to you."

"Yeah, sure," Cristobal said.

"Thanks. I'll see you soon," Charlie said, then entered the address in his GPS and drove out of the parking lot, following directions as he went.

But he wasn't the only one investigating. Detective Cristobal ran a quick search to see what the man was all about, and the more he read, the more impressed he became. Former army ranger. Highly decorated hero. Solved some high-profile cases, and he was licensed to practice in the state of Colorado. He had no quarrel with any of that, so he logged out of his search and went back to work.

As Charlie was driving, his thoughts shifted to Annie and he wondered if this was one of her good days or if she was upset. It used to happen more often, but not so much anymore, and in a way that bothered him. The reality of her world was a steady slide downhill, and he didn't like the distance—the emotional distance—between them. He did, however, trust Wyrick to take care of his business while he was gone, including his concerns about Annie.

But he set personal thoughts aside as he reached the precinct. He turned off the street into the parking lot and parked, then grabbed his briefcase and cell phone as he hurried inside. He was escorted into Missing Persons and directed to Detective Cristobal's desk.

"Detective Cristobal, I'm Charlie Dodge. Thank you for seeing me on short notice."

"Of course," Cristobal said. "Please take a seat."

Charlie sat in a chair at the end of the detective's desk.

"So, how can I help you?" Cristobal asked politely.

"By sharing as much of your investigation with me as you can. I understand there was a digital video from the traffic cam where his car disappeared en route to an appointment. I would appreciate a copy, and if not, at least the opportunity to view it."

Cristobal nodded. "I can do that. Truthfully, we're at a standstill right now. We've chased down every lead we had and exhausted our resources, and we still don't know if he left on his own or was kidnapped. The family has received no requests for money, and we've been getting a lot of pressure from them for answers we don't have."

"Was he into anything kinky that you know of…or in any way connected to organized crime?" Charlie asked.

Cristobal shook his head. "Not that we're aware of. Carter's a shark when it comes to his business, but everything was aboveboard. That's not to say he didn't make enemies, because his holdings are vast and diversified, but we didn't uncover any serious verbal threats to him, either."

"People like him don't just disappear," Charlie said.

"Agreed," Cristobal said. "And yet, he did. If you'll wait a few minutes, I'll get you the copies you requested. Would you like a cup of coffee?"

"Yeah, sure, that would be great. I got off the plane less than two hours ago, so I'm short at least a gallon of my daily caffeine quota."

Cristobal laughed. "I know what you mean. Do you take cream or sugar?"

"Just black," Charlie replied, and then checked his phone as Cristobal walked away. There were no updates from Wyrick, so he sat back in the chair. He was good at waiting.

A couple of minutes later, Cristobal returned with the coffee and two big chocolate chip cookies on napkins.

"It was someone's birthday today, and she brought cookies to share instead of cake. They're good. I got myself a second one so you wouldn't feel bad eating in front of me," he said and then grinned.

Charlie laughed. "Thanks."

Cristobal nodded as he sat back down and took a big bite.

Charlie had a quick sip of the coffee, hid his reaction to the bitter taste, then set it aside.

"Can I ask you some questions while we wait?"

"Sure," Cristobal said.

"Jason Dunleavy told me his uncle's car was on the traffic cam footage and then it disappeared."

"That's correct."

"So, what's up with the skip? Is that just a dead spot, no camera in that location?"

"Oh, there's a camera there, but when we investigated, it had been disabled. Someone shot it out. It's happened before in different locations around the city."

"How long had it been disabled?" Charlie asked.

"Actually, less than twenty-four hours," Cristobal said and took another bite of his cookie.

"That's too big a coincidence for me to believe it wasn't intentional," Charlie said. "Either someone wanted it out so he—or they—could snatch Dunleavy, or Dunleavy wanted it out himself so he could disappear."

Cristobal nodded. "We think so, too."

Charlie managed another sip of the coffee and nibbled at the cookie to be polite, while he ran through different scenarios in his mind.

"Okay, what about family connections? Did you find anything about any of the would-be heirs that seemed suspicious?"

"No, and that's all in the case file you'll be getting. We personally interviewed each one on a separate basis, and they all seemed genuinely upset that he had disappeared, and none of them are having any kind of financial difficulties."

"Not even Jason?" Charlie asked.

Cristobal frowned. "No. Why would you ask that?"

"Because when I met with him earlier, he had white residue on his tie. I made a comment that he'd missed some, and he didn't even pretend to deny it was a blow."

"That's something we didn't know," Cristobal muttered.

"If none of them are in financial difficulties, then maybe all that means is Jason Dunleavy has the money to indulge his habit," Charlie suggested.

"Maybe," Cristobal said.

"Since you're being so generous with me, I'm going to give you a heads-up about the secret room in Dunleavy's office."

Cristobal frowned again. "What secret room?"

"It's behind the bar."

"How the hell did you find that out?" he asked.

"I thought Dunleavy's desktop looked staged, and there were no business files to be seen. I asked if he had other computers, and the secretary hedged on answering until I

reminded her that I'd been given access to any and everything pertaining to Carter Dunleavy. So she walked to the
bar, pressed a secret panel and the door opened. There was a
whole bank of computers in there running nonstop."

"Son of a bitch," Cristobal muttered. "We'll be paying them
another visit. Did you find anything on them?"

"I don't know yet, and they might be encrypted. I have
my assistant checking files as we speak."

"Is he good enough to decipher encrypted files?"

Charlie resisted the urge to roll his eyes, which was his first
instinct regarding anything Wyrick did.

"*She* is hell on wheels with every damn thing she does. She
can hack anything, write programming for anything tech-
nical and has a pilot's license. She can fly anything, and has
actually rescued my ass a couple of times since she came to
work for me. Just before I left to come here, she took down
an assailant who was after a client in my office. Nailed his ass
with the Taser she keeps in her desk."

Cristobal grinned. "Sounds like she'd make a good cop."

"She doesn't like rules, so that might be a problem," Charlie said.

Cristobal laughed out loud, and then they sat in mutual silence as they finished the cookies.

Charlie took one last sip of the bitter coffee and set it aside
just as a clerk delivered the files and a digital copy of the traffic cam video.

The detective checked that it was all there and then handed
it over.

"I trust you'll share the info if you make any discoveries,"
he said.

"Count on it, and thank you."

"Of course, and thank you for the heads-up about the other
computers," Cristobal said. "I'll walk you out."

Charlie gathered up the info and put it in his briefcase, then followed Cristobal out of Missing Persons and down the hall to the elevator.

"Good hunting," Cristobal said as he pressed the down button.

"And you," Charlie said, then got on the elevator.

The ride down was swift and he was soon exiting the building. It was past noon now, but with the lunch hour came an increase in traffic. Once inside the car, he started the engine and turned on the air conditioner, then sat and read the initial police report, noting the location where they'd lost Carter on the traffic cam. The urge to see the area where Carter had disappeared was even stronger than his hunger, so he set the address in his GPS and drove away.

He'd been in Denver before, but it had been years ago, when he and Annie were celebrating their fifth wedding anniversary. Now driving through the streets again, recognizing restaurants and landmarks that they'd seen together, made this harder than he'd expected.

"Shit happens," he muttered, and made himself focus on the task at hand.

On Fifteenth Street, the GPS warned him he had an upcoming turn north onto Wynkoop Street, which was the road Carter would have taken to get to the Chop House Restaurant, where the lunch meeting he was supposed to attend was being held. But it was at that very intersection where the traffic cam had been disabled. Where Carter Dunleavy had disappeared...

As Charlie approached the intersection, he began assessing what else was there, and noticed the close proximity to an Amtrak station. He turned onto Wynkoop and headed toward the restaurant, but as he did, he also realized there were hotels and even a parking garage nearby—likely for access to Amtrak, but it was something he'd consider if he wanted to hide a car...

Now that he'd seen the location, he entered the address of his hotel, the Grand Hyatt on Welton Street, and drove back to his hotel. He was sick of riding, first in the plane and now in the rental car, and was more than relieved to get back to his room.

The lobby was full of women checking in, and a good number of them already in the bar visiting. Most likely a convention, he thought, as he rode the elevator up to the ninth floor. He exited, quickly oriented himself and followed the signs until he found Room 910.

The room was spacious, and the bed felt comfortable. He pulled the curtains back to let in some light and then unpacked the bag he'd left before and took out his laptop. The first thing he wanted to look at was the traffic cam footage.

He took off his shoes, ordered lunch from room service and then got out the files Detective Cristobal had given him. As soon as he had the make, color and license plate number of the car Carter Dunleavy had been driving, he quickly located it on the footage and followed Carter's progress. He saw the car on Fifteenth, still heading toward Wynkoop Street, but then he was gone. There was no further footage showing the car, and it didn't appear on the traffic cams on Wynkoop. But he'd seen the area, and there was no way there'd been some kind of on-site kidnapping without dozens of witnesses.

Charlie was leaning toward the idea that Carter was on the run, or that he'd been hijacked before he ever left the parking garage at his office and had been a hostage the whole drive through the city.

So now he'd seen the footage. It was time to read the police files and see where searches had been made and the people who'd been cleared so far in the investigation. He took his laptop and the files and lay down on the bed, propped himself up with the pillows and began to read. He was still reading when room service knocked and delivered his lunch. As soon as he had the room to himself again, he sat down at the table to eat, still reading files and making notes as he went.

Wyrick had all the data downloaded from Dunleavy's computers and was sorting through it as she went, moving some info onto files for Charlie to read. She'd been in Charlie's apartment before, but no farther than the living room, and having the entire place as their office was quite comfy. She had access to a full kitchen, a half bath and food delivery. With him gone, she could even spend the nights here and save herself some driving time to and from work if she wanted, but there were projects she was working on at her place that needed her attention, so that idea was quickly nixed.

And she didn't want to get too comfortable in his space and let him think she was suddenly going to be nice to him. The last thing she wanted him to know was that she thought he was sexy as hell. Not that it mattered. After her fiancé had walked out when she got sick, she was done with men, and Charlie was deeply and forever in love with his Annie.

Wyrick wasn't man bait anymore, but she was alive. She knew she looked like an android. No hair. No boobs. Over six feet tall in boots. So she played the tough bitch to the hilt and put away the woman she'd been. Now if she could find a way to outrun her past, her life would be just about perfect.

When lunchtime rolled around, Wyrick ordered Chinese through Grubhub and kept working. Forty-five minutes later, the doorbell rang. She hit Save and ran to answer.

The delivery guy was one she'd seen before. He eyed her warily as he handed over her food.

"You moved."

She frowned. He'd gotten personal.

"Something like that," she said and shut the door in his face.

She took the bag to the kitchen and began drawing out all the containers, then removed the chopsticks that came with the order. As she pulled the chopsticks apart, she flashed to a Thanksgiving dinner when she was a child, pulling the wishbone with her mother to see who got to make the wish. She allowed herself only a few minutes to process the spurt of sadness for her five short years of childhood before she set old memories aside.

"Suck it up," she told herself, then began opening the boxes and taste testing spring rolls, orange chicken, shrimp with snow peas and sweet-and-sour pork.

She'd purposely ordered more than she could eat, so she would have leftovers to take home, and she'd made an online grocery order, which she'd pick up at Walmart after work. Since delivery was straight to her car, it eliminated the need for her to mingle with the masses.

She was finishing up the shrimp and snow peas, and had all she wanted of the spring rolls. With most of the orange chicken and sweet-and-sour pork left over, she was good to go for a couple more meals and wrapping it up when her cell phone rang.

She wiped her hands and looked to see who was calling. When she noticed it was from her stockbroker, she answered.

"Hello, Corney, what's up?"

Randall Corne ignored her. She knew the *e* in his name was silent.

"Nasdaq is up. That's what's up. You made a huge killing today, as did your hub company on the Dow. The Dunleavy Corporation fell again today, due to the continuing mystery of Carter Dunleavy's disappearance. I was wondering if you want to buy in. Their stock is lower than it's been in years, and you know that'll change once the status of the company is—"

"I'm going to stop you right there," Wyrick said. "I am semi-involved with the Dunleavy Corporation at the moment, and buying now when I know more about the status than I should would make buying stock in the company illegal. So I pass."

"Oh. Uh… I had no idea you—"

"Thanks for calling, Corney. I need to get back to work."

She disconnected, then sighed. Passing on that tip had been painful. The Dunleavy Corp was a healthy company, and the diversification intrigued her, but this was a no-brainer. She was knee-deep in Carter Dunleavy's business. Buying into it would be all kinds of wrong.

She put her leftovers in the refrigerator, then poured herself a glass of iced tea and took it to the dining room table.

The afternoon passed slowly as Wyrick continued to sort through data from the computer downloads. But it wasn't until she began going through Carter's bank statements that she noticed one particular draw for five thousand dollars cash that happened every other Thursday. The more she searched, the more was revealed. That five-thousand-dollar draw had been going on for more than ten years. That was ten thousand dollars a month. A hundred and twenty thousand dollars a year—for ten years. Granted, it was peanuts to Carter, but it was also indicative of blackmail money to someone else. She made a note to call Charlie and have him check Carter Dunleavy's planner to see if there was any specific notation on Thursdays, then glanced at the time. It was already after six, and thanks to her latest move, she had a long way to drive to get home.

It wasn't as if she expected to find a smoking gun on the first day, so she saved everything, shut down the office and locked up as she left Charlie's apartment. She stopped at Walmart for her grocery pickup, waiting impatiently for it to be brought to her car. When she saw a delivery girl approaching, she popped the trunk.

The girl unloaded the sacks, then shut the trunk and came around to the driver's-side window. Wyrick signed off on the grocery delivery and handed her a twenty, which put a huge smile on the girl's face. Wyrick drove away, wondering what it was like not to have enough money.

She drove out of the parking lot, then back to the nearest on-ramp. Soon she was weaving her way in and out of traffic on the freeway, keeping a wary eye on the cars behind her to make sure she wasn't being followed.

An hour and twenty minutes after leaving Charlie's, she arrived at her new place and went around to the back of the old mansion and walked into the apartment. It took a couple of trips to get everything carried inside, but it wasn't until she set the security alarm on her car and locked herself into the apartment that she finally relaxed.

She stored the Chinese leftovers in the refrigerator, then began putting away groceries. As soon as she was finished, she went straight to the bathroom to shower and change. She turned on the shower, and then faced the full-length mirror on the back of the bathroom door.

She saw the obvious—her height and taut, well-defined muscles. The missing hair and breasts were hardly noticeable for the red, green and black dragon tattoo covering her entire chest and belly. The dragon's lower body and part of its tail wrapped around her back and across her lower right hip, then curled around her right leg, ending just below the knee. It was a powerful, bordering-on-mystical image, and it made her feel like the badass she presented to the world.

The water was obviously hot now, because the steam was slowly misting over her image in the mirror. She leaned in to adjust the temp, then stepped in beneath the flow, pulling the shower curtain behind her as she went.

The air conditioner kicked in as she was getting out of the shower, which prompted her to dry off quickly and get dressed. She was in a pair of shorts and a T-shirt as she went to the kitchen. Two meals of Chinese food in one day didn't appeal to her, so she scrambled eggs and toasted an English muffin instead, then ate it curled up on the sofa, watching the evening news.

After rummaging through her recent purchases for something sweet to end her meal, she settled for a handful of chocolate kisses and got her laptop, logged on to Merlin's Wi-Fi and began checking on her holdings. She pulled up the new game she was writing for her media company. It was for an Xbox game called *Clown Hell*. She was still tinkering with the title, but right now it alternated between *Happy Bites the Dust* and *Hammering Happy*. She hated clowns.

CHAPTER FOUR

It was evening by the time Charlie waded through the police files and was studying Carter's daily planner, checking the log of appointments he'd had during the past year. He was trying to find patterns in the schedule, looking for the ones that stood out. But without knowing anything about the man, he wasn't making much headway.

What he needed to do next was interview the family members. He couldn't decide whether to talk to them separately or confront them when they were all together, but his gut feeling was that someone in that family knew something. And without ransom requests, unless that someone—family or not—hated Dunleavy enough to kill him, the man was on the run.

He wondered if Wyrick had found anything and thought about calling her, then decided against it. If she'd found something, he'd already know it. She was the most direct and upfront person he'd ever known. The only thing she hid from him was her personal life, and as curious as he was about what made her tick and why she kept moving from one apartment to another in Dallas, none of that was his business.

His eyes were burning from so much online reading, and

his back ached. Old war wounds never let him forget they were there. He glanced at the time. He had a dinner reservation here at the hotel and the prospect of food was calling him, so he got ready and went down.

The lobby was still full of women, all with lanyards around their necks and some kind of logo on the dangling badges. The women had overrun the lobby seating, which made him wonder if there'd be a line at the restaurant. He was suddenly glad he'd had the foresight to make that reservation.

He headed down the hall to where the restaurant was located and could already hear the chatter. As he turned a corner, he saw a long line of guests waiting to be seated.

He walked past them and up to the hostess.

"Good evening, sir. How can I help you?" she asked.

"I'm Charlie Dodge. I have a seven o'clock dinner reservation."

The hostess scanned the list and picked up a menu.

"Yes, Mr. Dodge. This way, please."

Charlie heard voices behind him, but none of the women seemed bothered by the fact that he was being seated while they were still waiting. They seemed more interested in him.

The hostess put him at a table for two, then handed him the menu.

"Your waiter will be here shortly. Enjoy your dinner," she said.

"Thanks. What's with all the women? Is it a convention of some kind?" he asked.

Her all-business attitude shifted as she suddenly smiled. "Yes, and so exciting. They're all romance writers."

"There are a lot of them," he said.

"It's a national convention. I've already met some of my favorites. Enjoy your meal," she said again.

He opened the menu, but was still thinking about the comments he'd overheard as he was walking past the lineup.

Something about good on a cover. He was relieved. It was better than being good *under* covers, which was what he'd first thought they'd said.

He gave the menu a once-over but knew what he wanted to eat. Prime rib, done medium well, and a baked potato swimming in butter.

In Carter's absence, Jason Dunleavy was presiding at the family dinner table. Hanging on the wall behind him was a portrait of their ancestor Sean Dunleavy, who'd immigrated from Ireland a bit over two hundred years earlier. Sean had the good sense to catch the eye of the daughter of a railroad baron and married into money, which began their story here in Denver.

Jason was well aware that their Irish bloodline ran deep and true. Except for the difference in clothing styles, he could have sat for the portrait. All of the Dunleavy clan had the same high foreheads, straight noses, blue eyes and thick red hair.

It was just after eight o'clock when the first course was served—a light and flavorful vichyssoise, one of Jason's favorites. As soon as everyone was served, they began to dine. Edward Dunleavy's lack of sight did not deter him from tackling the soup, and Jason's mother, Dina, was taking tiny spoonfuls, as if she was afraid she might gain a little weight.

Jason shook his head at his mother's simpering behavior, while choosing to ignore Kenneth Miers, the so-called fiancé sitting beside her, although he had yet to see Miers put a ring on her finger.

He wished his uncle Ted didn't live so far away. He hadn't seen him since last Christmas. However, Ted had been the one to recommend Charlie Dodge, so he was grateful for that.

Dina was through with her soup and put down her spoon as she leaned back in her chair. "Jason, darling, you had a meeting with Charlie Dodge this morning. What did you think of him?"

Edward paused, tilting his head toward the sound of his sister's voice.

"Who's Charlie Dodge?" he asked, but it was Jason who answered.

"He's the private investigator I hired to find out what happened to Uncle Carter," Jason said.

Edward frowned. "I didn't know you were going to do that."

"The police are at a standstill. They have no new leads, and our stock is dropping every day Uncle Carter's whereabouts remain unknown," Jason said.

"Oh," Edward said. "I didn't realize that. I don't know what we'd be doing right now if it weren't for you. Neither Dina nor I are capable of tending to the corporation."

"It's not a problem, Uncle Edward. This is what Uncle Carter has been training me to do for years, so it's not like I'm starting from nowhere," Jason said.

"I say, what do you know about this man, Dodge?" Kenneth asked.

Jason looked up, saw his mother brushing a stray lock of hair away from Kenneth Miers's forehead and frowned.

"Uncle Ted recommended him. He's been treating Dodge's wife for Alzheimer's for several years now."

Kenneth barely hid a smirk and whispered something in Dina's ear.

She giggled, then glanced at Jason and flushed, obviously recognizing her precarious position. Staying on Kenneth's good side without antagonizing her son was nearly impossible because the two men didn't like each other.

Jason ignored his mother's unspoken request not to comment. "Kenneth, you do not have a say in any decisions that are made regarding our family business, but since you felt the need to comment, I think you should share it with the table," Jason said.

Dina gave Jason another pleading glance, which he also ignored. It made her mad enough to say something to him. "Really, Jason. You needn't be rude. Kenneth and I are only months from marriage."

Jason sighed. "It wouldn't matter if you were already married. Kenneth will never have voting rights in this family, or the corporation, and you know it."

Kenneth shrugged. "No problem, Dina, darling. I'll answer your son's request." Then he looked straight at Jason and smiled. "I merely made a comment about the competence of an investigator in that age bracket. I mean, Alzheimer's is a disease of the elderly, so exactly how old is this PI? If he qualifies for Medicare, I think you need to reconsider your choice."

"*You* need to think again," Jason snapped. "There are many cases of early-onset Alzheimer's. His wife is still in her forties. As for Dodge, he's a former army ranger. He has a sterling reputation in Dallas, where he lives and is much in demand. After meeting him today, I wouldn't want to piss him off."

Then Jason rang the bell for the servers, who promptly appeared. "We're ready for the next course," Jason said, ignoring the embarrassed expression on Kenneth's face.

But it was the sad tone of Edward's voice that shifted everyone's focus.

"I hope Mr. Dodge succeeds," Edward said. "I miss my brother."

Charlie had gone straight from his prime rib and potato to the hotel bar. Not because he particularly needed a drink, but because he wasn't ready to go back to the room and think about Annie. Today was her birthday, and while she didn't know or care, he did. He was too far away from Dallas to coax her into a bite of birthday cake.

He ordered a whiskey neat, downed it like medicine and signaled for the bartender to do it again. After that, he tossed some money on the bar and got up with his drink. The bar was full of even more romance writers, and he felt their curiosity as he moved through the room. He found a table at the back and sat down, waved away the waitress and sent a text to the director at Morning Light Care Center.

Today was Annie's birthday. Did she have cake? Is she okay? If there is any immediate need she might have, I'm out of state on a case. You can contact my assistant. I'm sending you her name and phone number. But if there is any kind of change in her health or condition, I still want to know.

He hit Send, then leaned back in his chair and took a sip of his drink. He got a reply within minutes, stating that Annie was fine, that she'd eaten her meal and part of her birthday cupcake. The staff sang "Happy Birthday" to her and thanked him for the info regarding his assistant. It wasn't as good as seeing Annie, but it eased his guilt at not being there.

About thirty minutes later, a waitress appeared with another whiskey on a tray and set it on his table, along with a note.

"I didn't order that," Charlie said.

The waitress pointed at a table of women in the middle of the room who were waving at him.

"They sent it and this note."

Charlie picked up the note.

Enjoy the drink with our compliments for being such a fine specimen of manhood. If you'd ever like to be on the cover of a romance novel, just let us know.
Betty, Jules, Robin and Tish
—Colorado Romance Authors

Charlie looked up. The women were grinning from ear to ear.

He chuckled, picked up the drink and toasted them, then downed it neat. That was one drink more than his usual, which meant it was time to quit. He set the empty glass back on the note, then walked out of the bar.

Wyrick had fallen asleep with her laptop open and was deep into a nightmare from her past.

"Look at me, darling, and smile."

Five-year-old Jade turned toward her mother, grinning broadly as she waved at the camera, before the merry-go-round took her away.

She was on the shiny black horse with the red saddle and reins. It was her favorite, and she rode it every Sunday. Her hands were tightly wrapped around the pole as she leaned back and closed her eyes, imagining that she was riding in the surf down at the beach. She could smell the salt air, the hot roasted peanuts and the sickly sweet scent of cotton candy. The squawk of gulls fighting over a bit of bread from someone's discarded hot dog was as familiar to her as the sound of her own voice. The music of the merry-go-round was so loud it almost drowned out the noise of everything else, but she didn't care. She and Mama were going to get taffy when the ride was over. It was what they did every Sunday afternoon at the pier.

She was coming back around to the place where her mother always stood, but when Jade lifted her hand to wave, Mama wasn't there! An odd little spurt of fear shot through her as she rode out of sight, then she told herself Mama would be there next time. Only when the carousel came around again, and then again, and there was still no sight of her mother, she officially panicked. Now the music and the ride were beginning to slow down, and her panic was rising. She didn't know what to do. She didn't know how to get home.

All of a sudden, two men wearing clown masks leaped onto the ride, pointed at her and shouted, "There she is!" They started run-

ning through the children on the ride, darting between the brightly colored horses forever in midgallop in an effort to get to her before the ride stopped. The children began to scream and cry, and parents were in a panic, too, trying to jump on the merry-go-round to save them.

Jade screamed as the clown men came closer.

Then there was an arm around her waist as someone grabbed her from behind, threw her over his shoulder and jumped off the ride, jarring Jade so hard she bit her tongue. Now she was not only screaming in fear, she could taste the blood.

She was crying, "Help, Mama, help!" when she heard a gunshot and then more people screaming.

Wyrick's eyes flew open, her heart pounding.

"It's the dream. Old news. I'm safe. I'm safe."

She threw back the covers and hurried to the kitchen, turning on lights as she went. Out of habit, she went through the whole apartment, making sure no one was hiding anywhere and that the door and the little transom-like windows near the ceiling were locked.

It was just after 4:00 a.m. and there was no way in hell she was going back to sleep now, so she put on a pot of coffee. Knowing caffeine on an empty stomach would only hype her up more, she dug through the refrigerator until she found the leftover sweet-and-sour pork, and stuck it in the microwave. When the ding sounded, she got a fork and took the food into the hall. She sat down with her back against the wall, giving her a clear view in both directions, and started eating.

After a couple of bites, the horror of the old nightmare began to fade. Needing something else to replace it, she began thinking about the files she'd been working on and wondered if it was too early to text Charlie, then decided it was and finished off the food. The aroma of the fresh-brewed coffee drew her into the kitchen for that much-needed shot of caffeine; she took the coffee with her as she went back down the hall to shower.

By the time she got out, she'd recovered her emotional equilibrium. She drank another cup of coffee while she answered more emails and was out the door before sunrise, heading to Charlie's apartment to begin the day.

She'd had a brainstorm as she was getting dressed, and was anxious to return to the Dunleavy case. She eyed her sleeveless red tank top, satisfied that it revealed just enough of that dragon tattoo to be interesting, then put on the black bolero jacket, a pair of skintight black pants with a red pinstripe and her black ankle boots.

Her face was bare of any kind of makeup except the black eye shadow beneath her brows that faded down into red on the lids, and the red on her lips.

The red on her mouth had been applied in two focused slashes like the work of an artist with a definite point of view.

The morning was already showing promise of the hot day to come as she got in the car and drove away from Merlin and his mansion. There was a front moving into the state from the northeast, so there was a possibility of thundershowers later in the day, which would lower the temperature.

As always, she noted the cars that stayed behind her, and if any got too close or followed her too far, she accelerated and lost them in traffic. When it was time to exit the freeway, she drove one exit beyond the one she needed, then doubled back on city streets until she drove up into the parking garage attached to the high-rise and finally parked on the level next to Charlie's floor.

Within minutes she was inside his place and disarming the security alarm. She sniffed the air as she turned, then frowned. The rooms held a faint aroma of cold coffee and her lunch from yesterday, so the first thing she did was carry out the trash. When she came back, she sprayed some air freshener, then started a pot of coffee, and at 8:00 a.m. she sent Charlie a text.

Carter Dunleavy has been withdrawing five thousand dollars every other Thursday for more than ten years. Don't know what he does with it. Am running searches to see what pops up. Check Carter's planner to see if there are any notations to explain this. Keep your phone charged.

She poured a cup of coffee and took it with her into the dining room where they'd set up the office, logged on to the main computer and got to work.

Charlie emerged from his morning shower and was drying off when his phone signaled a text. He wrapped the towel around his waist and hurried into the bedroom to get it.

It was from Wyrick. He hoped she'd found something he could use. After reading the text, he thought this just might be the beginning of a much-needed lead.

The order to keep his phone charged irked him, mostly because she had a point. He'd let his battery go dead when he was on a case a few months ago, and had to admit the dead battery had been an issue.

He'd been trailing a runaway teen and had tracked him into the swampy bayou country of East Texas. He'd even glimpsed the kid once before he disappeared from sight, but in his haste to catch up, Charlie slipped on wet ground and dislocated his shoulder. Then the kid doubled back on him, got to Charlie's boat first and drove it away, leaving Charlie stranded. That was when he realized his phone was dead.

He'd tried twice to jam his shoulder back in place, and the second time he tried it, he passed out from the pain and woke up with a fever.

Another day came and went with him wandering through

the morass of moss, swamp grass and gators. Because of the fever, he'd long since lost his sense of direction, and spent a second night sleeping in a tree, hoping he didn't encounter any snakes.

Then he dreamed about seeing a man waving a white flag from a window in a bombed-out house in Iraq. When he woke up, he made a distress flag out of the T-shirt he was wearing and tied it to the end of a tree branch near the edge of a bayou. He settled down near the water, as close as he dared, hoping someone would see it.

He'd never expected it to be Wyrick, but seeing her chopper coming in low over the trees hours later had been one sweet sight. When she'd signaled that she saw him, he was overwhelmed with relief. Another two hours later, she returned, manning a boat with a rescue team aboard, and ever since, treated him as if he was incapable of rational behavior.

Some days she grated on every nerve he had, but today was not the day, and the message was his first lead. Satisfied that he now had a starting point, he dressed and went down to breakfast.

After ordering, he sent a text to Jason Dunleavy, letting him know he wanted to speak with the family and asked when and where it would be convenient to do this.

He received a brief response that stated he could come to the Dunleavy estate around 10:00 a.m. today and gave him the address. Charlie sent a brief acceptance and laid the phone aside.

Again, the tables were packed with more conference attendees, but they weren't bothering him. He settled into reading the *Denver Post* on his iPad, and didn't see the woman approaching his table until she spoke.

"Excuse me for interrupting your breakfast," she said as he looked up. "You don't know me, Mr. Dodge, but I know you.

I'm Alicia Falco, Jimmy Bradshaw's aunt, and I couldn't miss this opportunity to thank you in person for finding him."

Charlie remembered the seven-year-old boy he'd rescued from kidnappers several years back, and stood to greet her.

"Ms. Falco, it's a pleasure to meet you. How is Jimmy doing now?"

Alicia nodded. "He's great. Today is his tenth birthday. I almost didn't come to the conference, and then changed my mind at the last minute. Now I'm so glad I did. I just wanted you to know that our whole family is indebted to you for finding him before he was harmed."

Charlie smiled. "It's what I do, Ms. Falco. My best to you and all your family, and tell Jimmy I said happy birthday."

Alicia Falco had tears in her eyes. "It will be my pleasure," she said and then went back to her table.

Charlie's breakfast arrived, and he continued reading the paper as he ate, unaware that his name and reputation were spreading through the conference. The attendees who'd seen him last night began asking Alicia Falco how she knew him. He was unaware that many versions of him would be showing up in writers' new romance books in the coming year.

A short while later, he went back up to the room to get his briefcase, making sure he had charging cords for his phone and iPad. He got the red Equinox from valet parking, put the address to the Dunleavy estate in his GPS and drove away.

CHAPTER FIVE

Jason's abrupt request to Charlie Dodge did not sit well with the family. They'd all been at breakfast together when Charlie's text came, and after he responded, Jason made the announcement.

"That was Charlie Dodge asking when it would be convenient to come and talk to the family. As you heard me say, he'll be here at ten this morning, so don't anyone leave the house until this is over."

The moment he said it, he saw the look of disapproval on his mother's face, but his uncle Edward's enthusiasm was welcome.

"I don't know what I'd be able to do, but I'm readily available to assist in any way that might help us find Carter."

Dina was outright angry.

"You might have asked us before you agreed to his request," she said. "Kenneth and I made plans to go antiquing in Colorado Springs today."

"Really, Mother? You think your little outings are more important than finding your brother?"

Dina flushed. "No, of course not, but—"

Kenneth patted her arm. "It's okay, darling. We can go tomorrow."

"But that estate sale you wanted to attend was this afternoon!" Dina said.

"I know, but there'll be other sales."

"You are so generous," Dina said.

"Jason, are you going to be here, too?" Edward asked.

"Yes," Jason said.

"Well, if that man is going to show up that soon, then I need to get ready," Dina said and took a last sip of coffee.

"I'll go with you," Kenneth offered.

A few moments passed, and then Edward lowered his voice.

"Jason, are we alone?"

"Yes, sir. Why?" Jason asked.

"I didn't want to say anything in front of Dina. I love my sister, but she's a bit unstable these days and I didn't want to prompt one of her bouts of hysteria."

"I know. Mother hasn't been herself since she began seeing Kenneth. I suspect he's just using her to live a cushy lifestyle, and I'm guessing she knows it, too, but doesn't want to admit it."

Edward sighed. "I feared as much, although subtleties often escape me because I can't see facial expressions."

"Well, they're gone, so what's up?" Jason asked.

"What do you think has happened to Carter?" Edward asked.

Jason sighed. "I wish I knew. None of this makes sense."

Edward's voice was shaky with emotion. "Since there were no ransom demands, I fear something terrible has happened. Maybe someone abducted him out of revenge. I know he made enemies."

"I have similar worries," Jason said. "But that's why I hired Charlie Dodge. I think he has a better chance of finding him than the police."

"I hope so," Edward said, then pushed his chair away from the table and felt for the cane hanging from its back. "I'm going up to my room. Will you call me when he arrives? I'll come down straightaway. Where do you plan to meet?"

"I think the library is best. Plenty of seating and more comfortable than the living room, which is far too ornate and formal for this meeting."

Edward nodded, then left, tapping his cane from side to side as he went.

Jason made a call to notify his office that he'd be late coming in.

Wyrick started another pot of coffee, and while she was waiting for it to finish brewing, she sat down at the computer. In all the information she'd gleaned from the computer downloads, she had a listing of Carter's credit cards and a year's worth of purchase records on every card. But she'd never run a scan to see if there were other cards with the same Social Security number or with variations of his name, and she hadn't checked to see if he had any mailing addresses beyond his office and home.

She was nothing if not thorough, and a little obsessed with perfection, so she began the searches feeling a sense of anticipation, hoping to find a smoking gun and give Charlie more leads to follow. She paused once to get coffee, then settled in to work.

Water dripped from the showerhead of the bathroom, but Buddy Pierce was oblivious. He was in the adjoining bedroom, sleeping off a night of drinking, and couldn't hear the drip for his snoring. But when somebody pulled into the driveway of the house next door and began honking the horn, it startled him awake.

"What the hell?" Buddy muttered, then rolled over and glanced at the clock. It was nearing ten.

He threw back the covers and swung his legs off the bed, scratching his head, then his whiskers, then his balls, before stumbling toward the bathroom.

He came out, debating with himself about going back to bed or getting dressed and going out to see what kind of gig he could hustle up. He needed money. When his cell phone began to vibrate on the nightstand, he grabbed it to answer.

"Hello?"

"It's me. What are you doing?"

"I just got up," he said. "What's wrong?"

"The family hired a PI to find Carter."

"So maybe he will find him and bring him home. I'm tired of messing around trying to make something look like an accident. I say we just shoot him outright and be done with it," Buddy said.

"That's a possibility. But the PI has to find him first."

"Yeah, right, so keep me updated," Buddy said.

Then the call disconnected.

As Buddy was thinking about returning to bed, his belly growled. No more sleeping. It was time to get dressed.

Charlie arrived at the Dunleavy estate with ten minutes to spare, and slowed down to take in the opulence of the place. It wasn't a house. It was a castle.

The medieval architecture of the home surprised him, and the landscaping within the grounds reflected the Irish countryside. Everything was lush and green, and if he wasn't mistaken, the touches of color toward the back of the property looked like heather. As he entered the circular drive and parked, he half expected to be met at the door by a man in plaid, with a pair of Irish wolfhounds at his heels. He picked up his briefcase and wasted no time getting to the entrance to ring the bell.

A moment later, a woman who could have passed for actress Helen Mirren's double opened the door.

"Charlie Dodge to see Jason Dunleavy," Charlie said and handed her his card.

"Yes, sir. Please follow me. The family is waiting for you in the library."

He couldn't help but gawk at the interior decor as he followed her down the massive hall. It fit the Irish-castle theme in every way, right down to a suit of armor and a family crest hanging above it. He didn't know how long the Dunleavy family had been in America, but they hadn't let go of their Irish roots.

Then the woman took a turn into a doorway and paused just inside the threshold.

"Mr. Dodge is here," she said and then left.

Jason approached, his hand extended in greeting.

"Thank you for seeing me at such short notice," Charlie said as they shook hands.

"Thank you for being so proactive in beginning your search. Let me introduce you to the family," Jason said and led Charlie into the room where the family was seated.

Charlie laid his briefcase on a nearby table, then turned to the people staring at him with varying degrees of distrust. It didn't faze him. In this situation, distrust was fair enough. It was pretty obvious as to who was blood kin because they all had the same red hair and blue eyes. The man with a proprietary hand on the woman's shoulder was the odd man out with his dark brown hair and even darker eyes.

Jason began introductions with the only female in the room.

"Charlie, this is my mother, Dina Dunleavy Reed. She's

the only girl born in this generation of Dunleavys. My father, Devon Reed, passed almost fifteen years ago."

"Ma'am," Charlie said, ignoring the displeased expression on her face.

The man beside her straightened, obviously expecting to be the next one introduced, and then flushed an angry red when Jason passed over him and gestured toward the older man.

Charlie saw the white cane at the side of his chair. This would be the brother who was blind.

"And this gentleman to my right is Uncle Edward. He's the eldest in the family."

"Sir," Charlie said and touched Edward's arm and then the back of his hand.

Edward immediately smiled, grasped Charlie's hand and shook it.

"A pleasure to meet you," Edward said. "My nephew sings your praises. My hope is that you are successful in bringing my brother safely home. We have always been very close, and I miss him."

"Yes, sir. This case has my full attention, and it will until I have an answer for your family."

Jason was moved that Charlie had made a special point of greeting his uncle.

Charlie turned his full attention to the dark-haired man at Dina's side and waited for Jason to introduce him.

A muscle twitched in Jason's jaw. "And this man is my mother's friend Kenneth Miers."

Dina frowned. "We're *engaged*," she said emphatically.

Jason shrugged. "Sorry. I keep forgetting. Maybe when he puts a ring on it, so to speak, I'll remember."

Kenneth's embarrassment was evident, but he kept his cool. However, now Charlie knew son and boyfriend did not like each other.

"Mr. Miers," Charlie said, acknowledging the introduction,

and then took the floor. "Thank you all for your attendance. I'll keep this brief, but I will be recording it."

He moved back to his briefcase, pulled out a voice recorder, turned it on and set it on a coffee table in the middle of where they all were seated.

"My first question is—"

Dina immediately interrupted. "I'm sorry, but I'd prefer you sat down. You're exceedingly tall and it's uncomfortable having to look up."

The tone of her voice was condescending.

Charlie's eyes narrowed. "I am not here to pander to anyone's comfort. I was hired to find your brother, not worry about your dissatisfaction that I'm here."

Dina's lips parted in shock.

Kenneth seemed ready to defend her, then obviously noticed the glint in Charlie's eyes and changed his mind.

"Now that I have your undivided attention… I'd like to say, before I begin questioning you, take none of this personally. I don't know anyone here, so these are questions I ask every member of a family in a case like this."

"Ask away," Edward said.

"Do any of you have any disagreements with Carter, whether personal or business related? Jason, I'll start with you," Charlie said.

Jason leaned forward. "I have none. Uncle Carter is like a father to me. He's my mentor and taught me everything I know about the family business. I not only like him, I love him, and I'm sick at heart about what may have happened to him. I think it's the not knowing that's the worst. We *have* to find him. The company's stability depends on it—and so does the family's."

Edward raised his hand to speak next, and no sooner had he begun than his voice started to tremble with emotion.

"Because I can no longer see, I am unable to help with

the family business. I've never had an interest in running it. I used to paint, portraits mostly, but no longer. I don't even know what we own or how it works. I have no earthly reason to wish my brother harm. He's my best friend, and like I already told you, I miss him."

Then he pulled out a handkerchief and blew his nose.

Dina glared at Charlie, daring him to challenge her.

Instead, he changed the subject. "Jason, how is your uncle Ted involved in the business?"

"Other than getting the same percentage of money from our shares in the corporation, not at all. He's wealthy in his own right due to his medical practice. I'm sure you know it's a successful one, since your wife is one of his patients." Then he looked straight at his mother. "It's your turn, and the longer you pout, the longer Mr. Dodge is here."

Dina sniffed, then stared at a point on the wall just past Charlie's right shoulder as she spoke.

"Carter and I are the closest in age. We don't fight. But we often have disagreements. However, they have nothing to do with the business."

"I see. So if Carter is dead, who steps into his shoes?" Charlie asked.

"Why, my son, of course. Carter trained him for that," Dina said.

Jason shrugged. "I'm the logical choice. The way this is set up, no one *but* family has final votes. The board of directors is a functional entity, with Uncle Carter holding the final vote. When it comes to really major decisions, we vote within the family first, and in those situations, Uncle Carter's vote has no more power than mine or Mother's or Uncle Edward's. Whichever way we vote is how Uncle Carter always votes in the board meetings. It's a little unorthodox, but the Dunleavys hold the highest number of shares, and those are never sold. When someone in the family dies, then that person's shares are divided equally among the remaining family members, so that none of us ever has more voting power than another. Yes, their monetary shares will increase their income, but no one in this family is hurting for money."

Charlie listened, but he was also watching faces and expressions, and every time voting was brought up, Kenneth's expression shifted just enough to notice. It was Charlie's guess that it galled the man to know he would never hold power within the family.

"There's one other question I need to ask. During my initial investigation, I discovered that Carter withdraws exactly five thousand dollars every two weeks. That's ten thousand a month, and this has been going on for about ten years. If he's being blackmailed, it would definitely be an angle to follow up on. Do any of you know about this?"

Edward chuckled. "Oh, that's Carter's poker stake. He's been playing poker with some of his friends for years. Sometimes he wins. Sometimes he loses, but it's his getaway from the daily grind of the job."

Charlie smiled. "Ah…poker. Well, that explains the money angle. By chance, do you know the names of the men he plays with? He might have mentioned problems he was having to one of them."

"Some, but not all," Edward told him.

"I can get you a list," Jason said. "I sit in on a game now and then."

"Much appreciated," Charlie said. "Thank you for taking the time to meet with me. Before I leave, how many people do you have on staff in the house on a daily basis?"

"Five, with others who come and go as needed," Jason said. "Do you want to speak with them, as well?"

Charlie was surprised by the offer. "Yes, if I might. It wouldn't take long. Just a couple of questions, without family present."

Dina gasped. "They know nothing about our business. I don't see the need to—"

Jason rolled his eyes. "Mother! Just stop. The help know everything. They see us. They hear us. They follow along behind the messes we make and clean them up. If they've learned anything that might help us find Uncle Carter, then I want to hear it." Jason motioned to Charlie. "Follow me. I'll take you straight to the kitchen. You can talk to them there, and when you're finished, Ruth Fenway will show you out. She's the housekeeper, and the one who answered the door."

Charlie gathered up the recorder and his briefcase, then paused.

"Thank you for being so forthcoming. I'll stay in touch," he said.

As soon as they reached the kitchen, Jason nodded at the chef, then spoke to Ruth. "Would you please ask the girls to come to the kitchen? Mr. Dodge wants a word with all of you."

"Yes, sir," Ruth said. She took a cell phone out of her pocket and sent a group text.

Jason pointed out the chef. "Charlie, this is our chef, Peter Curtis. He's been with us for almost ten years now."

Curtis nodded but kept on working.

Within minutes, three women came hurrying into the kitchen, looking wild-eyed and in a panic, clearly afraid they'd done something wrong.

"You're not in trouble," Jason told them. "This is Charlie Dodge. I hired him to find Uncle Carter. He wants to speak with all of you. If you know anything, please tell him. Be honest. We need to find my uncle."

The trio nodded and visibly relaxed.

"Charlie, from left to right, that's Louise, Arnetta and Wilma."

"Thanks," Charlie said, and as soon as Jason cleared the

doorway, he took out the recorder again and began another line of questioning.

"I'm going to throw these questions out, and if any of you know anything, please speak up. Now, are any of you aware of anything that might explain his absence?"

"No, sir," Louise said.

"Me, neither," Arnetta said.

"I don't, either," Wilma added.

"Okay…let me ask this a different way. Has anything odd happened here in the past few weeks? Anything that was out of the norm?"

Ruth raised her hand. "About a month ago, the family gathered in the library after dinner. They were having their favorite nightcaps when Mr. Carter suddenly became ill. Miss Dina had me call an ambulance, and they took him to the ER. They kept him overnight. Mr. Carter was back the next morning, but without any explanation to us. We assumed it was something other than food poisoning because no one else was ill and they all had the same meal."

"But what about the after-dinner drinks?" Charlie asked. "You said they had their favorite drinks. Do you mean they all choose different ones?"

Ruth nodded.

"Who makes the drinks?" Charlie asked.

Ruth shrugged. "First one of them, then another. There's no set routine for that."

Charlie shifted focus. "Is there any fighting among them that they don't show in front of visitors?"

"No, sir," Ruth said.

"Miss Dina and Mr. Carter squabble a lot," Arnetta added. "But it's nothing more than brother-and-sister squabbles. They don't get angry, just disagree. It never lasts."

"The day Carter disappeared, he drove himself to work.

Did he carry anything out of the house when he left, like a suitcase or hunting gear?" Charlie asked.

They all shook their heads.

"Do you know why he drove himself that day?"

Wilma shifted nervously from one foot to the other. "I don't...but I did overhear him calling the car service and telling them not to come, that he was driving himself."

Charlie had a feeling they knew more than they realized. He just needed to ask the right questions.

"Who takes care of Carter's clothing? You know, laundry, dry cleaning, repairs...that sort of thing."

Louise raised her head. "I mostly do the hand sewing, like hems that've come undone or loose buttons. But his clothes are sent out to be washed and cleaned. I'm the one who deals with that."

"Have you noticed anything missing? Like casual wear or suitcases?" Charlie asked.

"I don't know, sir. I really haven't been in his room other than to dust and clean since he went missing," Louise said.

"Louise, would you do me a favor?" Charlie asked. "Would you please run up to his room right now and look through his things. See if you notice anything that strikes you as odd. Check and see if he has socks and underwear missing. Look for jackets and shoes that aren't there. Look for missing luggage. I'll wait."

"Yes, sir," Louise said and left the kitchen at a hasty pace.

"Would you care for a cup of coffee while you wait?" Ruth asked.

"I made strawberry tarts yesterday. There are some left, if you care to have them with your coffee," Peter offered.

"I will if you'll all join me," Charlie said.

Within a couple of minutes, they were having coffee and strawberry tarts together at the long worktable while Charlie listened to their chatter.

About ten minutes later, Louise returned, and Charlie knew when he saw her face that she had news.

"What's gone?" he asked.

She put a hand to her chest to calm her racing heart, then took a breath.

"Two suitcases are gone. So are underwear and socks. His shaving kit is missing. None of the clothes he wears to work have been touched, but the clothes he hunts and fishes in have been sorted through. It took me a while to figure all that out, but at a guess, I'd say there are at least two weeks' worth of casual clothes missing, including shoes. And he always had an iPad in the drawer next to his bed. He read books on it and used it to answer personal email, as well. It's gone."

Charlie's hunch had paid off. This was leaning more toward the likelihood that Carter wasn't kidnapped, but on the run. Now he had to figure out where he'd gone and why he was running.

"This is great. You've been very helpful," he said, as he turned off the recorder. "Now I need all of you to do me a favor, and it's very important."

They glanced at one another, then back at Charlie and nodded in agreement.

This was gut instinct on Charlie's part, but it was strong enough not to ignore.

"Don't tell any of the family what you've told me, because if Carter felt he had to leave this house to stay safe, then I don't want anyone in the family to know he did this. If he felt safe, they would all have known why he's gone. Understand?"

They nodded.

He saw the shock in their eyes and was satisfied they'd keep quiet.

"Peter, Louise missed out on the coffee and tarts. I think she deserves a little break, too, don't you?" Charlie asked next.

"Absolutely," the chef said, setting her up as Ruth took him back to the front door.

"Thank you for your time, ma'am," Charlie said.

Ruth nodded. "Of course. We all like working for Mr. Carter. We've been most upset about his disappearance. I hope you find him."

"I'll find him," Charlie said and went back to his car.

He'd heard his phone signal a text while he was having coffee, but he'd purposely waited until he was alone to read it. Jason had come through for him. It was the list of names and contact info for Carter's poker partners.

He emailed the text to his office, along with instructions for Wyrick to check them out. Even though these guys were supposedly old friends, when losing large sums of money was involved, friendships often went begging.

The next item to check off on Charlie's list was exploring the area around the intersection where Carter had gone missing. He had the police reports on every place that was searched, but looking at them from a different perspective could yield new leads, so he set the address in his GPS and drove there.

CHAPTER SIX

Dodge Investigations was receiving the usual influx of requests for Charlie's services, which kept Wyrick busy making notes about each one for Charlie to review. She already knew which cases he would take, and the ones he'd pass over, but it wasn't her job to inform these would-be clients.

Despite the searches she'd made this morning, she hadn't found any new answers or leads, so when she received his email with a new list of names to research, she abandoned the sandwich she'd been eating and started with the basic background checks. She was still at the computer when the doorbell rang.

She frowned. Without knowing Charlie's personal habits, she had no way of knowing if he often received visitors. As a result she was cautious as she went to look through the peephole. When she saw a courier's uniform, the first thing she thought was, *They found me again*, but she still opened the door.

The courier nodded. "Afternoon, ma'am. I have a package for Charlie Dodge."

"I'll sign for it," Wyrick said.

He handed her the iPad.

She signed her name, then took the package and shut the door. It didn't have a return address, so she laid it at the back of the kitchen counter where she'd been putting his mail, and returned to the poker players.

Charlie headed toward the area around the Amtrak station, found a nearby place to park. He put on sunglasses and his Texas Ranger baseball cap, grabbed his gear and made his way to the DaVita Hotel parking garage.

The yellow pullover shirt he was wearing hung loose outside the waistband of his jeans. He liked the shirt because it was comfortable. But between his imposing stature and long lanky stride, he realized he stood out like a flashing beacon in the foot traffic.

He intended to cover the whole area around the intersection where they'd lost track of Carter, but he'd decided his first destination would be the garage adjoining the DaVita Hotel. During the initial police search, they'd come across two black Lexus cars in the garage like the one Carter Dunleavy had been driving. Neither had Carter's license plate number. According to the police file, one had Just Married written on the back window, with ribbons and deflating balloons tied to the bumper. The other had Wash Me written in the dust on the lid of the trunk.

What he hadn't found in the police files were any notes about checking the camera footage inside the parking garage, or notes on whether or not the people who owned those cars were in the hotel. That omission didn't sit well with Charlie. He was a careful man. It was what had kept him alive in Afghanistan, and it was what made him so good at the job he was doing now. He knew the cars wouldn't still be there, but he wanted to see their locations and—if it still existed—the footage from the hotel's security cameras.

The stoplight was red as he got to the intersection, so he

paused near the curb, waiting for the walk signal. There were about a half-dozen others also waiting, including a little boy who looked up at Charlie and was so obviously taken aback by his height that he kept staring.

Charlie pulled his glasses down just enough to make eye contact and winked.

The little boy grinned.

The light changed, and the little boy's mother tightened her grip on his hand as they hurried across the intersection. Charlie pushed his glasses back in place and stepped off into the crosswalk on his way to the parking garage.

He took off his sunglasses when he entered the garage and stuck them in his shirt pocket as he oriented himself to the layout. According to the police investigation, one Lexus was on the second level and the other on the third, so he started walking.

Once he reached Level Two, he reread the report to confirm where the first Lexus had been parked, and began looking for security cameras as he went. Minutes later, he found the location and scouted the area for the cameras; he made notes before continuing up toward the third level.

Along the way, he saw people parking and leaving the garage in haste, most of them likely in a hurry to catch the train. There were others coming to get their cars and drive away. Several people eyed him curiously, and a few women who were walking alone seemed nervous, even anxious, when they saw him. The mere fact that he was a man and that this was what frightened them made him sad, and at the same time, pissed off at men in general who'd caused them to feel that way. He didn't make eye contact and kept referring to his iPad in an effort to reassure them that he had a purpose for being there and was not a predator.

When he finally reached the third level, he was just getting ready to start searching when his phone rang. It was Wyrick.

"Hello."

"It's me. I finished a basic search on the poker players and attached it to an email. I could have sent you that info in a text, but you also received a package via courier today. I assumed it would be a personal package since this is not our official office, and no one knows we're working from your home. I felt it necessary to let you know this arrived, in case you were awaiting receipt or need whatever is in it."

Charlie frowned. "I'm not expecting anything. Who's it from?"

"There's no label or return address," Wyrick said.

"Will you do me a favor and check with the courier service to verify if it really came through them?"

"Already did," Wyrick said.

Charlie sighed. *Of course you did. Why did I even ask?* "And?"

"Yes, the package came through the service. Yes, the courier was valid. No, they wouldn't reveal the sender's name because he or she requested it go anonymously."

"My curiosity says open it, but I don't want to put you in any danger in case it's from an old enemy or a disgruntled client aiming for some kind of payback," Charlie said.

"I beat cancer. I'm not afraid of a package."

Charlie grunted beneath his breath. Sometimes the rawness in Wyrick's voice gave away how much she had suffered.

"Fine. Do what suits you," he said gruffly.

"I don't like secrets," she said. "Hang on. I'm putting you on speakerphone."

She headed into the kitchen to get the package and laid the phone down beside it. She'd been using a knife from his flatware as a letter opener and quickly slid it under a loose edge of the envelope flap and, with one swift cut, opened the end.

"The envelope is open. Nothing blew up. I'm dumping the contents on the table," she said and upended the package. "There's a letter and another package in Bubble Wrap. I'm going to undo the Bubble Wrap and see what's there."

"Okay," Charlie said.

Wyrick cut the tape and unrolled the wrap. "There are several pieces of what looks like really nice jewelry. Hang on a sec and I'll open the letter."

The moment Charlie heard her say "jewelry," the hair stood up on the back of his neck. *It couldn't be. Not after all these years.*

"The letter is handwritten. I'll read it to you, okay?

"Dude. I stole this from you, but the cops picked me up on outstanding warrants before I could pawn it. I been in prison ever since, thinking about the loot I hid at Mama's, and told myself if it was still there when I got out, I was giving it back. I been out a month. Took me a while to find out where you live now. All's I want to say is I'm sorry. I'm trying to do better. This was my first good thing.

"That's it. Someone with a conscience. Not a lot of that around," Wyrick said.

Charlie was stunned. "What's the jewelry look like?"

"Um, there are three, no, four necklaces, three with gold chains, one with silver. A couple of gold bracelets, one that's braided and another with a small chain clasp. And two rings. One cocktail ring with a jade cabochon, and one that's just a flat gold band."

He took a deep breath to steady his voice. "Is there an engraving inside the band?"

"I'll look," Wyrick said and tilted it. The moment she saw the words, she knew this must have belonged to Annie. Her voice unintentionally softened. "It says 'Forever in my heart.'"

"Son of a bitch," Charlie said. "Returning this might have

relieved the thief's conscience, but he gave it back too late to matter to Annie."

For once, Wyrick was at a loss for a smart comeback. "What do you want me to do with the jewelry?"

"Hell if I know," Charlie said. "I guess, just put it back in the envelope, then hide it in my bathroom, behind the stack of towels in the linen closet. I'll deal with it when I return."

"Yes, sir," Wyrick said. "Anything else you need?"

"Not right now," Charlie said and hung up.

It was the first time that he'd been the one to end a phone call, and she could tell he didn't even realize she'd called him "sir."

Wyrick carefully wrapped everything back up and headed for Charlie's bedroom. She knew where it was, but she'd never been inside, so opening the door felt like trespassing.

She walked straight toward the bathroom, opened the linen closet and put the package where he'd asked, then walked out.

Her heart hurt. It must be hell to love so hard without having it returned. Or in Charlie's case, no longer having it returned. She hadn't been engaged long enough to know what loving that hard meant.

She walked back through the kitchen to get a cold Pepsi, then walked to the windows overlooking the street in front of the apartment building to take her first drink. The pop was ice-cold and it made her teeth hurt and burned the back of her throat as it went down. Her eyes watered. But they weren't tears. It was the cold Pepsi that did it.

Don't you cry. Don't you dare cry for that man, Jade Wyrick. He's your boss and that's as far as it will ever go.

Charlie was in shock. He kept remembering how crushed Annie had been when she realized her mother's jewelry and the ring he'd given her before he left for Afghanistan had been stolen from their home. Ten years ago. A lifetime. When Annie was still Annie, before Charlie lost her.

When he finally shifted focus enough to know he was standing in a parking garage, it took him a few seconds to even remember why he was here. The sound of screeching tires brought him out of the funk he was in, and he quickly looked around to make sure he wasn't about to get run over.

Anxious now to check the last parking space and move on, he refreshed his memory as to where the other black Lexus had been parked, and started looking for the aisle. He eventually found it on the other side of the third level. As he turned the corner, he stopped, stunned by the sight of a very dusty black Lexus with the "Just Married" sign still on the car. The Mylar balloons were still there, too, tied to the bumper, lying flat on the concrete.

"What the hell? The police investigation took place over two weeks ago, and *this* is still here?" he muttered.

He squatted down in front of the license plate for a closer examination. Within seconds he saw new scratches around the holes where it had been screwed in place, but they shouldn't have been there. This wasn't a new plate someone had just put on, and the expiration sticker was only months away. This couldn't be right. He pulled out his phone and made a call. It rang three times before someone answered.

"Detective Cristobal."

"Hey, this is Charlie Dodge."

"How's it going, Charlie?" he asked.

"Oh, it's going. I have a question. I've been retracing the steps that were taken during the initial investigation after Carter went missing. I'm in the DaVita parking garage, and I just found something odd."

"Like what?"

"Remember the black Lexus on the third floor with the 'Just Married' sign and balloons?"

"Yeah. The tag number didn't match the Dunleavy Lexus," Cristobal said.

"That Lexus is still here, with all the 'Just Married' paraphernalia. And I'd bet a steak dinner that the tag on the car isn't the one that belongs to it."

"The hell you say!" Cristobal muttered.

"It's an older tag, but there are new scratch marks where it's screwed on. Did anyone run the tags when the cars were initially found? And did anyone check the DaVita Hotel to see if the owners of the cars were registered there or had taken the train? I'm asking because there's no mention of that in the reports."

"There should've been. Give me the number. I'll run it right now," Cristobal said.

Charlie read it off to him and then waited. He could hear the click, click, click of the keys as Cristobal entered it into the DMV database. A couple of minutes later, the detective was back.

"It belongs to a 2010 Lincoln, not a 2017 Lexus. Son of a bitch! I need a VIN and the interior dusted for prints. Do you mind hanging out a few minutes until I can get some people there?"

"No problem. I'll wait. I need to know if the car belongs to Carter, too. And I have one more question. Did anyone get the footage from the security cameras inside the garage? Because that's not in the report, either."

"I'll have to check Evidence. I'll get back to you. Thanks for the info."

"No problem," Charlie said again and settled down to wait for the police.

It wasn't long before the first police car rolled up, followed by a second one. They asked Charlie for identification to make sure he was the man Cristobal had mentioned, and then they all waited for the investigators to arrive from the crime scene detail.

As soon as they did, the site became a hive of activity. One of the investigators got the VIN, and when they ran it and realized the Lexus was Carter Dunleavy's personal car, they called for a tow truck to take it to their lab for processing.

The instant Charlie learned it was Carter's Lexus, he left. Cristobal called him as he was walking back to his car.

"Hello."

"Charlie, it's me. We don't have the footage. And we did have someone checking all of that out, but I just heard that the detective got sick during the investigation. He was on his way to the ER when he had a stroke. Whatever leads we might have gleaned fell through the cracks because he hasn't been able to speak since," Cristobal said.

"That's a tough blow for him. And just so you know, they're towing the car back to the lab. The VIN checked out. It's Dunleavy's personal car. I don't know how long they keep security footage, but if I find out anything more, I'll let you know. Oh…one other thing. I interviewed the family this morning," Charlie said.

"And?"

"I didn't sense anything about them that would lead me to believe anyone was lying. However, I asked to interview the staff as well, and when I did, it occurred to me to send the maid who tended to his clothing up to his room. I asked her to check for missing luggage and anything else she could think of, and I got a hit. Two suitcases, several changes of clothing, all of it stuff he used for hunting and fishing, along with an iPad from a nightstand were missing. I think he's running."

"Son of a bitch!" Cristobal said. "I know this makes us look like a bunch of screwups, but this isn't business as usual."

"I can see that, and I think it went off track with your de-tective's sudden stroke. Look, it's just me, focusing on only one man, not a city of troubles. I'll be in touch if more happens," Charlie said.

"Same here." Cristobal disconnected.

After finding an employee of the parking garage and explaining he was part of the investigation surrounding Carter Dunleavy, the other man gave him the name and phone number of the person to talk to about the security setup in the garage.

Charlie moved out into the sunlight before making that call.

"Security, this is Mauldin."

"Mr. Mauldin, my name is Charlie Dodge. I'm a private investigator working with the Denver police on the Carter Dunleavy case. I just located Carter's black Lexus in the DaVita parking garage. I need to know about the availability of security footage."

"What the hell?" Mauldin said. "They already checked two weeks ago and the car wasn't there."

"Well, it's there now. It appears the tag had been changed, and the crime scene crew is towing the car out of the garage as we speak."

"Oh. I'm sorry to hear this," Mauldin said. "So how can I help?"

"Would you still have footage of the day Dunleavy went missing?"

"Normally, we keep it for several weeks, and then it's deleted. If someone hasn't jumped the gun and deleted it early, we should still have it. I'm going to put you on hold while I go check."

"Thanks," Charlie said and moved into the shade of the building to wait. He was thinking about the stolen jewelry when Mauldin came back online.

"Mr. Dodge, are you still there?"

"I'm here, and it's Charlie. Do you have footage?"

"We do. Our office is in the DaVita Hotel. I'll wait for you in the lobby. Look for a middle-aged man in a rumpled gray suit."

Charlie laughed. "And I'll be the tall guy in a Texas Rangers ball cap and a yellow shirt."

"A man after my own heart. I was born in Waco. See you soon."

Charlie had already seen the hotel, so he started walking toward it and within minutes was in the lobby. As promised, a man wearing a rumpled gray suit lifted his hand. Charlie pocketed his sunglasses and went to meet him.

"Mr. Mauldin, I appreciate this courtesy," Charlie said.

"Call me Stu. I'm happy to do anything I can to help the case. Follow me. I have one of my staff setting up the viewing for you now."

When they entered the security area, it was immediately obvious that there was nothing shortchanged with their security system. He'd seen some of the best setups, and this one was state-of-the-art.

"This is amazing," Charlie said.

Stu nodded. "We also cover security for the train station, as well as the hotel and parking garage." They continued through the front entrance and down a hall to a bank of offices. Stu led him into a room on the right.

"Charlie, this is Rachel. She's one of our best in the technology department. She'll take you through whatever parts of the footage you want to see."

Charlie eyed the young woman, privately thinking she didn't look old enough to be the best at anything, then reminded himself it was the younger generation that *was* the best with technology.

"Rachel, I appreciate your help," he said as he sat down in the chair provided for him. He took off his cap and laid his things aside.

"My pleasure, sir," Rachel said. "If you're ready, we can begin. If at any time you see something you want replayed, just tell me, and we can take it slower."

"So, is this the day of the disappearance?" Charlie asked.

"This begins with the day he went missing on the traffic cam."

"Okay, proceed." Charlie scooted closer to the monitor.

The first few hours of footage were quickly scanned, revealing nothing but daily traffic, with more cars coming into the garage than going out. When he finally saw a black Lexus appear at the entrance, he pointed.

"That's a Lexus, but the time is off compared to when they lost him on the traffic cam. I still want to watch, though."

She clicked on a few keys and a second screen popped up on the monitor so they could trail that specific car as it headed onto another level.

"There it is again," Charlie said as the next camera picked it up. "Is this the second level?"

"Yes," Rachel said.

And when they saw the car pull into an empty parking space, Charlie leaned back a bit, watching as the driver, who turned out to be a woman, got out and hurried away.

"Yes, wrong Lexus. The one I need to see goes up to the third level."

Rachel took the second screen down and they went back to watching the entrance.

They continued to scan footage and got closer to the time Carter was picked up on the traffic cam.

"It should be showing up here soon," Charlie said.

And he was right. Less than a minute of footage later, another black Lexus entered the parking garage, also taking the aisle leading to the next level. Rachel was already on it, tracking the progress as she changed from camera to camera. Once the Lexus reached the third level, Charlie's gaze was so focused on the monitor that he forgot where he was. He wanted that first look at Dunleavy. He watched the car being parked and then the driver getting out.

Almost immediately, Charlie frowned. The driver looked nothing like the pictures he'd seen of Dunleavy.

What the hell? "That's not Carter Dunleavy," he said.

His mind was spinning as he watched the driver lean over the back of the car and begin to write on the window. Then he circled the car and finished what he was writing, leaning over from the other side. Charlie grunted. The driver had written "Just Married," with some kind of giant marker. He opened the back door, reached in and pulled out a handful of Mylar balloons, which he began tying to the bumper. As soon as he was finished, he looked around quickly, as if making sure he hadn't been seen, then walked a few cars farther down, unlocked the door to a white Ford Escape, got in and drove away.

"Stop," Charlie said. "Is there any way to catch the car that's leaving to see if we can get a tag number on it?"

"I'll try," Rachel said and once again began switching camera footage.

Each time they saw the vehicle, it was facing the camera as it passed. They watched it pull up to the exit—and then it was gone.

"The tint on the window was too dark to see the driver," Charlie said, "but there was a fairly good shot of him from the side when he first exited the Lexus. Could you possibly print a copy of that for me?"

"Yes, but I can't do that right here. If you don't mind waiting, I need to run back to my office."

"I'll wait," Charlie said, still surprised by what he'd just seen.

This was a slick switch, but it only deepened the mystery. Was Carter in on this, or had it been a ruse to keep the cops from looking for real kidnappers? When did Carter leave the Lexus, and did he leave it by choice? Or was he never in it at all?

He was still trying to figure out scenarios when Rachel returned and handed him the print.

"Thank you," Charlie said. "Detective Cristobal is going to be as confused as I am by this revelation. As I told you, I really appreciate your help. And if you wouldn't mind, please don't mention this. Until Dunleavy's disappearance has been solved, we don't want to alert the wrong people about what we know."

Rachel smiled. "Sir, I work in Security. We know nothing, see nothing. Mr. Mauldin will be informed of the results, but it stops with him."

"Right," Charlie said.

"Unless there's anything else we can do for you, I'll walk you out," Rachel said.

"No, that's all."

"Then follow me." Rachel led Charlie back into the lobby. "Good luck," she said, then left him on his own.

Charlie took his sunglasses from his pocket as he went to the front entrance and put them on as he walked out into the sunlight. It was time to get back to his car and let Cristobal know what had just happened.

He reached the SUV and started the engine as he made the call.

"This is Cristobal."

"It's me," Charlie said. "I just finished looking at security footage from the parking garage, and you're not going to believe what I saw."

"Oh, hell, what now?" Cristobal muttered.

"The man who drove Carter's Lexus into that garage was not Carter Dunleavy."

"What? Are you sure?"

"I'm positive. Unless Dunleavy lost forty pounds and grew taller, it's not him. The footage shows the man writing 'Just Married' on the back window, then tying Mylar balloons to the bumper. As soon as he's finished, he walks a few cars down, gets into a Ford Escape and drives away. You might want to pay a visit to the hotel and see the footage for yourself. It's possible you'll see something I missed," Charlie said.

Cristobal grunted. "We're the ones who've been missing the point, but it was all part of the overall confusion, and this only makes it worse. If these people were kidnappers, why take the car to the parking garage and risk being caught on a security camera? After what you said about the missing clothing and now this, I think you're right. He's running. But why?"

"I have some other interviews today. If I learn anything new, I'll give you a call. I'm guessing there are people who know exactly where Carter is and are helping him hide," Charlie said.

He disconnected, then drove back to the hotel. At this point, he was a stranger to Carter's friends, and making cold calls to people who were likely close to Carter Dunleavy would gain him nothing.

He turned on the radio as he drove, searching until he found a country station, and let music replace the empty feeling in his heart. The stolen jewelry showing up after so many years had resurrected old memories. Sad memories.

Because of someone's change of heart, he had the ring back, but he was never going to get Annie back. They didn't have a future together anymore. He went from job to job, telling himself it was to pay for her care. But the truth was he'd rather be working than alone in the apartment.

When he finally reached the Grand, he pulled into the parking lot rather than valet parking, gathered up his gear and got out. It was close to 2:00 p.m. when he entered the lobby, so he made a detour to the coffee shop, picked up some deli food because he'd missed lunch and ordered the largest coffee they had.

A couple of minutes later he reached his room and went inside. He could tell that the maids had come and gone because his bed was already made, so he wasn't going to be disturbed. He put everything on the bed except his food, which he left on the table, and went to wash up.

As he was drying his hands, he glanced up into the mirror, eyed a few strands of gray hair at his temples and realized he was beginning to look like his father. Then he hung up the towel, went back to the table, kicked off his shoes—and ate everything he'd purchased without tasting a bite.

CHAPTER SEVEN

After Charlie finished eating, he opened his laptop to look at the report Wyrick had sent him on Carter's poker buddies. In typical Wyrick fashion, she'd gone above and beyond on the background checks, including a DMV photo of each man, plus photos pulled randomly from the society pages of the *Denver Post*.

It was immediately obvious from her reports that none of the five had money troubles, so losing money to Carter in a poker game would not have been an issue. He had contact information for each of them, and as he was going through the report to jot down the names and numbers, one of the men looked familiar.

He checked the name, Rom Delgado, again, wondering if he'd met the man somewhere in the past. He was still staring at the photo when he realized where he'd seen him. The parking garage! He pulled out the photo from the security footage to compare with the one from Wyrick's report. He didn't have a clear view of the man's face in the parking garage picture, but his gut was telling him that he'd found the man who'd helped Carter disappear.

He reached for his phone.

Rom Delgado was in his home office when his cell phone rang. He picked it up, glanced at the caller ID and frowned. It was an out-of-area exchange, but so few people had his cell number that he answered it anyway.

"Hello, Rom speaking."

"Mr. Delgado, my name is Charlie Dodge. I'm a private investigator hired by the Dunleavy family to find Carter Dunleavy. Do you have a moment to speak with me?"

Ah, that explained how this man had his number. Obviously the family had provided it.

"Of course," Rom said. "Carter is one of my dearest friends. We're all concerned."

"I'm going to be up-front with you in the hope you'll be honest with me. I know you helped Carter disappear. What I don't know is why he felt the need to do so at the expense of his family's feelings."

Rom felt like he'd been gut punched. Two weeks had come and gone since Carter's disappearance, and he'd thought he was in the clear.

"Not over the phone," Rom said.

"Then where do you want to meet? And I'll warn you, the police now know Carter didn't leave the Lexus in the garage, that someone else drove it there. They know because I told them."

Rom felt the second blow land as hard and fast as the first.

"It's not what you must think," he said. "Will you come to my home?"

"Give me an address," Charlie said, and Rom relayed it. "I'll be there within the hour."

Rom blinked. Dodge had already disconnected. He sat there a moment, then hit the call button on his phone.

Carter Dunleavy was on top of the world. At least it felt that way from his viewpoint on the back deck of Rom's mountain getaway high above Colorado Springs.

The mountains always called to him, but he'd never taken the time away from work to enjoy them like this, and if the attempts on his life had never happened, he would still be in Denver behind a desk. He'd had two good weeks up here, giving him plenty of time to contemplate his so-called accidents and the level of skill they required—or didn't. He was still in shock that any of this was even happening.

Carter had enemies and knew their faces, but nothing about this was professional, which was the route most of his corporate enemies would have taken. The final straw was having his brakes fail on a mountain road.

He'd been at a wake held for an old friend. Dina and Kenneth had also gone to the wake, but in separate cars and he'd left a few minutes ahead of them to get back into the city for a meeting.

When he'd first realized what was going on, it had been his driving skill that kept him from hurtling into the canyon below. But the faster the car went, the more panicked he became. There was only one way to stop, and that was to wreck it, so he drove straight into the side of the mountain.

He wound up with a bloody face from being hit by an airbag. Every muscle in his body hurt to the point that he was afraid to move, but the car was spewing and leaking fuel and water all over the road. He needed to escape, and then Kenneth and Dina drove up on the accident. It was Kenneth who got a tire iron from their car and popped open the door to get Carter out, and it was Kenneth who fixed the backseat of their own car so Carter could lie down until rescue services arrived.

Dina finally got herself together enough to sit down on the floorboard and hold his hand. She kept saying over and over how sorry she was that they'd argued, and that she really loved him with all her heart. All he could manage was to pat her hand and tell her he loved her, too.

The airbags had saved him from serious injury, but that accident really had been the last straw. Although he couldn't prove it, he suspected it was just the latest in a series of "accidents" he'd been having, and he'd begun planning a way to disappear. He'd wanted people to think he was dead, and had been counting on whoever was involved to show their hand by attempting some kind of takeover.

But the days had passed and turned into weeks, and so far, no one had made a move on the company. Jason was standing strong against the fluctuating price of their market shares. None of it made sense.

A shriek in the skies above his head shifted his thoughts once again to the beauty before him. He was looking up at an eagle, wings outspread as it soared above him when his burner phone rang. It could only be Rom.

"Hello, my friend. Do you have news for me?" Carter asked.

"I have some news, but not what you'll be wanting to hear," Rom said.

Carter heard regret in his voice. "What happened?"

"Jason hired a private investigator to find you."

"Really?" Carter sighed. "I shouldn't be surprised. He's a dutiful and loving nephew. So what's the problem?"

"This guy's been here two days and did what the Denver PD were unable to do in two weeks. He already knows you weren't kidnapped, and he knows I drove the car to the parking garage."

"Well, hell," Carter muttered.

"I thought we'd gotten a pass with that, but we didn't. He called to tell me he knows I was complicit in your disappearance, and he's told the police that it wasn't you driving the car. He's on his way here to question me further, and he's going to want answers. How do you want me to deal with this?"

"He's obviously good at his job. What's his name?" Carter asked.

"Charlie Dodge."

"When he arrives, I want to talk to him," Carter said.

"Are you sure?" Rom said.

"Yes. And then I'll have to make a call to the chief of police to keep you out of trouble."

"Don't worry about me," Rom said. "You're the one who's not safe."

"No, I got you into this, and I'll get you out. But I won't do any of that until I speak to Mr. Dodge."

"Okay. It's your life on the line."

"I know what I'm doing," Carter said. "And just for the record, you're officially off duty."

Rom frowned as Carter disconnected, then went to the wet bar and poured himself a shot of whiskey, downing it like medicine before walking out onto the balcony.

Being found out wasn't an actual surprise. He'd been prepared for it, but then as the days went on, he'd begun to think fate was giving him a pass. So it was happening now. It didn't matter. He owed Carter for bailing him out of financial difficulties years ago, and would do it all over again, if asked.

His wife saw him and waved from the tennis court. His son looked up, then waved and smiled, as well.

"I'm winning!" she said.

Rom gave them both a thumbs-up and went back inside to wait for the other shoe to drop.

★ ★ ★

Charlie's adrenaline was pumping. He was on the hunt and the first big lead had just fallen in his lap. He didn't waste time as he left the hotel and was in the neighborhood in which Rom Delgado lived in under twenty minutes. From the sizes of the estates he was passing, it was very obviously upscale and exclusive. Not on the level of Dunleavy Castle, but each residence was unique and architecturally stunning.

His GPS directed him to turn right in twenty-five feet, which took him off the street and up a drive bordered by two massive poplars pointing toward the sun. He continued on the winding drive, toward a decent replica of an Italian villa. Then he rolled to a stop and got out, carrying his briefcase as he went up the half-circle tier of stone steps, across a flagstone courtyard to the front door.

He rang the doorbell and within a few moments the door swung inward. Charlie eyed the tiny woman with flashing black eyes peering up at him.

"Charlie Dodge to see Mr. Delgado. He's expecting me," Charlie said.

"Yes, sir, come in."

Charlie stepped over the threshold and followed her down a hall and into a sitting room.

The maid paused in the doorway. "Mr. Dodge is here, sir."

"Thank you, Della," Rom said and came to meet Charlie with his hand extended. "Mr. Dodge, it's a pleasure to meet you."

Charlie nodded, shook hands and saved the smiles and pleasantries for someone he didn't suspect of collusion.

"May I offer you a drink?" Rom asked.

"No, but thank you," Charlie said. "What I need from you are answers."

Rom paused, then pointed to another, larger courtyard in the back that was visible beyond the French doors.

"Would you join me outside? Our discussion needs to be confidential. No curious ears at doorways out there."

Charlie was surprised. "Do you distrust your own staff?"

Rom chuckled. "I distrust everyone. Except Carter. Please follow me."

As soon as they were outside, Charlie started talking. "Where's Carter Dunleavy?"

Rom shrugged. "He's safe."

"I only have your word for that, and I don't trust people, either," Charlie said and then thought, *Except Wyrick, even though she doesn't trust* me *enough to tell me what's going on in her life.*

"What if you could talk to him? Would that suffice?" Rom asked.

Charlie frowned. "No, because I have no idea what Carter Dunleavy sounds like. I want to know the purpose of this stunt."

"After you called, I told him you'd discovered our little deception. He wants to talk to you," Rom said.

"I'm not sure the Denver police are going to call this fiasco a 'little deception,'" Charlie responded.

Rom shrugged. "Carter asked. I don't tell Carter no. So, will you please talk to him? He can explain everything to you, and then I think you'll understand."

Charlie grudgingly gave Delgado points for loyalty and was beginning to believe he might not be as full of shit as he'd first thought.

"Call him. I'll listen to what he has to say."

"Thank you," Rom said as he took his phone out of his pocket. "Come with me, please."

They walked out to one of the ornate benches in the courtyard, looked around to make sure they were still alone, then sat down and Rom made the call.

"Hello, Carter, he's here and reluctantly willing to speak to you. All you need to know is Charlie Dodge is the real deal. I think you can trust him." Then he handed the phone to Charlie.

"This is Charlie Dodge. Your family—in fact, everyone under your roof—is hovering on the point of grief, so start talking."

"And someone under that roof is trying to kill me," Carter said.

That explains a lot. Then Charlie remembered the housekeeper at the Dunleavy house telling him about the accidents Carter had been having.

"Are you referring to the incident your housekeeper mentioned when I was interviewing the staff?"

Carter sighed. "I should have known Ruth would have my back. Yes, that and more."

Charlie listened closely, hearing sadness in the man's voice, which was something he would expect if this story was valid.

"Why do you think it might be family?" Charlie asked.

"I can't totally say it's family, but it's someone there. Employee, family, somebody. No one else would have the access to me to make that stuff happen, except someone under my roof."

"Who in your family would have anything to gain by your death?" Charlie asked.

"The only thing they would gain are more shares and a raise in income. On the other hand, we're all indecently rich. Jason has a nasty little drug habit, but it's never become an issue, and I know for a fact that he doesn't owe his soul to some dealer."

Charlie was surprised Carter knew, but didn't comment.

"My brother Ted lives in Dallas and has a very lucrative medical practice, besides the money he gets from the corporation. He also—"

Charlie interrupted. "I know Ted. He's my wife's doctor, and the reason I'm even here. He recommended me to Jason, and I owe Ted a measure of loyalty for the kindness and care he gives her."

Now Carter seemed a little surprised at how their families were intertwined.

"I'm sorry your wife is ill," Carter said.

"Thank you," Charlie said. "I've been told that you and your sister, Dina, are often at odds. Is this true?"

Carter chuckled. "We've been fussing together since we began to walk. But it's nothing serious. Dina is spoiled. She was the only girl in the family and never wanted anything to do with the business side of the corporation. She's perfectly happy that Jason will be the next Dunleavy in the boss's chair."

"Jason is also the one who came looking for a private investigator," Charlie said. "He's worried about the falling prices of the market shares. He needs you—or a body—before the business implodes."

Carter sighed. "Understood, which is exactly what I would have done if I'd been in his shoes."

"What do you think of Dina's friend?" Charlie asked.

"Kenneth? I think he's a sponge who makes an attempt now and then at being a good guy, but he has no power in the family and never would, even if they were married," Carter said. "And of course, Edward is the last one I'd suspect. We're best friends and always have been. And he's blind."

"What are you going to do about this?" Charlie asked. "The police have to be informed that you're alive so they can end their search. You don't even want to know how much trouble Rom could be in for helping you do this."

"The chief of police is a friend. I'll make a call," Carter said.

"And I'll call Jason," Charlie said, "because he hired me and it's my job to let him know you've been found. Then it's up to you to tell him anything else you want him to know."

"Understood," Carter said again. "But I want to hire you

to find out who's trying to kill me. It's worth a million dollars to me."

There was a long moment of silence, and then Charlie cleared his throat.

"I identify the guilty party and you give me a million dollars?" he asked.

"Yes, but if that's not enough I—"

"It's enough," Charlie said. "I'll need a detailed account of all the incidents you believe were attempts on your life."

"Done. And I'll need your email address," Carter said.

"I'll have Rom text it to you. I have one more question. Are you going to stay hidden or are you coming home?"

"My instinct is to stay where I am," Carter said.

"Then there's another aspect to consider. Everyone is going to know you're alive now. And this could trigger your attacker to get serious and search you out. When the family finds out Rom helped you, will that give away where you are?" Charlie asked.

Rom had been completely silent until now, but the moment Charlie said that, he jumped up.

"Yes, it could," Rom said.

Carter heard him. "Rom's right. It could."

Charlie sighed. He'd taken this job because of Ted. He owed Dr. Dunleavy more than money. Ted was keeping Annie safe. The least he could do was keep Ted's brother safe until the guilty party was caught.

"I have a suggestion, if you're up for it," Charlie said.

"I'm open to anything," Carter told him. "I don't want to die."

"I'll take you to Dallas with me. I have a large apartment in a building with great security, and I have even more security in my apartment."

There was a long moment of silence before Carter asked, "Why would you do this?"

"Your brother. He's taking care of my Annie, so I'll take care of his brother until it's safe for you to go home."

Carter was silent again, obviously thinking, and then he spoke.

"So you live in Dallas?"

"Yes, but I flew here, and we can't fly back without giving you away. I'll have my assistant pick us up. She's a licensed pilot."

"She?" Carter said.

Charlie sighed. "Yes, and she's hell on wheels. And right now, my apartment is also my office, and she'll be there every day working. The building downtown where my office was located blew up due to a gas leak. The explosion took out a city block."

"I heard that on the news!" Rom said.

"What will she think about me in hiding at your place? Will she be frightened in any way?"

"Wyrick fears nothing," Charlie said.

"Wyrick? You call her by her last name," Carter said.

"Only because she refuses to answer to anything else. Look, you'll understand when you see her, but I'm telling you now, if you make even one joke about her appearance, I will toss you out of the chopper without a second thought."

Carter had to be wondering what he was getting himself into, but he must have decided it didn't matter if it kept him alive.

"It's a deal," he said.

"Is there room for a chopper to land where you are?" Charlie asked.

Rom tapped his shoulder. "Even better, there's a helipad, a hangar and a refueling station."

"Okay, Mr. Dunleavy, as soon as I coordinate a time with Wyrick, I'll let you know when to expect us," Charlie said. "You'll be off that mountain before sunset tomorrow."

"I can't thank you enough for this," Carter said.

"You're already thanking me to the tune of a million dollars. That's enough to satisfy me and take care of Annie. I'm going to tell Jason I found you as soon as we disconnect, then it will be up to you to call and say what you want to say. Just don't let on that you're leaving the state. Tell him you're in hiding and not coming back until I find out who's after you. I'll be in touch."

Charlie ended the call. "Now, Mr. Delgado, I'll need the address to find Carter on a map, so Wyrick can get a GPS location."

"Absolutely," Rom said. "It's on top of a mountain above Colorado Springs. I'll write it down for you."

They went back into the library, where Rom gave Charlie the info he needed, including Carter's phone number, and Charlie gave Rom his email address to pass on to Carter.

"This should do it," Charlie said. "And thank you."

"I was happy to be of service," Rom said. "I'll walk you to the door." As soon as they reached the front door, he shook Charlie's hand. "Thank you for helping my friend."

"It's what I was hired to do," Charlie said, and was back in his car within moments. As he was driving away, he called Jason, who answered on the second ring.

"Hello?"

"This is Charlie. I found your uncle."

Jason gasped. "Are you serious? Already! Where is he? Is he okay? What happened to him?"

"I'm going to let him fill you in on everything later. I told him I was calling you, and that it's up to him to tell you what he wants you to know. But he's safe and well."

"Oh, thank God!" Jason said. "I can't wait to share this with the family."

"Don't do that until after you talk to Carter."

"Why not?"

"You'll understand after you talk to him. I'll send you a final bill via email. Pleasure doing business with you," Charlie said and disconnected.

He glanced at the time. It was an hour later in Dallas, so it wouldn't be long before Wyrick would be leaving the office. He dug the address Delgado had just given him out of his shirt pocket and picked up his phone.

CHAPTER EIGHT

Wyrick had logged out of the computer and was closing down the office for the day, which also meant carrying the dishes she'd used to the dishwasher and starting it up. She was thinking about a long soak in the old claw-foot tub in her apartment when her cell phone rang. When she saw it was Charlie, she wiped her hands and answered.

"Dodge Investigations."

"It's me," Charlie said.

"I know. Caller ID. I'm simply being professional," Wyrick said, grinning to herself. She could just see Charlie rolling his eyes.

"Whatever. I found Carter Dunleavy. He was hiding out. Someone's trying to kill him. He thinks it's someone in his house," Charlie said.

"Whoa. That's cold," Wyrick said. "What are you going to do?"

"It's become necessary to move him from where he's hiding to a different location, so he's going to be staying at my place until we find out who's after him and why," Charlie said.

Wyrick was stunned, and the tone of her voice showed it. "Your place…as in here?"

"Yes. Is that a problem?" Charlie asked.

"No, nope, not at all. Just wondering why you suddenly decided to become a caretaker for your clients?"

"Carter's brother Ted is Annie's doctor. I owe him," Charlie said shortly. "I need to get Carter out of Colorado, but we can't use regular transportation without leaving a trail. I need you to—"

Wyrick interrupted. "Where do I pick you up?"

"I was about to tell you when you interrupted," Charlie said. "You'll need a chopper. Pick me up at the Denver airport. I'll turn in my rental car there. Then we're going to a place in the mountains above Colorado Springs to pick up Carter—"

"I have a chopper and you know it. I don't suppose you have coordinates…or a GPS location?" Wyrick said and then heard Charlie sigh.

"If you'd let me tell my story, you'd already have the address I was about to give you. I know you're perfectly capable of getting the GPS location to it yourself."

Wyrick didn't answer. She knew Charlie was pissed off at God, and pretty much the whole world for what had happened to Annie, but he never talked about it. So she was purposefully obstinate now and then just so he could let off a little steam.

"Are you still there?" Charlie asked.

"Obviously. I'm waiting for that address."

Charlie read it off to her, then listened to her read it back.

"Yes, that's it. Oh, there's a helipad and a refueling station where Carter's staying. When you have a time frame for picking me up at the airport, let me know."

"That was an unnecessary request," she said, and thought she heard a curse word a second before she hung up.

Since there would be company here tomorrow, she headed down the hall to the spare bedroom to check it out. The bed was made. There were clean towels in the guest bath, soap in the shower and an assortment of guest items in one of the drawers, including a new toothbrush and a tube of toothpaste. He was good to go.

She went back through the apartment, turning off lights, then grabbed her things and set the security alarm as she hurried out the door.

She glanced over her shoulder as she walked to the parking garage. She hated how this made her feel, and tried not to run.

When she finally stepped out into the garage, the heat from the wind slapped her in the face.

Texas in the summer never let a sun worshipper down.

Once she was inside the car with the cool air moving, she searched Spotify for music and went through her playlist for anything by Carrie Underwood to sing her home.

Humming under her breath, she took an on-ramp to get on the I-35 freeway and wasted no time melding with the speeding cars. She was thinking about what she needed to do regarding the flight tomorrow when she looked in the rearview mirror. The same gray sedan that had pulled onto the on-ramp behind her was still there. She frowned, then sped up and moved into a passing lane, shooting past six cars before getting back into one of the central lanes. She looked into the rearview mirror just as the same gray sedan pulled in behind her again.

"Damn it!" Wyrick muttered. "I am not in the mood for this. What do they think they're trying to prove? I know they're watching me. I know they're following me, and they know I know it. So is this a scare tactic, or are they waiting to see what it takes to really piss me off?"

She wasn't about to lead them to Merlin's, so she began signaling to get off at the next exit. She stayed far enough ahead to make the driver think she didn't realize he was there, then drove down the exit ramp to the stop sign and took a left.

Just as she suspected, the gray sedan exited, too. She kept driving, looking for a large parking lot or a mall. A few blocks farther, she noticed a large strip mall in the distance and gunned the engine, putting some distance between them as she whipped into the entrance. She took the first empty parking place she saw, which happened to be in front of a bakery, then got out, running over to a group of large shrubs a few feet away.

Within a few minutes, the same gray sedan pulled into the parking lot. She could see it going up and down the aisles looking for her car. She knew when he saw it because he sped up, then drove right past where she was standing, pulled up a few feet away from her bumper and got out. She watched him get down on one knee behind her bumper and put something beneath it, and as soon as his back was turned, she stepped out from behind the bushes and got a perfect shot of his car and the license plate. She ducked out of sight just before he got back in the car and drove away.

She watched him leave the parking lot first and came out of hiding, then went straight to her bumper and found a GPS tracker. She pulled it off and began looking for a place to plant it.

When a delivery van with a big happy face on the side parked in front of the Happy Face Florist, she considered it a sign. Her Happy the Clown game… Happy Face Florist. The moment the driver got out of the van and went inside, she ducked behind it, put the GPS tracker beneath the bumper and then went back to her car and drove home.

Mack Doolin was patting himself on the back for finally outsmarting Jade Wyrick. Cyrus Parks had been breathing down his neck because he'd been unable to find her after the explosion. Giving Parks this news was going to buy himself some breathing room. He made the call. The phone rang a couple of times, and then Parks answered.

"You better have good news for me," Cyrus said.

Mack laughed. "I do. I got a tracker on her car. She won't be so jumpy if she can't spot me in the traffic, plus I can follow her all the way to work and home without her knowing it."

"That is exceedingly good news," Cyrus said. "Well done. Your fee will be transferred in the morning. Stay on her. I want you to find out where she's living now."

"Will do. Have a great evening," he said.

Parks hung up without comment.

Mack frowned and then blew it off. He didn't want the man for a friend. It was all about the money.

Once Wyrick knew the jerk was off her tail for the evening, she drove straight to Merlin's. But it wasn't until she drove through the gate on her way to the house that she finally relaxed.

Merlin was outside puttering around a large flower garden as she pulled up and parked. She sat for a moment, watching him deadheading roses, and wondered if it was just coincidence that he looked like a Disney version of Merlin the magician. Maybe it was simply the long gray hair and the chin-length beard. Then she gathered the bag with her things and got out.

Merlin heard her slam the car door, looked up and waved. She waved back. Moments later, she was inside.

She turned the dead bolt, dumped her bags by her workstation and sat down at her computer. She logged in to get the GPS location for the address Charlie had given her, then got the flight coordinates.

"Child's play for a genetically modified genius," she murmured and picked up her phone to call her flight mechanic. After a couple of rings, he picked up.

"Hello."

"Benny, it's me. How long would it take you to get the Ranger ready for a flight out tomorrow morning?"

"Not long. I just finished a thorough overhaul yesterday. The engine is clean as a whistle. I refitted some seals, so all she'll need is fuel and the usual preflight check. How early do you plan to leave?"

"I'm going to say 8:00 a.m., and I'm flying to Colorado Springs. As soon as I've picked up passengers, I'll do a turnaround. Without any incidents, we should be back at the hangar shortly after noon."

"Yes, ma'am. I'll have it ready to go."

"Thanks, Benny. See you in the morning."

Having crossed that off her to-do list, she headed for her bedroom. Dinner would come later. She couldn't wait to get her makeup off and her clothes changed.

Jason didn't have long to wait for his uncle's call. Less than thirty minutes after his conversation with Charlie, his cell rang again. He didn't recognize the number.

"Hello?"

"Hey, Jason."

"Uncle Carter? Is this really you?"

"Yes, it's me. I owe you an explanation for scaring the family like this, but there was a reason, and at the time, disappearing was the only thing I could do until I had a chance to think."

"Oh, my God. I am so grateful to hear your voice. We've all been sick with worry. What the hell happened?"

"You know all those incidents I've been having…thinking I had food poisoning, slipping on that water at the top of the stairs, then having my brakes fail coming back from Ian Siegrid's after the wake?"

"Yes, but... Wait! What do you mean, *thinking* you had food poisoning?" Jason asked.

"Remember when they decided to keep me in the ER overnight, so I sent you home?"

"Yes, I remember, but you were released the next day and caught an Uber home without even calling us for a ride," Jason said.

"Only I didn't have food poisoning. When the tests finally came back, there were traces of arsenic in my system."

Jason gasped again. "Oh, my God! Are you serious? I can't believe this is happening. I would have sworn our employees were loyal to the bone."

"So would I, and later, after the car I wrecked was hauled away, I got a call telling me my brakes failed because someone had made a tiny cut in the brake line. I've also had that same car try to wreck me twice on the freeway. My home is no longer safe. Someone under my roof is trying to kill me."

Jason gasped. "No! I don't believe it! We would never—"

"I didn't mean to imply it was family. I said someone under my roof. There are ten to fifteen people there daily. Some on the grounds and some inside. I don't know who it is, but I just hired Charlie Dodge to find out."

Jason's voice was shaking. "Okay. But what do I tell the family? And what do I tell the police?"

"I'll call the police, and you can tell the family and staff the truth. Maybe it will trigger the guilty party to reveal himself. And tell the family I won't be taking calls. I can't use my cell phone without giving my location away."

"This is a nightmare, Uncle Carter. I'm sorry, so sorry this is happening. I'll make an announcement to the press tomorrow. At least this should settle the unrest in the corporation."

"You've done a fine job of holding down the fort. If you'll bear with me a bit longer, this should soon be over."

"We've got your back, Uncle Carter. Just stay safe."

The call ended. Jason was in shock. As he glanced up, he caught sight of himself in a mirror. He looked like he'd seen a ghost and he'd run his hand through his hair so many times during their conversation, that the cowlick at the crown of his head was standing at attention. He checked his watch, then called his secretary.

"Gloria, do I have any appointments?"

"No, sir. Your next appointment is at noon tomorrow. It's the charity luncheon at your golf club, remember?"

"Yes, right! Then I'm going home. I won't be back in the office until after the luncheon tomorrow."

"Yes, sir," she said. "Will that be all?"

"Yes, and thank you," he said.

Jason logged out of his computer, pocketed his phone and locked his daily planner in the desk. It was all part of his normal routine, but there was nothing normal about this day. They'd gotten their miracle, but at quite a price. Who the hell was responsible for this? Charlie Dodge was good—damn good. Maybe he'd pull off another coup and catch the sorry bastard who was doing this.

Jason left through a private elevator at the back of the office and went home. He couldn't wait to share the news.

Wyrick had hacking skills the government didn't even know existed, so running the plate on the car that had been following her was a piece of cake. Now she had a name, which made him her enemy. She had only two friends: Merlin and Charlie. Everyone else was either on her blacklist or her hit list. So far she'd only acted on the hit list in her dreams. But if they didn't back off, she wasn't making any promises.

"So, Mack Doolin, you've been made," she said.

She began taking his personal life apart, one website at a time, from being held back in fourth grade because he still couldn't read, to being kicked out of college for inciting a riot in his fraternity.

"Damn, Doolin. Just look at your bad self," Wyrick muttered, her fingers flying over the keyboard, clicking one site after another until the screen was full, and she'd come up to this very day and the credit card he'd used to buy gas—right before he began chasing her ass down I-35 again.

And through that gas purchase, she went to the credit card company, found the bank where he was a customer and saw the same money deposited into his account from a company she recognized all too well. It was a shell company belonging to Cyrus Parks and Universal Theorem.

Now that she knew for sure, she needed to decide what, out of several possibilities, she could do to cause trouble for UT.

Payback was a bitch.

But it would have to wait.

Charlie needed a ride.

Mack Doolin was congratulating himself on finally getting close enough to Jade Wyrick and her Mercedes to plant the tracking device. He woke up to a tidy sum added to his checking account and an ache for more. Now he needed to find out where she was living, and that bug he'd planted made it easy.

He started the morning with an iPad, a coffee to go and a bag of doughnuts as he headed for his car. As soon as he was inside, he activated the tracking app on the iPad and checked to see where she and her Mercedes were this morning.

Once the blip popped up on the screen, he fished a doughnut out of the sack, ate half of it in one bite and set out to find her.

It didn't take him long to realize she was hopping from one location to another with some rapidity, and figured she was running errands. He took a big swallow of coffee and finished off his second doughnut, then got serious about chasing her down, only it wasn't as easy as he'd assumed it would be.

Whenever he thought he was about to catch up, the blip would begin moving again. He'd speed up, knowing he'd spot the Mercedes soon, but it never happened.

And then the blip showed the car heading toward the freeway, and Doolin was certain then that he had her pegged. He took the on-ramp and shot through traffic, chasing the blip until he began to close the gap, positive he'd see the Mercedes. He planned to stay far enough behind that she'd never see him following her to work.

"Where are you, bitch? What have you and your fancy-ass car been up to this morning?"

He glanced down at the map on the screen, then changed lanes to get a better view of what was ahead of him—but there was no Mercedes. The app said she was there. She wasn't.

"What the hell?"

He accelerated into a passing lane, his focus on the traffic, and when he looked back down again and realized he was ahead of the blip, he glanced up into the rearview mirror. Still no Mercedes. Just a delivery van.

And that was when it hit him. All those stops he thought she'd been making. It wasn't her. It was this van!

"Son of a bitch! She not only found it, but planted it on another vehicle." He frowned. "Now what do I do?"

Jason drove home with mixed emotions. The family's elation would be short-lived when they heard the news, and he intended to make the announcement in front of family and employees alike. He could imagine the ensuing chaos. No one was getting a break when it came to being a suspect, although he'd bet his life there wasn't a single member of his family involved.

The closer he got, the more stressed out he became. He and

his mother had exchanged words last night. They had yet to kiss and make up and it wasn't likely that would happen anytime soon. Not with Kenneth feeding her irrational emotions.

Jason didn't get why Kenneth was doing that. His mother was so desperate for someone to take care of her and make her decisions that he didn't need to alienate her only son to do it. Jason would be more than happy to turn her mood swings over to a kind and loving companion. Not some sixtysomething dude looking for a permanent sugar mama.

Ah, well. That's for another day. Today's about the family revelation we prayed for.

He tapped the preprogrammed number to call home and waited for someone to answer. As he expected, it was Ruth.

"Dunleavy residence," she said.

"Ruth, it's me. Is the family home?"

"Yes, sir."

"How many members of the staff are on-site?"

"I'm not sure, because the gardening crew is here and they often vary."

"Okay. Whoever's there will suffice. I'll be home in about five minutes. Please notify the family to gather in the great room. Not the library, the great room. It's larger. And I want every member of the staff in there, too."

"At the same time?" Ruth asked.

"Yes, at the same time. I have an announcement to make."

"Yes, sir, right away," Ruth said, and as she disconnected, Jason was already planning how he'd break the news.

It pissed him off no end that his uncle felt he had to leave the safety of his own home to stay alive, and he intended to rake them all over the coals before he was done.

With that attitude in place, he turned up the drive toward home and drove behind the castle to the family parking garage.

This would put an end to Miranda using his missing uncle

as the excuse she needed to call him daily. They'd been seeing each other for almost a year, but she was getting too possessive and clingy. He needed to break it off with her. However, she was somewhere in Italy shopping for designer clothing and likely pretending she was someone other than the daughter of a butcher who'd turned his homemade sausages into a household name. Johannes's wealth funded her every desire, except Jason. He was the only thing her money couldn't buy.

He picked up his briefcase and, like all the family, went in through the kitchen. He liked seeing what was going on in the castle from the bottom up, and at the same time, get a whiff of what was cooking for dinner. Every evening, it was a game between him and their chef as to whether he could guess the entrée of the night. But Peter wouldn't be in there this evening. He'd be in the great room with the rest of the staff. Still, Jason sniffed the air and peeked in a couple of pots as he passed through.

When he finally arrived, the silence was telling. It was obvious his family didn't feel comfortable visiting among themselves in front of the staff, and the staff were just as uncomfortable mingling with the family.

When his mother saw him walk in, she stood abruptly, then started crying.

"You've come to tell us Carter is dead, haven't you?"

Kenneth immediately put an arm around her shoulders. "Don't borrow trouble, darling. Let's sit down and hear what he has to say."

Jason ignored his mother's outburst as he put his briefcase aside, then poured himself a shot of Irish whiskey and downed it straight.

"Yes, I have news. The man I hired to find Uncle Carter was successful. I got a call from him less than an hour ago. Uncle Carter is alive and well."

Jason knew his uncle Edward would be the first to raise a fist in victory, and he was.

"Thank God, thank God!" Edward cried, unashamed of the tears running down his cheeks.

His mother, Dina, was crying again, but this time they were happy tears. Even Kenneth seemed truly elated by the news.

The staff were celebrating in their own way, hugging and clapping each other on the back, smiling and nodding their heads in delight.

Jason let them have a moment, then raised his voice.

"May I have your attention, please?" And as the silence spread, he continued. "There's more. And I can't tell you how damn pissed off I am about it. The reason Uncle Carter disappeared was because he believes someone under his roof—and he meant the entire estate—is trying to kill him."

The gasp that ensued was so loud, Jason imagined he felt the oxygen being sucked out of the room. He thought his mother was going to faint, and every member of the staff was staring straight at him, as if they suddenly couldn't look into the eyes of the person standing next to them.

"No!" Edward cried. "I can't believe… I don't understand… Carter is the dearest man."

Jason went over to Edward and put a hand on his shoulder to console him.

"Yes, Uncle Edward, he's good to all of us, and we love him dearly. But in the business world, he has enemies. And if he's right, we'll find a connection between someone in this room or on the payroll for this estate who is connected to one of his known enemies, and when we do, heads are going to roll. I will show no mercy to the guilty parties or the families they leave behind when they realize they'll be spending the rest of their lives in jail."

Then Jason looked at the chef.

"It's prime rib with baby carrots and pearl onions."

The chef smiled. "Sir. I believe you peeked."

"Then I am right?" Jason asked.

"That you are," the chef said.

Jason nodded. "You can all go back to your duties now. Thank you for your patience, but don't forget what I said."

CHAPTER NINE

Carter Dunleavy was standing on the back deck of the cabin with a cold beer in his hand. He had yet to take a swallow, because he wanted a clear head to get this story told. He didn't know where Al Forsythe was at this moment, but he was calling him anyway, hoping the Denver police chief wouldn't let it go to voice mail.

Carter knew he had some big explaining to do, but his main focus was making sure Rom didn't wind up being blamed for anything other than doing his friend a favor. He set the bottle of beer on the deck railing and made the call. It rang and rang, and just when Carter feared it *was* going to voice mail, he heard the terse sound of Al's voice.

"Chief Forsythe."

"Hey, Al."

Forsythe's voice shifted into an angry rumble. "Who the hell is this?"

"Al, it's me, Carter."

"What the fuck? *Carter?* Where are you, how are you, and do you need help?"

"My location is still secret for the time being, but I won't be here much longer. Once the news gets out that I'm alive, it will alert the person or persons trying to kill me that I've come out of hiding. I'm fine. And I'm calling to beg your forgiveness for letting the ruse go on this long, but until recently, I was uncertain as to how to proceed."

"Someone's trying to kill you? And you don't feel confident that the entire police force in Denver, Colorado, can do anything about it?"

The anger in Al's voice was evident, and Carter couldn't blame him.

"It's not like that, Al. This has a more sinister undertone than even I first believed when the incidents began. I thought I had food poisoning, only to learn that the lab in ER found trace elements of arsenic in me. I've slipped on water at the very top of the stairs, and avoided breaking my neck by making one desperate grab at the stair rail. And the wreck I had just below the Siegrid home wasn't an accident. I found out later my brake line had been cut. And there were other, earlier things that I chalked up to my imagination. Until they upped their game…"

"The hell you say," Al muttered. "But you could still have trusted us. We would've put a twenty-four-hour guard around your house."

"That's just it, Al. At this point, I'm convinced it is someone on my estate who's doing this. I don't know if there's a personal agenda, or if they took money from one of my business enemies to kill me. I've done business with many people and made enemies along the way. Enemies who wouldn't shed a tear at my demise. So at this point, the most dangerous place for me to be is home."

"Well, that does screw the pooch," Al said.

Carter grinned. The euphemism was military slang from an old Tom Wolfe novel.

"To put it bluntly, yes, it does, and I have a favor to ask.

You're going to find out that Rom Delgado helped me escape Denver, but at the time, he thought he was only helping me hide. He didn't realize the extent of what my disappearance would do, but I did. It's all on me, and I'm asking for understanding and forgiveness. I owe a lot of cops an apology, too, and whatever man-hours it cost, counting overtime, plus bonuses for the cops and a generous donation to the orphans' fund. I will pay and gladly."

Carter knew that paying back the costs of a false police report was the usual penalty, plus discretion by the judge as to whether jail time would be served. But he figured no one would be putting him in jail for hiding from a killer.

"Yes, yes, I'll certainly pass the message along. Does Jason know?"

"Yes, he just found out," Carter said.

"Who told him?" Al asked.

"The man my nephew hired to find me. His name is Charlie Dodge, out of Dallas, and he is one hell of an investigator. I haven't met him, but I spoke to him. He's been working with your detective who is in charge of the investigation, so he hasn't been going rogue on any of this. Maybe you could call my nephew now. Maybe the two of you could hold some kind of press conference. Work out what you want to say, because if I can't go home, then I'm damn sure not coming back to Denver. I like to hunt ducks, but I don't intend to become a sitting duck for the hunter who's after me."

"Okay, and understood," Al said. "It took you long enough, but I'm glad to hear your damn voice. Next time we go to dinner, it's steak at your house. I've heard your chef, Peter, is Cordon Bleu all the way."

Carter laughed. "It's a deal, and thank you again for understanding. I would appreciate it if you'd call Rom and assure him he's not in any legal trouble, and that I misled him in my intentions."

"Yes, I can do that, but not until after the news conference," Al said.

"That's fair. I hope to see you soon," Carter said and disconnected.

Once Charlie got back to the hotel, he made a courtesy call to Detective Cristobal as well, but he'd already been contacted by Chief Forsythe. Charlie thanked Cristobal for being so cooperative and ended it there.

Hours later, he was in bed, half-asleep and trying—not for the first time—to watch the end of *Transformers: The Last Knight* before turning out the lights. Just as they were getting to the climax, his cell signaled a text. It was from Wyrick.

Barring complications, I'll pick you up at Denver International at 10:00 a.m. I'll text once I'm on the ground to tell you where. I'll be refueling there before pickup. Bring me a coffee and anything resembling a sweet roll.

Charlie blinked. "Damn woman."

He rolled over, set the alarm on his cell phone, allowing himself plenty of time to get to the airport and turn in his rental, then, God forbid he should forget, pick up refreshments for the pilot. When he looked back up at the TV, he realized the movie was over and he still didn't know how it ended.

So he sent a text to Carter Dunleavy, telling him the plan as it stood, and that he would call him again from the airport when they were en route to Colorado Springs.

Wyrick had dressed purposefully for the flight this morning. Her eye makeup was purple to match the formfitting purple leather she was wearing. She had long since been unable to startle Charlie with her getup, but she didn't dress to shock him anymore. It was just who she'd become. This morning, she would get her boss back, and breakfast to boot.

She left the apartment as the sun was coming up, feeling a sense of anticipation. She didn't mind spending the day in the air. Keeping an ever-cautious watch on her rearview mirror, she arrived at the private airport where she stored her Ranger, certain she hadn't been tailed. Benny was standing in the open doorway of the hangar, and the Ranger was out and ready for her.

She parked her Mercedes inside, set its security alarm and walked back out.

"Morning, Benny," she said.

"Morning, ma'am. Nice duds."

She grinned. Benny didn't give a shit about how she looked, which made her feel easier around him.

"I do what I can," she said.

"And you do fine. She's fueled up and ready to go. I'll walk with you through preflight check, in case you see something you don't like."

Wyrick tossed her bag in the back of the chopper before beginning her inspection. Once she was satisfied all was well, she slid into the pilot's seat to do a final run-through, then started the engine.

She put her headset on for radio contact, adjusted the fit and gave Benny a thumbs-up as she revved the engine. Once she reached maximum lift, she went straight up and made a quick half circle to get her bearings. Then she headed north for Denver.

The flight chatter on the headset was normal as she checked in with air traffic control at Denver Airport, informing them she was in the air.

They radioed back with an altitude setting, and told her they had her on radar.

Wyrick was good to go.

She was flying with the early-morning sun on her right, glancing every now and then at the panel before her, making sure there were no surprises brewing.

As she flew, her thoughts slipped back to when she began taking flying lessons, and how unhappy Universal Theorem had been with her for taking risks with her life when her work for them was so important.

She'd told them then, in a calm, steady voice, which they knew was the only warning they'd get before she reached meltdown, that she gave every waking hour of six straight days to the company, and that they didn't fucking own her—although she didn't really know at the time that they sort of did—but they acquiesced.

She blinked, coming out of that memory to ensure she was still on course, and popped a stick of gum in her mouth to keep from gritting her teeth.

Her life would make a damn fine suspense movie if the viewers were ready to suspend disbelief. She'd suspected some of what had happened, but never in a million years would she have believed the depths of what they'd done. All she knew was that the world as she'd known it had died on the day of the clowns.

It was how she'd compartmentalized the day her mother was murdered, and when she went to live with Cyrus Parks, the man who'd "rescued" her from the clowns and who claimed to be her father.

The men in clown costumes were blamed for her mother's murder, supposedly killing her in the act of trying to abduct Jade. They were arrested, arraigned and then conveniently died in jail before they ever made it to trial. It was all too neat for her peace of mind.

Wyrick shelved the memories, although they never really went away. She existed because of the madness of men and of science—a fact she couldn't outrun.

When she finally reached the airspace of Denver International, she radioed in for landing instructions. After she'd landed and was on the ground waiting for refueling, she called Charlie.

He answered on the second ring.

"Your ride is here," she said. "Do you have my breakfast?"

"Yes, I have your food. How do I get to you?"

"I have it covered. Write down this number."

"Wait a damn minute while I put your breakfast down," he muttered.

She grinned, but only because he couldn't see her.

"Okay, I'm ready," he said.

She rattled off a number, then followed up with instructions.

"Call that number. Someone from Airport Personnel will ask for your location, then they'll get you and escort you to where I am. As soon as we're refueled, we'll be out of here."

"Thanks. See you—" The line went dead.

"Shit. She hung up on me again," he grumbled, and resisted the urge to drop her breakfast in the trash.

Instead, he called the number, and before he was over his disgust, he was on his way to meet her, carrying the breakfast in one hand and pulling two piggybacked suitcases with the other. The young man from Personnel who accompanied him had little to say.

When he finally saw Wyrick in all that purple leather, standing beside the chopper with her hands on her hips in a "what took you so long" stance, he wondered what Carter was going to think of her. A couple of minutes later he handed her the coffee and a sack.

"Here's your breakfast."

She accepted the bag and the large cup of coffee, peeled off the lid and gulped some down.

"It's still warm, too. Thanks. I'm starved."

He frowned. "Why didn't you eat before you left?"

She'd already taken a bite of a cheese Danish, so she chewed and swallowed before answering.

"Because I didn't want to be late and let you down." Then she took another big bite, closing her purple-lidded eyes in sugar ecstasy, and chewed unselfconsciously in front of him.

In that moment, Charlie realized that as aggravating as she could be at times, she had never let him down. She went above what the job required whenever he asked without complaint. He should probably calm down a bit when she started needling him. He knew she wasn't cruel in any sense of the word. She just got under his skin, and the moment he thought that, it startled him. He'd didn't realize it was that personal.

Then she took another bite of the Danish, and as she did, a large flake of the icing caught on the edge of her lower lip. He started to point it out and then stopped. In staring at the sugar, he had unintentionally looked—really looked—at her mouth. He'd never bothered to examine that part of her before, because what came out of it usually bugged the hell out of him. But now that she wasn't talking, he was shocked to see how pretty it was. Really full, sensual lips.

"What are you staring at?" she snapped.

He blinked. "That big piece of sugar hanging on your lip. I'm making bets with myself as to whether you'll feel it and catch it, or it falls off without you knowing it was there."

Now Wyrick was the one staring, momentarily speechless. She snaked her tongue out and licked her lower lip, found the sugar and sucked it into her mouth and let it melt on her tongue…and obviously didn't see the shock that flashed in Charlie's eyes.

"Thanks. I would've hated to miss that," she said and dug into the sack again. "Thanks for bringing two when I only asked for one," she added.

"I'll deduct it from your Christmas bonus," he said.

She grinned.

Charlie wasn't sure he'd ever seen her grin before, either. Hell, this was a morning for surprises.

"When can we leave?" he asked.

She held up a finger and circled the chopper to talk to the guy refueling the tanks, then came back.

"He said about five more minutes and we'll be clear to fly."

"Then I'm calling Carter, so he'll have an idea of how soon we'll be there. How long do you think it will take?"

"Oh, probably twenty or so minutes by air."

"That close?" he said.

"Only as the crow flies. Or the chopper… You'd be driving mountain roads for a good two hours, maybe more, since you said it was on the top."

He nodded, then walked a distance away to make the call.

She watched him without thought as she downed the second sweet roll, and was fine until she focused on his wide shoulders, the narrow waist and muscular backside and legs. That was when she closed her eyes and turned her back on him to finish eating. Even though she had a lump in her throat. Even though she had to wash her last bite down with coffee that had finally gone cold.

Before he was through talking, the tanks had been topped up. She did a quick check of the chopper itself, and by the time she was through, he was at the passenger's-side door.

"Are we ready?" he asked.

She nodded. "Get in."

He tossed his suitcases in the back, then climbed into the passenger seat and shut the door. He was reaching for a headset as she got into the pilot seat.

He glanced at her again, but she was down to business as

she fired up the engine, then adjusted her headset and contacted the tower.

As soon as she achieved takeoff power, they were up and off. Now she was flying due south with the sun on her left.

Charlie seemed thoughtful, with little to say, which suited Wyrick fine. Neither one was interested in chitchat, so she left him alone.

Buddy Pierce was walking out of his house to his car when his cell phone rang. He checked the caller ID, then got in the car and started it before answering.

"What now?" he said.

"Carter Dunleavy has been found. He's onto us, too. He was in hiding."

"Is he coming home?" Buddy asked.

"Not yet. Not until they find who's behind the attacks."

Buddy frowned. "That's not good news. How am I supposed to finish the job now?"

"I don't know. I'm just giving you an update. If I hear anything different, you'll be notified."

"Okay. I'll be ready when you are."

The caller disconnected.

Buddy Boy drove away. Right now he had other business to attend to.

Carter Dunleavy was packed and ready to go, although he was going to miss the quiet and solitude of this place. He did one last walk-through of the house, making sure he hadn't left anything behind and taking care to leave it as pristine as when he'd arrived. He'd already emptied the leftover milk down the sink, brought the leftover food into the forest for the animals to eat, making sure not to leave anything near the house that would draw a bear's attention.

Now that he was finished, he carried his bags out to a bench in the shade of the small hangar. It was where he'd parked the car Rom had lent him to drive up here. He waited, watching the skies. When he finally saw the chopper coming, his stomach knotted. This was the next step he had to take, even if it took him farther away from home.

As it came closer, he stood. And when it got close enough to identify, he realized it was a Bell jet. The chopper looked like one of the Long Rangers, and it was coming in hot, although when the pilot went from flight mode to landing, it was done with finesse. That was when Carter remembered Charlie's pilot was a woman.

He couldn't see much of anything until the skids were on the helipad. The rotors were still spinning, but at a lower speed as two people got out and came to meet him. He picked up his bags and started toward them, but his eyes were on the pilot, and all he could think was that Charlie had found his own version of Wonder Woman.

She was a good six feet tall. No hair, but the most striking face he'd seen on a woman in years. And then he realized she had no breasts, and all of a sudden the missing hair made sense. She wasn't just some man's wet dream. She was a *warrior* in a whole other sense of the word.

"Good morning, Carter. Are you ready for your ride?" Charlie asked.

Carter shifted focus to get a better look at Charlie Dodge. Finally, he had a face to go with the voice. "I'm grateful for your help and ready for whatever play you call next."

"Good. This is Wyrick, our pilot, but as I told you, also my assistant."

Wyrick nodded.

Carter smiled at her. "She's also a damn beautiful woman, but you neglected to mention that. Ma'am, it's a pleasure to meet you, and I am grateful to you, as well."

Wyrick's mouth opened, but she was so clearly surprised

by what he'd said that she probably expected him to laugh it off as some kind of a joke. And then she must have realized he was serious.

"Since you're the first man who's hit on me in a while, I'll give you a pass for the unnecessary compliment. It will not, however, get you to Dallas any faster, so I suggest we all do something useful, like loading your dandy little ass into my chopper so we can be on our way."

Charlie must have seen the startled look on his face and arched an eyebrow, as if to remind Carter he'd been warned, but he barely noticed the gesture. He was busy grabbing suitcases and following Wyrick like a scolded child trying to get back in his mama's good graces while Charlie brought up the rear.

As soon as they'd stowed luggage and settled him into a window seat in back, Wyrick flashed him one more hard look.

"Do you get airsick, Mr. Dunleavy?" she asked.

"No."

"Okay, but don't try to be a hero. There's a bottle of Dramamine in the pocket on the back of my seat. If you throw up in my chopper, you get to clean it up."

"Yes, ma'am," Carter said and buckled himself in.

Charlie closed the doors on his side and got in. Wyrick was already in her seat, headset on, buckled and ready for takeoff.

"Buckle up, Boss," she said.

They went straight up and made a little circle in the air as she got her bearings. "Next stop, Dallas."

CHAPTER TEN

Back in Denver, sunrise in the Dunleavy household came with mixed feelings. They gathered for breakfast knowing Carter was alive and well, but somber at the thought of why he'd left so abruptly.

"Good morning, family," Jason said as he walked into the room.

Edward was carefully dipping a corner of his toast in his coffee and then eating it. A habit he'd had since childhood.

"Good morning, Jason," Edward said in return.

Jason grinned. "Hey, Uncle Edward. Don't you think you might try a little jelly on that toast at least once?"

Edward chuckled. "You know I like coffee toast better. What are you having?"

"I'm going for bacon and waffles. But I'm having maple syrup, not coffee, on mine," Jason said, as he began filling his plate from the buffet on the sideboard.

"You don't know what you're missing!"

Jason laughed. "Oh, you forget. I know exactly what I'm missing. I believe I was about ten when I finally asked you for a taste. You dunked that toast for me and I took a bite.

Never wanted to spit food out as badly as I did that toast, but I chewed and swallowed it anyway because I'd asked for it."

Edward shook his head. "I remember. That was before I lost my sight. I watched your face, and I knew you didn't like it. But you took it like a man and swallowed it. I knew then you'd grow up into a person who kept his word."

Jason patted his uncle's arm. "Thank you, Uncle Edward. I'd like to think you helped me grow into the man I am."

Edward sighed. "Given that I was never to father children, it was a joy to be with you."

Jason guessed that Dina was tired of the conversation being about someone besides her, judging by the way she greeted her son's arrival.

"Good morning, darling," Dina said, giving him a big smile.

"Morning, Mother. You're looking lovely this morning. What do you have planned for the day?" he asked, and forked two waffles, a pat of butter and a serving of bacon onto his plate, then poured maple syrup over the lot and sat down.

Dina eyed his food choices, but said nothing. Jason was still toned and fit, so all those carbs and sugars likely wouldn't do him any harm. And he did have bacon, so there was protein.

"Mother?" Jason said.

Dina looked up. "What, dear?"

"I asked what you were doing today, since you're all dressed up."

"Oh, I'm sorry, I guess I was off in my own little world for a moment." She reached over and patted Kenneth's shoulder. "Kenny and I are going window-shopping," she said. "Aren't we, lovey?"

Jason was chewing bacon, and watching the smirk on Kenneth's face as she called him lovey. He looked all too pleased with himself, which suddenly put Jason on money alert.

"Oh, shopping for anything special?" he asked, and cut a piece of waffle and popped it in his mouth.

Dina batted her eyes before she answered, and when her gaze shifted to the side of his face instead of meeting his eyes, he knew she was about to spend a boatload of money on Kenneth. It was no business of his what she did with her money, and Lord knew they all had more than they could ever spend, but he hated her being used like this. She had yet to answer.

Suddenly, Kenneth answered for her, as if he couldn't wait to get in a little dig at Jason.

"Your mother is buying me a car for my birthday. She is so amazing. I am such a lucky man."

Dina flushed, highlighting the faint sprinkling of freckles across her nose. "I want you to have it, so that's the end of that," she said.

Jason kept eating without comment. He didn't even ask what kind, which rankled Kenneth just enough that he told them anyway.

"We're going to look at Aston Martins. I've always had a fancy for a British-made car, and those suit me."

Jason nodded, and even though it was killing him not to comment, he never looked up.

Edward, oblivious to the sidelong glances and studied silences at the table, picked up the conversation.

"Jason, where are we on revealing the news of Carter's disappearance?"

"I'm not sure, but I'm going to phone Chief Forsythe this morning to see if he's planned a news conference yet. I want to be there to issue a statement on behalf of the corporation."

"Good idea." Edward nodded. "The news should settle the rumors and ease up on the falling stock prices."

"That would be my hope."

"If a time is settled on for today, do call home and let us know. I'd like to listen to it," Edward said.

"Of course I will," Jason told him as he continued eating.

Dina and Kenneth excused themselves first and left the room.

Edward soon gave up on his coffee toast and opted to go outside in the back courtyard and get a bit of sun. He mentioned that he thought he'd heard lawn mowers running earlier, and he did enjoy the scent of freshly cut grass.

That left Jason to finish up alone, which suited him fine. He got up to refill his coffee and served himself another couple of bacon slices to finish the meal.

By the time Edward came in from outdoors, Jason was gone. The room was empty, the dishes all cleared away, and he was ready for a morning nap on the daybed in his room, beneath a soft throw of Dunleavy plaid.

After everything else that was going down today, Jason had canceled his appearance at the proposed luncheon that was supposed to be today and was going back into the office to tie up a few loose ends. His. phone rang as he was driving. He took the hands-free call while negotiating around a wreck at an intersection.

"Hello, Jason speaking."

"Jason, this is Chief Forsythe."

"Chief, I was going to call you as soon as I got to the office, but you beat me to it."

"Oh, are you in traffic? I can call back," Forsythe said.

"No, I'm fine. Hands-free calling, you know."

"I guess," Forsythe said. "I'm no good with all that new technology. Look, the reason I'm calling is I'm setting up a news conference about Carter's situation. I'd like you to be there, as well. I'm sure the press will have questions that you'll be better suited to answer. I understand the delicacy of what's going on with this, and wasn't sure how you wanted to proceed."

"Yes, I'd like to be there. What time have you set aside, and where is it going to be held?"

"I'm thinking eleven o'clock this morning, on the courthouse steps. That gives us a better angle for the cameras if they're below us, and it's easier to see reporters' hands up for questions."

"Obviously, you're on top of how to set up a news conference to focus on what needs to be said. I'll get there ahead of time. Shall I meet you in the courthouse lobby?"

"Yes, that will be perfect, and we can walk out together from the front doors. See you then."

Jason disconnected with a tap of his finger and glanced at his dashboard clock. He'd only have about an hour at the office before he'd have to leave again. But this time he shouldn't be gone long. Work was piling up and he hated to fall behind.

And—of course—because Jason was in a hurry, traffic delayed his morning drive. He ended up taking a different exit just so he could get out of the snarl of angry drivers and speeding vehicles, and was still winding his way through city streets when his cell phone rang again. He tapped his Bluetooth to take the call before he thought to see who was calling.

"This is Jason," he said shortly.

"Darling, it's me! Are you on your way to work?"

Jason sighed. Shit.

"Yes, actually I am, and I'm in something of a hurry, sorry to say."

"That's perfect, then. We can chat during your drive without interrupting your day. I called to tell you I think I've found the perfect dress. I'm so excited."

"Perfect dress for what?"

She giggled. "Our wedding, you silly."

Jason's gut knotted. He'd let this get completely out of hand.

"Look, Miranda. We date. We've never talked about marriage. *You* talk about marriage. I did not give you an engagement ring. I did not propose. You're moving out of my comfort zone here."

There was a long moment of silence, and then another giggle, a halfhearted one.

"Oh, well, silly me. Then enough about shopping. Is there any news about Uncle Carter?"

Shit again. He was not her "uncle Carter." Jason felt like telling her about his uncle right now. She was in Italy, so it wasn't like she could go shout it in the streets before the news conference. Maybe if he did, she wouldn't have an excuse to keep checking in about Carter's disappearance.

"Actually, Chief Forsythe and I will be having a news conference later this morning, and with good news. But that's all I can say until an official announcement is made."

Miranda squealed in his ear. "That's wonderful! I won't press you for more, but I'm going to take this as *very* good news, and be grateful you shared it with me. I'm always in your corner. I don't want to be a bother, my love. I'll say goodbye and I'll see you soon. Since I jumped the gun on a bridal wardrobe, I'll be coming back a little sooner than planned. See you then. Love you much."

Jason ended the call with a frown and gave himself a talking-to. "I guess I'm going to have to give up good sex for the sake of my peace of mind. It's not a discussion I look forward to having, but I started it, so I'm the one who'll have to end it."

Whenever Chief Forsythe called a news conference, it always stirred all kinds of speculation as to why, but considering the continuing mystery about Carter Dunleavy's disappearance, most of the gathering media were guessing it had to do with that.

They were all at the foot of the courthouse steps, getting microphones set up and making sure they had a good view of the podium where the chief would stand to speak. One of the later-arriving news vans pulled up and began unloading equipment. A cameraman shouldered his camera for the live feed.

It was ten minutes to eleven when news began to spread through the gathering crowd that someone had seen Jason Dunleavy going into the courthouse through a side entrance. The news solidified their suppositions. This was about Carter Dunleavy. But was the news good or bad?

Jason called home to let his family know the news conference was being aired at eleven, and then got out of his car and headed into the building. Chief Forsythe was in the lobby when Jason appeared, and smiled as they shook hands.

"This is one news conference I'll be happy to hold," Forsythe said. "Good news is rare in my business."

Jason grimaced. "And a blessing for us. We were beginning to fear all hope was lost, but we never would've dreamed the answer would be something like this."

"I can only imagine. So, how far are you going to go with the revelation?"

"Uncle Carter said tell the truth. He said maybe it'll force the guilty party's hand in one last-ditch effort and he'll get himself caught."

The chief nodded in agreement. "This is going to open a whole new can of worms for us, but if that's what it takes, we're behind you one hundred percent. I'll make the announcement and then turn it over to you to add details. Okay?"

"Okay. Let's get this rolling. Obviously, it's not a pleasant subject for our family. Everyone is tense, and the staff is uncomfortable and silent around us. No one knows quite how to approach this. Maybe once I get this said, the knot in my stomach will go away," Jason said.

The chief gave him a thump on the shoulder, and then they were on the move. A couple of uniformed officers walked out ahead of them, and as Chief Forsythe and Jason Dunleavy exited together, they were soon flanked by a half-dozen detectives from Missing Persons. Off to the side, but included in the group, was Detective Cristobal, who'd been the lead on the case.

The hush that came over the crowd as the men descended the steps made Jason even more anxious, but if this—the one thing he could do for Uncle Carter and the family—brought justice, it would be worth it.

Chief Forsythe was imposing as he stepped up to the podium. He adjusted the microphone to his height, cleared his throat and then looked up and out at the crowd. There were far more people gathered than just media by now. Watching him, Jason couldn't help but wonder if the person or persons they sought were standing in that crowd.

And then Forsythe began.

"Thank you for coming, and I'm going to make this brief. Due to combined efforts of the police department for the city of Denver, including Detective Cristobal of Missing Persons, who was lead on the case, and Private Investigator Charlie Dodge, who was hired by the family a few days ago to aid in our search, I am happy to announce that Carter Dunleavy has been found and is alive and well."

The crowd cheered. Cameras were rolling and Forsythe held up his hand for silence.

"I am now going to turn the dais over to Jason Dunleavy, who has more to add to the story, so please hold your questions until he finishes."

Jason stepped up as the chief moved aside. He had a speech he'd prepared, but he'd already decided that reading what he had to say would lessen the impact. He wanted to be looking into the cameras focused on his face, counting on those responsible to learn that their little reign of terror was coming to an end.

"Good morning," Jason said. "Before I start, I want to take this time to thank all the people who've sent notes to our family, who've posted positive messages to us on social media and who have been praying for my uncle's safe return. The fact that he's alive and well was such a wonderful message to receive, and when he finally called me, and I heard his voice, I knew it was the truth.

"But there's a very startling, even horrifying reason he disappeared so abruptly, and it's something he hadn't shared with anyone. Not even us, his family. Carter Dunleavy ran because someone is trying to kill him. And the reason he didn't let anyone in on this is because he firmly believes the person responsible lives or works under his own roof. He hid because he no longer knew who he could trust."

The gasps of disbelief were followed by shouts from the media, asking to be recognized. Questions were being thrown at him from all sides, but Jason stood within his own silence until he was calm enough to speak in a civil tone.

Finally, he pointed at one of the journalists in front. "You, ma'am, in the blue suit."

"Katie Powers from the *Denver Post*. How will the rest of this investigation proceed? Is Mr. Dunleavy going to stay in hiding, and is your private investigator going to be part of the ongoing case?"

"My personal dealings with Mr. Dodge came to an end when he found my uncle, which is what I hired him to do. However, it is my understanding that Uncle Carter has asked Mr. Dodge to stay on the case on his behalf."

Jason pointed to another journalist and then another and another, each time answering without giving anything away, and when the question finally arose as to exactly what attempts had been made on Carter's life, he stopped the questioning.

"I'm not going to divulge any further information about

an ongoing investigation. My family thanks you, and I thank you for appreciating just how intensely these accusations have affected us. I ask for your continued support and prayers for my uncle until this nightmare has ended."

Then he stared straight ahead, into the cameras down below him. "Make no mistake. You will be caught. You will be brought to justice, and no mercy will be shown to any others involved."

Questions were still coming at him as he turned away from the bank of microphones, shook hands with Chief Forsythe, then had a private word and a handshake with Detective Cristobal before going back up the steps and into the courthouse.

Chief Forsythe ended the conference with one last thank-you and followed Jason's retreat.

Buddy Boy Pierce caught a news flash, while he was having a late breakfast at a little diner, that Chief Forsythe would be holding a news conference at 11:00 a.m. today, and that it was regarding the disappearance of Carter Dunleavy. That was less than an hour and a half away, and it was something he didn't want to miss. As soon as he finished his food, he drove back home to watch.

He was ready and waiting when it began—and when it was over, he was more rattled than he wanted to admit. He'd felt that face-to-face warning from Jason Dunleavy. And the fact that the PI found Carter so quickly when the police hadn't meant he was damn good at his job.

And now, knowing that Carter had just hired him to find the people behind the attacks made Buddy feel damn vulnerable. Yes, he'd once cut a brake line, and he'd cut him off in traffic a couple of times in hopes he'd wreck. But none of those actions would lead Carter to believe it was someone in his household. Buddy was beginning to wonder what the hell else was going on inside that castle that he didn't know about. He had his contact there, but as far as he could tell, that contact was not culpable in any attacks. And Buddy didn't count on being blamed for stuff he didn't do. He was still in a quandary when his cell phone rang.

"Hello."

"It's me, calling to tell you that Jason Dunleavy just—"

Buddy interrupted. "I saw it all. What I want to know is, who the hell else is working this besides me?"

"I don't have a clue what—"

The denial hit Buddy wrong. "Bullshit!" he shouted. "I'm not stupid. Nothing I did would give Dunleavy the idea that it was someone under his roof. I'm done with this and with you. I don't want anything more to do with this. I don't want that hotshot PI from Dallas on my trail. I'm out."

"You can't—"

"Yes, I can, and I just did," Buddy said and disconnected.

The remaining Dunleavys were still gathered around the television in the media room, humiliated that their family drama was being played out in such a public forum. Dina began wondering if she would be judged by the friends in their social circles, and Kenneth was concerned on Dina's behalf.

Edward had no concerns as to how he would be viewed. Most of the world had forgotten he existed.

The house staff had gathered in the kitchen to watch, as had a couple of gardeners.

Once, they'd been proud of working at the castle and being part of the extended service that kept the Dunleavy family in the luxury into which they'd been born. But now, because of this, there was a level of shame and distrust aimed at all of them. Until the guilty were found and arrested, every member of the staff was a suspect.

Several of the women were in tears. The men were red

faced and silent. And when the conference was over, they all looked at each other, nodded cordially and went about their business.

Only one in the group was long past nervous and drowning in guilt. *Why did I let myself become involved? No matter what happens now, my life is over.*

After staring at the back of Wyrick's bald head for the better part of thirty minutes, Carter Dunleavy finally fell asleep.

Wyrick was all business. She took a bottle of water Charlie quietly offered and drank her fill before handing it back.

"Thanks," she said.

"No problem," he said, then leaned against the headrest and closed his eyes, thinking about seeing Annie again. He opened them once when they hit a little air pocket, but one glance at the stoic expression of Wyrick's profile, and he relaxed.

He had expected the flight to take longer, but when she began contacting the control tower at Dallas International Airport to request landing instructions, he realized they were nearly home.

Carter roused when the chatter from tower to pilot began and he sat up, rubbing the sleep from his eyes as he looked out the side window. He'd seen Dallas from the air plenty of times, flying in and out because of his businesses, but he'd never spent one moment of his life in someone else's home. It had always been hotels, meeting rooms, conference rooms in big buildings. The fact that Charlie Dodge had extended the safety and comfort of his own home wasn't lost on Carter. He'd just met him, but he had a feeling that one day they were going to become fast friends.

And while Carter was thinking about friendship, Charlie was thinking about his car in airport parking, and wondering if he should have suggested Carter disguise himself in some way. Suddenly Wyrick's voice was in his ear.

"There's a small brown bag behind my seat. It has some things you might suggest Carter use to disguise himself until you get him home."

Charlie stared. "I was regretting I hadn't thought of that sooner. Once again, you have my back. Remind me to give you that raise."

He distinctly heard Wyrick snort. "I don't need a raise. Hand him the bag and see what you two can figure out. I'll be leaving you both on your own as I take my chopper back to the hangar, and believe me, that thought is not encouraging."

Charlie laughed, which startled her, because he usually took offense at everything she said. She frowned. She did not want him amused. She needed him to stay pissed. It would not be good to be friends, so she ignored both of them for the rest of the flight. Besides, other than requesting another guide from Airport Personnel to walk them out of the landing area, her job was done.

Charlie heard her setting up the escort as he was helping Carter, and for the first time since she'd walked into his office to apply for the job opening, he felt nothing but respect for the woman she was.

Once she landed, she kept the rotors spinning and got out long enough to help them unload.

Carter paused. "Thank you for this," he said.

"Thank Charlie," Wyrick said with a shrug. "He's the one who sent me."

"This way," Charlie said as the guide picked up one of their bags to lessen their load. He got Carter started, then turned around.

"See you at the apartment tomorrow. You can take the rest of today off."

"Is your client safe yet?"

"You know he's not."

"Then I'll be back at your apartment later," she said and got into the chopper before he could argue.

Charlie hefted the suitcases he was carrying, and hurried to catch up while Wyrick focused on taking off.

She flew straight back to her hangar, landing a little after 1:30 p.m.

Benny came out as she began to descend. The moment the skids touched the landing strip, she started shutting everything down. There was a pain between her shoulder blades, another throbbing between her temples, and the knot in her belly wasn't anywhere close to easing.

Part of it was tension from the flight up and the turnaround so close behind. Part of it was thinking about being in the same apartment with both Charlie and Dunleavy and trying to work, but most of it was what was happening to the wall she'd built between her and the boss.

It didn't feel as high as it once had, and she needed the separation. There was no room in her life for attachments, even friendship. It was far easier to stay grounded when she wasn't focused on anything but survival.

Damn Charlie Dodge. He got under my skin when I wasn't looking.

All she could do now was maintain her usual distance. The good thing about wishes and broken hearts—they were hidden from view.

She got out, stretching tired muscles as she took a big breath of Texas air. Even though she was too far away to get a scent of the city, she imagined a faint smell of woodsmoke and barbecue.

"Did you have a good flight?" Benny asked.

"Yes. The pickup and delivery were both successful. I'll be heading out as soon as I get my car."

"Yes, ma'am, and I'll get the Ranger cleaned up, serviced and pulled back inside. Have a safe trip to the city."

Wyrick put all her things inside a shoulder bag and went

into the hangar to get her car. A couple of minutes later she emerged, shifted into a higher speed and took off from the landing strip like a bullet shot from a gun.

Charlie and Carter caught an airport van that took them to where he'd parked his Jeep, and as the van departed, they began loading up their luggage.

"You don't have to do this," Charlie said.

"It feels good to stand up and move around a bit," Carter said, scratching beneath the wig he was wearing. "Is it far to your place from here?"

"We'll get there shortly. Do you need a bathroom break or something to drink before we take off?"

"I'm good to go, but I'm getting hungry. How about you?"

Charlie grinned. "I could eat. There are a couple of pretty decent places on the way home to pick up some fast food if you have a taste for fried shrimp and hush puppies, or a chopped brisket sandwich with a little Tex-Mex heat in the barbecue sauce."

"I'd pick the chopped brisket, since you asked," Carter said.

"Then get your dandy little ass into the Jeep and we'll be on our way."

Carter laughed at the reference. "Your Wyrick is pure nitroglycerin just waiting for a quake to set her off."

"Oh, she's not mine in any sense of the word. Sometimes I think I work for her, and I did warn you."

Carter shook his head. "You can't warn someone to dodge lightning," he said and got in the Jeep.

Charlie drove out of the parking lot through the tollgate, then straight to the barbecue joint he liked best. The chopped brisket sandwiches disappeared in rapid order as Charlie ate while he drove, taking an exit ramp off the freeway. It wasn't until he entered his parking garage that he remembered the stolen jewelry that had come while he was gone. And that his dining room was now his office, and Wyrick would soon be back in her spot, fielding calls, managing appointments and weaving her own magic spell on his computers, coaxing hidden information from the worldwide web.

"We're here," Charlie said, as he pulled into his parking spot. "It's not quite castle-worthy, but it's where I come to lick my wounds from daily bouts with Wyrick."

Carter laughed again. The more he was around Charlie Dodge, the more he liked him. A hard man with a soft heart was rare. A loyal man, even rarer.

Charlie grabbed all the garbage from their meal on wheels and dumped it in a garbage can near the door, then went back to get some of the luggage. Between the two of them, they got everything inside in one trip.

Charlie dropped his things so he could disarm the security alarm.

"Carter, consider this your home for the time being. I know I don't have to tell you not to order food or anything else with your credit cards. Anytime you want something to eat other than what's here, tell Wyrick. She has a credit card for the business, so it won't call attention to you in any way. Come with me and I'll show you to your room."

Carter picked up his bags and followed Charlie, who was turning on lights as they went.

"Here we are—last room at the end of the hall," Charlie said as he opened the bedroom door and turned on the light. "You have your own bathroom. The remote for the television is on the nightstand. The closet has plenty of room to hang up your clothes, and the dresser is empty, so use all the space you need. If you like to read, I have a pretty good selection of mystery and suspense novels in the living room. I'm not a fan of e-readers. I still like to hold a book."

"This is a wonderful room, Charlie. It already feels comfortable."

"Considering the mess your life is in right now, this was an easy fix. Wyrick will be here later. She's determined to finish out the day. I have emails to go through. Just make yourself at home anywhere in the apartment. There are cold longnecks in the fridge. Wyrick doesn't like my beer choices, so I'm sure they're still there."

"I'm somewhat tempted to try this bed and take a nap."

Charlie grinned. "Knock yourself out," he said and left, closing the door behind him.

But while Carter was kicking off his shoes, Charlie headed for his bathroom. He found the package Wyrick had hidden for him, unfastened the Bubble Wrap and went through the jewelry, one piece at a time. Everything that had been stolen was there. He still couldn't believe it, and wondered why in the hell this happened *now*, when Annie would never know or care.

Maybe that was the lesson to be learned. There'd been a time in his life when the loss of that jewelry had been a tragedy for Annie. The loss now was her hold on reality.

He took the package to his office and put it in the safe, then unpacked his things and stowed his suitcases. He left his room sock-footed, making no sound as he moved through the apartment, settling back in the vibe of home. It all looked the same, but it didn't quite feel the same. Maybe it was knowing Carter was down the hall.

And then he passed the office setup in the dining room again and remembered Wyrick had been in here every day he'd been gone. He sighed.

That was what it was.

Female energy.

Where he ate.

Where he slept.

This was the impetus he needed to find new office space as soon as possible.

CHAPTER ELEVEN

Charlie wasn't the only one picking up a late lunch on the go. Wyrick ordered a chopped pork sandwich and a large sweet tea from a little place not far from Charlie's building. Lady Luck had left her a parking space close to the deli as she walked inside to pick up her order.

Her entrance went unnoticed until she began weaving her way through the tables to get to the counter. She heard the mumbling, and then the undertones of voices stating their opinions about how she looked. She pulled off her sunglasses, hung them over the neckline of the shirt beneath her jacket as a waiter stepped up to the cash register.

"How can I help you, sir?"

"It's ma'am, and I'm picking up an order to go for Wyrick."

The waiter blushed. "I'm sorry, I didn't mean—"

"Just get my food," she said and was reaching for her wallet, when she heard the sound of a chair scraping against the wooden floor, then footsteps coming up behind her. Every instinct for self-preservation was on alert. But before she could react, someone grabbed her by the arm and yanked her around to face him.

"You ain't no woman."

The waiter came running from the kitchen. "You! Sit back down and leave her alone!" he cried, but the man ignored him.

Wyrick was about two inches shorter than the man who'd accosted her, but she was younger and leaner.

"Take your hands off me," she said.

"You're just some queer, and I don't like—"

Wyrick punched him in the nose. Blood spurted. He cried out and clutched his nose with both hands.

Wyrick calmly paid for her food, then picked up the sack and started out the door. She was reaching for the knob when she heard a roar of rage.

"Look out, lady!" the waiter shouted.

Wyrick dropped her sack and raised her arm to deflect the first blow, but she wasn't fast enough to deflect the second as the man swung an empty beer bottle at her face. She ducked, getting a glancing blow rather than a direct hit as the bottle shattered against her head.

Wyrick staggered backward into a wall, then pulled a handgun from beneath the back of her jacket and jammed it between his eyes.

"You wouldn't be the first man I shot," she said softly, watching the color draining from the bully's face.

"I called the police!" the waiter said.

"I'll wait," Wyrick told him.

It was only minutes before she began hearing sirens, and when they got louder, the bully shifted nervously.

"Don't fucking move," she said calmly and shoved the barrel a little harder against his forehead.

He groaned.

The cops came in on the run, and when they saw her holding a gun on a man, they pulled their own weapons and ordered Wyrick to drop hers.

She laid it on the floor, then raised her hands.

"I have a permit to carry," she said. "It's in my wallet. May I show you?"

"Yes, ma'am," an officer said and nodded after she showed him.

"It's not her fault," the waiter said. "She was just trying to pick up an order when this guy assaulted her. All she did was fight back. When she punched him in the nose and then tried to leave, he grabbed a beer bottle, chased her down and hit her with it."

Wyrick's head was throbbing as she pointed to her sack of food. "May I get that? It's my food," she said.

One of the officers picked it up and handed it to her.

"Your head is bleeding. You should sit down," he said.

She didn't argue. The waiter came with a handful of wet paper towels and a bottle of water, and a woman sitting at a table in the back stood up.

"Officers, I'm a nurse. May I help her?"

"Yes," he said.

Wyrick was beginning to shake from the adrenaline rush. When the nurse took the wet towels and began cleaning away the blood to assess the damage, Wyrick didn't move.

The officers on scene were taking witness statements, and by the time they were through, they had a clear picture of what happened.

"What are you going to do with him?" Wyrick asked as they walked her assailant out the door in handcuffs to the waiting ambulance.

"He has a rap sheet, and what he did to you violated his parole. He's going back to prison."

"Can I go home now?" she asked.

"As soon as the EMTs check you out," the officer replied.

"I don't need an ambulance," Wyrick insisted.

He frowned. "You took a pretty severe blow to the head. You might have a concussion."

"I'll be fine," Wyrick said and was reaching for her food

when another cop walked in. He saw her, did a double take and headed straight toward her.

"Aw, man. Last time I saw you, you'd just taken a man down with your Taser. Where's Charlie working now that the building blew up?"

"At his apartment."

"Who's her boss?" the first officer asked.

"Charlie Dodge," he said.

Everyone in Dallas PD knew who he was and now they were really staring—as if to say, *So this is his badass assistant!*

"I'm going now," Wyrick said. She picked up her food and hurried out the door.

She put the sack on the floorboard of the passenger side, then started her car before eyeing herself in the mirror on the back of her visor.

"I did not see this coming," she muttered as she drove away. She was sad right down to her bones, but it would pass.

When she finally arrived, she entered the parking garage, drove through the ever-circling aisles up, all the way to the ninth floor, and parked beside Charlie's Jeep.

Once she killed the engine, she sat in the resulting silence for a few minutes, mentally shedding the emotions of what had just happened, then looked at herself in the rearview mirror. There was no way to hide the bruise on her cheek or the small cut on the side of her head. She hated the reality of who she was and glared herself down. Then she picked up her food and her shoulder bag and got out.

Work—and Charlie—were waiting.

When Wyrick reached the apartment door, she never even thought about knocking. She'd been coming and going at will while Charlie was gone, and without thinking, she just used her key and walked in.

Charlie was in the kitchen when the front door opened,

and the moment Wyrick stepped over the threshold, she realized what she'd done.

"Sorry. Didn't mean to startle you. You've been gone ever since this became the office. It appears I've overlooked the fact that it's also your home. Want me to go back out and do this again or what?"

Charlie eyed the defiant look on her face. "I'm not going to dignify that remark with an answer. You came to work, so do your thing."

She shut the door and started for the kitchen with her food, jaw set.

She realized he'd seen her face. He tried to clasp her arm, but she stepped out of his reach so fast, he froze.

"What happened?"

"Nothing."

"That is not nothing," he said. "Your head is cut and there's a bruise on your cheek. Did you fall?"

"No," she said and turned her back on him.

"Whatever's wrong, I didn't cause it, and don't pretend we haven't just spent the better part of the day in a helicopter together."

Before he could finish what he'd been going to say, his cell phone rang. It was the break Wyrick needed to walk away.

"Hello," Charlie said.

"Charlie, this is Officer Dial from Dallas PD. Is your assistant with you?"

Charlie's head came up. "Yes."

"Keep an eye on her and make sure she doesn't have a concussion. She took quite a blow to the head."

Charlie tensed. "I saw it, but she's not talking."

Dial sighed. "She was in Billy's to pick up a to-go order when some jackass didn't like her looks. He called her a few names, then grabbed her by the arm and yanked her around to face him. She punched him in the nose and started to leave with her food, but he came after her with a beer bottle. After he hit her, she pulled a gun on him. That's when we arrived."

Charlie was alternating between shock and rage when he realized Wyrick was looking at him. Their gazes locked.

"I'll make sure she's okay, and thanks for calling," Charlie said. He laid his phone down and moved toward her, then stopped when they were face-to-face. "I'm so sorry."

Wyrick was drowning and wouldn't let anyone save her. He needed to back off.

"This kind of thing is nothing new," she said. "I'm going to eat before I get back to work."

Charlie felt her rejection as strongly as if she'd physically pushed him away. If that was how she needed to play it, then he wasn't going to change her rules.

He turned on his heel and headed down the hall to Carter's room. The door was ajar, and Carter was reclining on the bed watching TV.

Carter saw him and hit Mute. "What's up?" he asked.

Charlie closed the bedroom door. "I'm going to be out for a short while. I need to check on Annie before I get back to work. Wyrick just got here. She stopped to pick up some food on the way and someone jumped her."

Carter sat straight up in bed. "What the hell? Jumped her? What for? Is she okay?"

"It has to do with her looks. Could you keep an eye on her once in a while until I get back? I need to make sure she's okay. Someone broke a beer bottle over her head. She refuses to talk about it, and I need to know she isn't concussed. I won't be long."

"Oh, my God!" Carter said. "Yes, of course I will. I won't say anything to her, but I'll make sure she's upright and breathing."

Charlie gave him a thumbs-up and went back to where she was working.

"Carter is in his bedroom watching TV. Use the business credit card for anything he needs or wants. Now that you're here, I'm going to see Annie."

Wyrick listened without comment, but when he was finished, she got herself something cold to drink and sat down to eat. Charlie left without looking back.

For Charlie, the moment he pulled the door shut between them, he felt like he was running out on someone in need—then let it go. Annie was his. She was the one he should be dwelling on. He thought about the jewelry that had been returned to him, and wished he could put the gold keepsake ring back on Annie's finger. But since that wasn't possible, he'd settle for seeing her. And as always, as soon as he started driving toward Morning Light Care Center, he developed a knot in his stomach, and the closer he got, the tighter it wound.

Later, he would realize how close he'd come to never seeing Annie again, because the wreck that began only two cars ahead of him was sudden and violent.

It took every driving skill he'd ever learned not to wind up in the ensuing pileup, as he braked and swerved all the way onto the shoulder of the multilane freeway.

Metal began flying as one car rolled, and the other one was hit by more cars as drivers tried to dodge the car that had rolled. Moving traffic immediately slowed down as Charlie called 911.

Drivers were pulling to a stop and getting out, running toward the half-dozen smoking cars now piled up across three lanes of I-35. Charlie stayed where he was, eyeing the growing chaos with unease.

And then he saw something through the smoke that made him abandon every instinct he had for self-preservation.

A toddler was crawling out of the first overturned car. She was covered in blood and obviously dazed, because the moment she stood up and saw the smoking mass of crumpled cars, she started toward them.

Within seconds Charlie was out of his Jeep and running, faster than he'd ever moved, praying with every beat of his heart that he wouldn't be too late.

She was three steps away from the spilling fuel of one car, and the sparks popping out of the one next to it, when Charlie scooped her up and kept running. He was on the far side of a Greyhound bus when the sparks finally ignited the fuel, which then flamed and traveled right back into the wrecks. The resulting explosion rocked the ground where he stood, and the traffic disaster had become an inferno.

Charlie looked down at the little girl in his arms, trying to figure out if the blood was hers or belonged to someone she'd been with.

Earlier she hadn't uttered a sound, but now she was crying, "Mama, Mama, Mama," with one little hand clinging tightly to his shirt collar.

Charlie cradled her against him and began talking softly in her ear. "I got you, baby girl. You're okay… You're okay."

He could hear sirens now, and an approaching chopper nearing the crash site. Media swarmed these accidents like vultures circling a fresh kill. He could only imagine what the scene must look like from above. The fire was growing, as each wrecked car caught fire.

Charlie looked down at the baby again and moved farther away from the intensity of the heat. He wasn't going to visit Annie today. He was meant to be here, to keep a baby girl alive. He'd lived through too many incidents in Afghanistan that should have killed him to question providence anymore.

He glanced back, relieved to see traffic was already being rerouted onto the exit ramp they'd just passed. In the distance, he could see the flashing lights of fire trucks and ambulances speeding toward them, and police cars coming at breakneck speed.

As soon as he could, Charlie made his way back to his car and got a bottle of water and a couple of wet wipes. He pulled down the tailgate of his vehicle, reached inside for a quilted sleeping bag and unrolled it. He sat down with the baby, who was crying more loudly now and becoming more aware of everything.

"Mama, Mama," she sobbed as Charlie wiped the blood from her hands and face, then held the bottle of water to her lips.

"Want a drink, honey? It's water. Want a drink of water?"

The baby sucked back a sob and opened her mouth. Charlie tilted the bottle and dribbled a little bit in, then waited to see if she could swallow. And she did.

When she reached for the water bottle, he poured a little more in her mouth and repeated it until she pushed the bottle away. He was screwing the lid back on when the baby made a sound as if she'd just swallowed another sob, then laid her face against his chest, her little head tucked beneath his chin.

And so Charlie sat, holding the baby as close against him as he dared, waiting for paramedics to reach them.

Wyrick had finished her sandwich and was getting ready to call new clients to set up appointments, when Carter came running up the hall.

"Turn on the television! Now!"

Wyrick raced to the living room, grabbed the remote and aimed it at the television.

"What's happening? What channel?" she asked.

"Anything local! Charlie's on TV."

"You aren't serious?" Wyrick muttered as she tuned in to KXAS, the NBC affiliate, and immediately saw the burning footage of a multicar pileup on I-35.

Ambulances were on scene, as were fire and rescue. The

news anchor was firing off updated information as it was coming in.

"…and we've just been handed an update to the video we aired earlier. The man who saved the toddler has been identified as Charlie Dodge, a well-known private investigator from the Dallas area."

"There!" Carter cried. "They're running it again. All I have to say is your boss sure can move."

Wyrick felt the blood draining from her face and sat down to keep from fainting. The video began with Charlie leaping out of his Jeep and running all the way to the baby. Her heart began to pound when she saw sparks and smoke coming from beneath the hood of a nearby car, and then in one smooth move Charlie grabbed the little girl in his arms and kept running without missing a stride.

The video lost sight of them when he ducked behind a Greyhound bus trapped in stalled traffic, and then everything exploded. She jumped and then shouted.

"Oh, my God. Oh, my God!"

"There's more, just wait," Carter said.

Wyrick could hear the news anchor's voice, but not what he was saying. She was too focused on the man who emerged out of the smoke carrying a bloody baby against his chest. The film ended after the baby tucked her head beneath his chin.

"Does Charlie have children?" Carter asked.

Wyrick shook her head.

"Pity," Carter said. "He'd be a natural."

Wyrick stood, handed Carter the remote and went back into their office. She picked up her cell and activated the locator app she'd put on his phone before he left for Denver.

He was on the move now, which meant the paramedics must finally have taken the child. She found the street he was on and the direction in which he was driving, and realized he was on his way back.

She sat down in front of the computer and started to call

him, then stopped. If she had to talk right now, she was pretty sure she'd cry, so she sat quietly until she'd cleared herself of emotion, then went back to work.

Carter came back to where she was working and handed her a cold bottle of Pepsi.

"No, thanks. I'm fine," Wyrick said.

"No, you're not, but I won't tell your boss. Since I doubt I could persuade you to drink on the job, I suggest caffeine. Good for dealing with shock."

He set it on the coaster beside her and walked away.

Wyrick picked it up, unscrewed the lid and took a long drink, feeling the burn as it slid down her throat. By the time Charlie returned, she'd recovered. She saw the blood all over him and blinked, before she made herself look away.

"You were on television. Is any of that blood yours?"

"Really? It was a mess, and no, none of this is mine," Charlie said.

"Is the baby okay?" she asked.

Charlie eyed her closer, thinking he just heard a break in her voice.

"They think so. The blood all over her was her mother's. Her mother didn't make it," Charlie said. "Are you still okay?"

She nodded.

"Okay, then," he said and walked down the hall.

Wyrick heard his bedroom door open and close, and then the place was silent again, like it used to be when she was here by herself. She took a deep breath, answering the rest of the afternoon emails before shutting everything down and letting herself out.

Before she got in her car, she checked it for trackers, then left the parking garage. Her head was throbbing and she needed to be alone.

Mack Doolin saw the film footage of the accident. He knew Charlie Dodge. He knew Wyrick worked for him, and he also knew Dodge's office had been in the building that had exploded.

It occurred to him that Charlie might be doing business out of his home for the time being. Only he didn't know where Charlie lived. But it gave him a new angle on trying to run Wyrick down. This was the new break he'd been waiting for. The sooner he got the information he needed as to where she was living and working, the sooner he'd have another payday.

The mood within Dunleavy Castle was somber. *Suspicion* was the key word of every day, and it was getting on Dina's nerves. Now that she knew Carter was alive and safely hidden, her anxiety had shifted to impatience. She wanted all this drama to be over with, and their lives to go back to normal. Kenneth was talking about moving out of the family home when they married, and Dina was excited at the idea of looking for property.

The Aston Martin Kenneth had chosen for his birthday present was a powder blue convertible, and they were taking it for a drive tomorrow. Maybe they'd look at homes for sale while they were at it.

Ruth was overvigilant now on behalf of the family, scowling at everyone who came and went within the castle walls.

Edward was mostly himself. Since learning Carter was alive and well, he had no quarrels about anything.

But it was Jason who was feeling the pressure. He wanted his uncle back at work, so it would loosen his workload, and that wasn't going to happen until the people responsible were behind bars.

And if that wasn't enough of a headache, Miranda was coming back to Denver. He really, really needed to put a stop to dating her. There were countless other women he could see who weren't campaigning to become his wife.

Dinner at the household came and went, and as was the

family's habit, they'd gathered together in the library afterward for a nightcap.

Kenneth was bartending. A shot of bourbon for Jason. A gin and tonic for Edward, and Dina wanted a martini. Kenneth made another for himself, and then they settled into their own spaces to bring the day to an end.

Jason was sitting beside Edward, listening to him tell some tale about a childhood escapade he and Carter had pulled when they were young. He laughed in all the appropriate places and urged his uncle to share more stories, but he was watching his mother and Kenneth from the corner of his eye. Their relationship was all one-sided, which irked him no end. Kenneth was attentive when he got his way, and pouted like a toddler when he was thwarted. Jason couldn't imagine what his mother saw in him, then guessed it was the companionship, more than anything else. He sighed and looked away. He didn't like to think of her as lonely, and it wasn't his business to interfere.

Edward finally ended his story and settled into his chair, sipping his gin and tonic.

Jason was thinking about retiring for the night when he got a text. He glanced at his phone and resisted the urge to curse. Miranda was at the airport. That meant tomorrow he'd be inundated with messages from her, all wanting to know when they could meet. He didn't respond, but he had a decision to make.

"It's been a long day. I think I'm going up," he said.

"I'll go with you." Edward set his glass aside.

"Good night, Jason, darling," Dina said.

"Good night, Mother."

"Aren't you going to tell Kenneth good-night, as well?" Dina asked.

Jason left without answering, then wished he had spoken to Kenneth, because he could hear his mother apologizing profusely for his behavior.

When Charlie came out of the shower and found Wyrick gone, he stood in the dining room, looking at the makeshift office, and knew he needed to get her out of this space. For whatever reason, she was as uncomfortable being here as he was with her presence.

His phone began ringing, and he reached across the kitchen counter to pick it up. "Hello."

"Charlie Dodge?"

"Yes, who's speaking?" he asked.

"This is Jamie George from KDFW here in Dallas. We were wondering if you'd be available to make a statement regarding your amazing rescue during the pileup today."

"No. Thanks for calling," he said and disconnected.

Not five minutes later his phone rang again, and this time it was an on-the-spot reporter from WFAA Dallas, requesting the same thing, and again, Charlie turned him down.

After that, he let the calls go to voice mail and devoted the rest of the evening to Carter. They ordered in from an Italian restaurant, and when it arrived, shared the end of the dining table to eat their dinner.

Their conversation started out randomly, but it didn't take long for Charlie to get down to the business of finding Carter's inept assassin.

"From all you've told me about the attempts on your life, they don't feel professional. It's more like someone just taking random opportunities and acting in the moment. Do you agree?" Charlie asked.

Carter nodded. "Yes, and I think that's why it took me so long to realize the incidents were more than accidental."

"I've been thinking about the arsenic you ingested. Are you sure it happened after dinner?" Charlie asked.

Carter nodded again. "Any earlier and I would've become sick before or during dinner. It was afterward that I felt ill."

"Do you remember who was pouring drinks that night?" Charlie asked.

"Not really."

"Okay, then what do you usually choose as your nightcap, and does anyone else favor it, too?"

"I like a Gibson. That's gin and dry vermouth with an onion. My dad was a fan and it rubbed off on me, and no, nobody else has them. I'm always the one who—" Carter paused. "Oh! The pickled onions. They're kept in the little jar beneath the bar. Nobody ever has them but me."

"Good job," Charlie said. "You might have just solved the question of how you ingested the arsenic. But we need to see if the same jar of onions is still behind the bar. I'll call Jason later. I don't want him to know where you are, so all I'll say is that we're staying in touch because I'm working on your case."

Carter laid down his fork and leaned forward, resting his elbows on the table—something he probably wouldn't have had the freedom to do at home.

"If it was the onions, then it was most likely a woman. Other than the chef, I don't have male household staff," Carter said. "But if that's so, the brake line then becomes an anomaly. I don't know any woman capable of doing that, and there wouldn't be a man anywhere near the library to poison the jar of pickled onions."

"So maybe there are two of them," Charlie said.

Carter sighed. "I can't believe I'm even having this discussion. I made enemies, but none I ever thought hated me enough to try and kill me."

"What about ex-girlfriends or ex-wives with a grudge?" Charlie asked.

"I had one long-term relationship that never panned out, but that was years ago, and I never married. I guess the job is my lover. Jason is the player in the family. He always has a girl or two on call."

"Are they the kind of girlfriends he brings home to dinner with the family?"

"No," Carter said. "Although they often want to be. He's been seeing a young woman for some time now who has her sights set on him. She's the daughter of Johannes Deutsch, the man who founded Deutsch Sausages in Denver. Of course they're sold nationwide now, and her father is very rich in his own right, so it's not as if she's out to snag Jason because of his money. They have plenty."

"No one's mentioned her before," Charlie said.

"That's because she'd been in Europe for at least two, maybe three months."

"What's her name?" Charlie asked.

"Miranda Deutsch."

Charlie made a mental note to have Wyrick do a little research on her, as well.

As soon as they finished the meal, Charlie began cleaning up and sent Carter into the living room to watch television. After the kitchen was tidy again, Charlie went into his office to call Jason. It was after ten o'clock in Dallas, but an hour earlier in Denver. Not too late to make the call. He was staring at a photo of Annie on his desk when Jason finally answered.

"Hello."

"Jason, this is Charlie."

"Is everything okay?"

"As far as I know," Charlie said. "The reason I'm calling has to do with your uncle's case. I've been checking in with him on a regular basis, and during one of our updates, I asked him about the night he was poisoned. I wanted to know who pours drinks, and who drinks what, and it occurred to him that he's the only one who has a Gibson for a nightcap."

"Yes, that's true. No one else in the family cares for them. Why?"

"I want you to go down to the bar and see if there's an opened jar of pickled onions still there. If so, confiscate it and have it tested for arsenic. It would've been impossible to contaminate any of the liquor without endangering the whole family, but the jar of onions would work, since he's the only one who has them."

"The onions! Yes! That makes perfect sense. And anyone in the household knows he's the only one who has them with a drink," Jason said.

"If the jar is unopened, leave it, but get in touch with me. After the first attempt failed, whoever did it might have removed the tainted jar, and we don't want to let on that we know," Charlie cautioned.

"I'll go down now and text you back, one way or the other."

Charlie put the phone down to wait for the text, and reached for Annie's picture. She was looking into the camera when he'd taken it, and the smile on her face was so real. It had been a long time since she'd looked at him that way.

Back when she still saw him—knew him—loved him…

"I miss you," Charlie said. "I miss us."

Jason's text came a few minutes later.

New jar. Never been opened.

Charlie sent a text back.

When it didn't work, they disposed of the evidence. Keep this to yourself.

He pocketed his phone and joined Carter.

* * *

Wyrick hadn't been home more than five minutes when her cell phone signaled a text. It was from Corne, her stockbroker.

Your gaming enterprise is paying off. The release of your latest game shot sales up through the roof. You scored a little over twenty million today alone.

She sighed. Money was easy to make. Life was what was hard. She sent a thumbs-up emoji to let him know the message was received, then laid the phone aside and went to shower and change. The ritual was necessary. It was an emotional signal to herself that was now free to be her true self. No leather, no makeup. No lies.

This was where she lived her truth, and she held fast to the adage that the truth would set her free.

CHAPTER TWELVE

Buddy Boy Pierce was feeling all kinds of relief now that he was off the Dunleavy job. He was feeling so good that he was thinking of taking a little trip down Tijuana way. Maybe it would give things here a chance to cool down.

He'd ordered pizza over an hour ago and was wondering where the hell it was when his doorbell finally rang.

"It's about damn time," he muttered and picked up his wallet as he headed for the door.

But it wasn't the pizza delivery.

"You! What the hell? I already quit. I've had my say."

"But I haven't."

Buddy frowned, and then he saw the gun—and the silencer.

"No, no, no, I wouldn't—"

The pop was as minimal as the little bullet hole between Buddy's eyes. But the blood and brain matter that hit the easy chair behind him was messy as hell. Now Buddy was on the floor, and the shooter was gone.

A few minutes later, the pizza delivery guy drove up, grabbed the pizza box and took off toward the house. He was already up the steps and on his way to the door when he realized it was ajar.

"Pizza delivery!" he called out, and when no one came, he pushed the door aside just enough to peek in. He saw a body on the floor, and the bullet hole between his eyes.

He choked, then gagged at the sight of all that blood and threw up off the side of the porch. After he caught his breath, he pulled himself together and called 911.

Wilma Short hobbled toward the door of her apartment, grateful to be home. The moment she was inside, she kicked off her shoes. Her feet hurt. They always hurt at the end of a day's work at the Dunleavy estate. Ruth kept telling her to get better shoes, but Ruth was always full of suggestions that irked Wilma. There was nothing wrong with the shoes she had. Her feet just hurt after running errands through that damn castle all day. But now she was home and grateful for her small apartment, and the first thing she was going to do was have a long soak in a hot bath.

She started the water running, and then went back into her bedroom to get a pair of sweatpants and a T-shirt to put on after she got out.

Steam was rising from the tub as she undressed. She clipped up her hair and stepped into the water, closing her eyes in quiet ecstasy as she settled down in the tub.

"Oh, my Lord, this does feel good."

She leaned back, resting her head against the rim of the tub as the heat soaked into her tired bones. She'd been thinking for days about what a mess she was in. She still couldn't believe she'd let herself be swayed into anything as reprehensible as setting up accidents for Carter Dunleavy, then waiting for them to happen. Getting paid big money to do it had been the great persuader, but she obviously wasn't good at it, because he was not only alive, but onto the fact that someone wanted him dead.

Wilma sighed. She'd never really wanted him dead. She just wanted that money more, so she lay within the silence and the heat, letting her mind drift. The failures weren't her fault. She'd done exactly what she'd been paid to do, nothing more, nothing less.

She was on the verge of dozing off when she heard a noise, then decided it was the dishwasher changing cycles.

Less than a minute later, she heard it again, and this time sat up, the water dripping from her bare breasts as she slowly climbed out of the tub. She was reaching for a towel when the door swung inward.

Wilma screamed, "You! How did you get in? What are you doing here?"

"I had a copy made of your door key. I thought you'd be glad to see me."

"Well, I'm not!" Wilma shouted. "Get out of my apartment!"

"Now, Wilma. We had an agreement. I gave you a lot of money to do one little thing, and you haven't been successful. I came to let you know I won't be needing your services anymore."

"Good," Wilma muttered. "I've been the one taking all the risks, and I'm glad it's over."

"It's not over by a long shot. I don't need you anymore, but I can't leave a witness alive."

Wilma gasped when she saw the knife. "No! Get out, get out! I won't tell. Why would I incriminate myself?"

"Sorry, I can't take any chances."

"No! I won't tell!" Wilma cried and tried to escape, only to be hit in the back of the head with a fist. She fell backward into the tub, and water sloshed up and then all over the floor. Momentarily stunned by the blow, she sank beneath the water, and as she did, the assailant slashed the main arteries in both wrists.

Wilma regained consciousness when she inhaled the water, and came up coughing and gasping for air. She couldn't see for the soap and water in her eyes and was reaching toward the side of the tub when she felt a hand on the top of her head, holding her in place.

"What are you doing?" she screamed, clawing and pulling on the hand, and then the wrist, trying to get free. "Have you lost your fucking mind?"

It took her a few minutes to realize the water was turning red, and then she let go of the assailant and stared at her arms, following the blood flow to the slashes on both wrists.

"What have you done? Why? Why?" Wilma moaned as she grabbed her washcloth, trying to stop the gushing from the open arteries.

"I have done nothing. You, on the other hand, just committed suicide because of a guilty conscience."

"I need help. Call 911," Wilma said and began trying to climb out of the tub, but slipped and sank under the water again. This time when she surfaced, she was light-headed.

"Help me," Wilma begged. "Please."

"Sorry, no can do. But don't worry. You left a note explaining your regret about what you tried to do."

"Nooo—" Wilma's resistance was weak, and the hand was back on her head now, pushing her down beneath the water.

Red bubbles broke the surface as she still struggled. In her last conscious act, she dug her fingernails into the hand holding her down, breaking the skin and bringing blood drops to the surface.

The struggle ended. The assailant backed up, eyeing the bloody water all over the floor, and realized there'd also be footprints. Without hesitation, the assailant seized Wilma's towel to smear the existing footprints into the water, then exited the apartment barefoot, carrying bloody shoes.

A short while later, Wilma floated up to the surface, eyes wide and fixed, her hair matted and clumped from the clip that had come undone.

The next morning was management's monthly pesticide spray for the hallways and storage rooms of the entire apartment building. They sprayed inside the apartments every three months, but Wilma had requested that her apartment be sprayed today. Twice she'd seen a cockroach since the last spraying and she'd known all too well that where there was one, there were others.

Juanita Fargo, the building manager, knocked once, and when no one answered, used her passkey to enter. The pest control technician followed her inside.

"Make it snappy," Juanita said. "This is the only request we had for an apartment to be sprayed, and I need to get back to the office."

"Yes, ma'am," the tech said.

He always began at the back of an apartment and worked his way forward, so he started down the hall to do the bedroom first.

Within seconds of his departure, Juanita heard a scream, and then the man came running back up the hall, his eyes wide with shock.

"There's a dead woman in the bathtub!"

Juanita ran to look, but got no farther than the bathroom door before she saw all the blood and the body. It was Wilma Short!

"Oh, my God. Oh, my God," she said and ran out of the apartment with the man from pest control right behind her. Once in the hall, she paused long enough to call 911. A man's voice calmly answered.

"Nine-one-one. What is your emergency?"

"There's a dead woman in one of the apartments I manage. We found her floating in the bathtub, and there's blood everywhere."

"I have your address. What is the apartment number?" the dispatcher asked.

"It's Apartment 233."

"Please wait on scene for the police to arrive, and don't touch anything."

"Yes, okay," Juanita said and then saw the pest control technician standing a few feet away, the horrified look still in his eyes.

"I'm sorry you saw that," Juanita said. "Don't spray any further in this wing. Just complete the rest of the building. The crime scene people will likely be taking samples of everything in this area and we don't want to contaminate anything with pesticide. I don't know how long I'll be detained here, but if you need me to sign the work order when you've finished, text me and I'll come down to the office. And don't leave the building. The police will likely want to speak with you."

"Yes, ma'am," he said and gratefully moved to another wing of the second floor to resume his job.

Homicide Detective Calvin Bruner was just coming in to work when he got the call about a body in an apartment and rerouted himself to the address. Police and ambulance were on scene when he arrived, and he quickly followed a cop up to the apartment.

"That woman is the manager who found the body," the cop said. "Her name is Juanita Fargo."

"Thanks," Calvin said and went to talk to her.

"Ms. Fargo, I'm Detective Bruner from Homicide. I understand you're the building manager."

"Yes," Juanita said. "This is horrible, so horrible. Wilma

Short was a really nice lady. She'd been renting from us for almost five years. Never caused a bit of trouble."

"How did you come to find the body?" Bruner asked.

"Today is spraying day for this month, and Wilma wanted her apartment sprayed. We found her when I let the technician in."

Bruner frowned. "Did he spray any part of the apartment before that?"

"No. He always starts at the back of an apartment and comes forward. He had no more than walked down the hall into her bedroom when he saw the body in the bath. He cried out, then came running. When he told me what he'd seen, I ran down to look and got no farther than the bathroom door. Neither of us went in, and I sent him on his way to finish the rest of the building."

Detective Bruner nodded, making notes as he spoke.

"Was Ms. Short married?"

"No," Juanita said.

"Boyfriends?"

"Not that I know of."

"Do you have any information on her that would give us the names of emergency contacts or her next of kin?"

"Yes, some of that is on her lease. If you'll stop by the office when you're done here, I can give you what I've got."

"Thanks," Bruner said.

"Can I go now?" Juanita asked.

"Yes, but I'll be down later to get that info from you."

"I'll have it ready," Juanita said, then glanced into the apartment and shuddered. "I'm so sorry. I can't believe this happened, and on our property."

She left the floor, moving as fast as she could toward the stairwell.

Bruner eyed a uniformed office standing guard near the door.

"Is there any sign of forced entry?" he asked.

"No, sir," the cop said. "Nothing we could see, but there's a suicide note on the bed."

Bruner slipped some disposable booties over his shoes and went inside. The apartment was very small, but clean and well kept. He moved down the hall to the single bedroom and then toward the bath.

He grimaced at the sight of the body. The water was red. She'd bled out in the tub, which could mean it was a suicide, but there was a lot of water and a bloody towel on the floor. It didn't look so much like a suicide anymore. To Bruner, it looked like someone had been in here with her and tried to erase footprints with a towel on the way out.

He turned around to look at the note on the bed beside him, then leaned over to read it without picking it up.

I can't live with the guilt any longer. Tell the Dunleavy family I'm sorry I tried to harm Carter. He was always so mean to me, I just wanted to pay him back.

Bruner straightened up with a jerk. "Oh, shit. Carter Dunleavy!" This note was for a suicide, but again, it appeared to him that she might have been murdered. He'd heard Jason Dunleavy's speech at the courthouse and immediately got the drift of what this might mean. "Double shit," Bruner cursed. "Someone wanted her silenced."

The crime scene crew arrived. He could hear them talking, and then they were behind him.

"Dang, Bruner. You got here fast."

"I was on my way in when I got the call. This doesn't look like a suicide to me, not with all this bloody water on the floor and a bloody towel all the way over here. It looks like she might have put up a fight. Maybe we'll get lucky and find a bloody fingerprint on the damn towel. However, the note on the bed connects this woman to Carter Dunleavy's disappearance, so don't miss anything. Carter Dunleavy is friends with the chief, and this may be connected to whoever is trying to kill him."

"We'll get the goods. You get the man," the tech said.

Bruner nodded, then backed out and left them to it. He pulled the booties off his shoes out in the hall and went downstairs to get the victim's information and see about talking to the pest control man who found the body.

Ruth was in the kitchen with Chef Peter when her cell phone rang. She took it from her pocket to check the caller ID and then frowned.

"What in the world?" she muttered.

"What's wrong?" Peter asked.

"It's the police department. I'd better take this." She stepped away from the noise of a blender Peter had running. "Hello? Ruth Fenway speaking."

"Ms. Fenway, this is Detective Bruner from the Homicide Division. You're listed as the emergency contact for Wilma Short."

Ruth's heart skipped a beat. "Yes. I'm the housekeeper at the Dunleavy estate, and Wilma is an employee here. Has something happened to her? We've been wondering because she's usually here by now."

"I'm sorry to have to tell you this, but Wilma's body was discovered in her apartment this morning."

Ruth screamed, and Peter came running.

"No! Oh, no!" Ruth said and started to cry.

"Ma'am, do you know if she had any next of kin?"

"She has a mother in a nursing home, but the woman isn't in her right mind. You can't be giving her that kind of news."

"No, ma'am, of course not. So that's her only living relative?" Bruner asked.

"Yes," Ruth said and took the handful of tissues Peter gave her.

"Had she ever been married?" Bruner asked.

"Not that I know of, and she never mentioned boyfriends, either. Oh, my God, I can't believe this!" Ruth wailed.

"Is Mr. Dunleavy still on the premises?" Bruner asked.

"Yes, sir. The family will be coming down to breakfast anytime now."

"Ask him to call me. Can you take down my number?"

"Yes, just a moment while I get a pen and paper." Ruth ran back into the kitchen, dug a pad of paper and a pen from a drawer. "Okay, I'm ready," she said.

Bruner gave her his cell phone number and repeated his name.

"I've got it," Ruth said.

"Thank you," Bruner said and ended the call.

Ruth's hands were shaking, and Peter was still beside her, waiting for answers.

"What happened?" he asked.

"Wilma's body was found in her apartment this morning."

Peter gasped. "No! Oh, my God! What happened? Why?"

"The detective didn't say, but he asked for Mr. Jason to call him." Then Ruth's eyes welled up all over again. "I can't believe it! This makes no sense. No sense at all."

Peter hugged her. "This is terrible news. I'm so sorry."

Ruth nodded. "So am I. I need to find Mr. Jason and give him the message."

As Jason had predicted, Miranda was blowing up his phone this morning, but he was more intent than normal on dressing with care. He'd called a meeting to speak with the board members, making sure they understood the situation regarding his uncle.

But Miranda's calls kept repeating until finally he knew

he'd get no peace until he spoke to her in person, so he answered the next call.

"This is Jason."

"Darling! Finally! I've been calling forever."

"I know, and we need to get something straight here. I'm not running just one business in Uncle Carter's absence. There are three huge ones, plus subsidiaries. I'm busy. So when I don't answer, I would assume you'd understand I'm not taking calls."

He heard her take a deep breath, then felt the rage behind her words as she answered.

"That is a horrible welcome home. It's not what I expected from you. You've already backtracked on our wedding plans, and now you're treating me like a call girl begging for a trick."

He hesitated long enough to let her make what she chose of it before he answered.

"You can't backtrack on something that never was, and I do not want to hear another word about a wedding, understand? I never asked you to marry me. I never hinted at an engagement. Honestly, Miranda, I think we need a break from each other. You want way more from me than I'm going to return. We were good in bed together. That's about it for me."

The scream was earsplitting, and the curses that came after it were right out of the gutter. He grimaced as he disconnected. That wasn't pretty, and he didn't enjoy it, but he was glad it was over.

He went back to the mirror to adjust his necktie when someone began knocking at his door. He came out of his bedroom suite into the sitting room.

"Come in," he said.

The door opened. It was Ruth, and he could tell she'd been crying.

"Ruth! What's wrong?"

"Oh, Mr. Jason, Detective Bruner from Homicide just

called me. Wilma was found dead in her apartment this morning, and Detective Bruner said he needs to speak to you as soon as possible. This is his number."

"Wilma dead? I'm so sorry, Ruth. This is terrible! Oh, wait! You said Homicide. Do they think she was murdered?"

"I don't know. Detective Bruner asked me about any relatives she had, and of course I told him there was only her mother, who's in a nursing home. She doesn't recognize people anymore, so there was no need to notify her. I guess Arnetta, Louise and I were the ones closest to her."

"Maybe Bruner will have more answers for us. I'll let you all know if I find out anything new."

"Thank you, Mr. Jason. Oh, and breakfast is ready."

"Thank you, Ruth. I'll be down soon."

"Yes, sir," she said and hurried away.

Jason looked down at the name and number on the paper and then went back to get his phone. When he made the call, it was quickly answered.

"Detective Bruner, Homicide."

"Detective, this is Jason Dunleavy. Our housekeeper just informed me of your call. Why did you need to speak to me?"

"There was a note left on Wilma's bed that was obviously meant to suggest she committed suicide, but there'd been a struggle in the bathroom, and it appeared someone tried to clean up bloody footprints walking away."

"So you're saying she was murdered?"

"It's beginning to look like that. Either way, it still affects the case we have on your uncle Carter Dunleavy."

"Dear God, I'm sick just thinking of the fear and horror she must have felt, but why does it affect Uncle Carter's case?"

"There was no forced entry, so we're assuming it was someone she knew, and that brings me to why I needed to speak to you. The note that was left behind claimed that Wilma was confessing to being the person who kept making the attempts on your uncle's life."

Jason staggered backward, then dropped onto his bed.

"What? No! Why? Did she say why?"

"Something about him being mean to her all the time and she was sick of it and tried to kill him."

"Well, that's not true. I can state that for a fact. Uncle Carter handpicks the people who work here. We appreciate the staff and they're treated with consideration, respect and kindness."

"Okay, but I've talked to Detective Cristobal, who handled the missing person report, and everyone agrees with your uncle's belief that the attacks on his life had to be partly an inside job. Maybe Wilma was part of it, and someone was unhappy she hadn't succeeded, so he got rid of her to protect his identity."

"I just can't believe that," Jason said. "I'll be contacting Charlie Dodge to give him this information, too. Uncle Carter hired him to find out who was behind it all."

"Cristobal mentioned him," Bruner said.

"So, what do we do?" Jason asked. "And what about Wilma's body?"

"It'll be in the ME's office undergoing an autopsy. All of this is early days, but because of the note, we needed to let you know. I do not believe the danger to your uncle has, in any way, been neutralized."

"Thank you for informing us," Jason said. "And please keep us updated. Uncle Carter's life depends on what we learn."

"Yes, that's understood," Bruner said. "We'll stay in touch."

Jason disconnected, then sat staring at the floor in disbelief. What did they really know about Wilma, other than that she was an only child with a mother in a nursing home and that she'd been a good member of the staff?

Shaking his head, he pocketed his phone and went down to

breakfast. The family had to be told, and the staff also needed to know what the police believed. This day was steadily getting worse and he still hadn't had a cup of coffee.

Kenneth and Dina were the first ones into the breakfast room, but neither one of them paid any attention to Ruth's quiet demeanor or red-rimmed eyes. She was staff and of no importance.

Edward entered next, his white cane tapping the way, and as he did, Ruth hurried toward him.

"Good morning, Mr. Edward. May I escort you to your seat?"

Instead of saying yes, as he usually would, he paused.

"Ruth, I hear sadness in your voice."

"Yes, sir," Ruth said. "This way, sir." And she led him to his chair. "Would you prefer eggs or pancakes this morning?" she asked.

Edward sat, but he wasn't satisfied to let it pass.

"Pancakes with Peter's blueberry syrup, please, and a strip of bacon." Then he added, "I'm sorry for whatever has troubled you."

"What troubled Ruth is going to be troubling all of us," Jason said, as he entered the breakfast room in hurried strides. "Good morning, everyone. Ruth received sad news this morning. One of our staff passed away last night."

Dina gasped. "Oh, dear! Who?"

"It was Wilma," Jason said. "And I received a message from the detective who notified Ruth. He asked me to call him, which I just did."

Ruth carried the food to Edward. "Your pancake is in the center of the plate. It's buttered and has blueberry syrup as you requested and it's cut into squares. I put two pieces of bacon on the plate. They're at nine o'clock. You need to eat both of them."

Edward smiled. "Yes, ma'am," he said and carefully felt for the plate to verify its placement and took a deep breath as he smelled the fresh coffee Ruth was pouring.

Kenneth got up to fix a plate for Dina while Jason stood, waiting for a moment to speak.

"What's the big mystery about Wilma's passing?" Kenneth asked.

"She didn't just pass away. They're thinking she was murdered," Jason said. "And according to the detective, there was a supposed suicide note left on the bed, but they're not buying it."

Dina frowned. "Really, Jason! We're eating here."

Jason slapped the table, rattling the crystal. "Fuck breakfast! A woman we know was murdered, and Detective Bruner thinks Wilma was involved in what happened to Uncle Carter. Like I said, there was a suicide note, but the police dismissed that theory. Bruner suspects the person paying her to dispose of Uncle Carter was displeased that none of those incidents killed him, so *she* was killed to shut her up."

Ruth grabbed at her heart in disbelief and fainted at the end of the breakfast-laden sideboard.

Jason groaned. He shouldn't have blurted that out so callously. He picked her up and carried her out of the breakfast room and down to the staff lounge.

Peter turned to see who was entering, then ran toward them.

"Ruth! Oh, no! What happened, Mr. Jason?"

"She fainted. I'm afraid there's more bad news regarding Wilma's passing. She may have been the one responsible for the attacks on my uncle here in the house and was killed to shut her up. At least that's their working theory."

Peter was obviously stunned, but before he could comment, Ruth moaned. She was coming to.

"She needs a place to lie down," Jason said.

"There's a daybed in our lounge," Peter offered.

"Right!" Jason carried her there.

Louise walked into the lounge just as Jason laid her down. She rushed to the bed.

"What happened to Ruth?"

"She fainted," Peter said. "Mr. Jason, we've got this now. Thank you for bringing her to us."

Jason backed off as they circled the bed to tend to Ruth. It felt weird to walk away, but he could tell they were uncomfortable with him in the capacity of helping them, instead of the other way around.

"This has been a terrible morning. Let me know if we need to call an ambulance," Jason said and returned to the breakfast room to get his phone.

When he started to leave, his mother cried out.

"Jason! Wait! What about your breakfast?"

"I've lost my appetite," he said and went into the office to call Charlie Dodge. Uncle Carter needed to know this, and Charlie was the link who could make that happen.

CHAPTER THIRTEEN

Charlie was making ham-and-cheese omelets for breakfast when the doorbell rang. He slid the pan off the burner for a moment and went to answer.

It was Wyrick. The cut on her head had scabbed over, and the bruise on her cheek was darker. But her eyes were flashing, and the jut of her chin was a mute warning not to mention the other issues. She needed a hug, but she sure as hell didn't want one, so he felt obliged to insult her instead.

"Use your damn key," he said and ran back to tend to the omelet before it overcooked.

Carter walked into the kitchen, saw the stony expressions on both Charlie's and Wyrick's faces, and wondered how on earth they managed to work so well together.

"Good morning, Wyrick," Carter said.

"Morning," she said, then turned her back and took off her turquoise bolero jacket with the black soutache braid, and hung it on the back of her chair. The turquoise eyeshadow with gold eyeliner was a definite statement, and the gold lipstick she was wearing sparkled. Her knee-length pants matched the jacket, with the same black braid running down the outside seam of each leg. Her black knee-high boots had three-inch heels. All she needed was a red cape and the kind of sword bullfighters used for the killing blow. The blouse she'd worn under the jacket was white and semi-sheer. She'd probably chosen it *because* the dragon tattoo on the entire front of her body was visible enough through the fabric for shock value. Charlie suspected Wyrick needed to unsettle them so they'd leave her the hell alone.

She saw a note from Charlie on top of her keyboard and picked it up.

"Who's Miranda Deutsch?" she asked.

Charlie slid an omelet onto a plate, then looked up. "Jason's girlfriend. She's been out of the country for several months, but since I didn't know about her before, I don't want anyone attached to the family in any way to be overlooked. Just run a basic background search."

Wyrick wanted a cup of coffee before she went to work, but given the small amount of work space in the kitchen, she waited for Carter and Charlie to exit.

The men took their plates to the other end of the dining table to eat, and as soon as they were out of the way, she filled her cup.

Charlie already knew she had a tattoo on the front of her body because he saw bits and pieces of it now and then, depending on what she wore. But this was a full-on view, and he was stunned. The colors of the dragon were startlingly beautiful, but the image was of danger, power and rage.

Like war.

He knew war.

He sat down without looking at her again.

Carter saw it and was intrigued, but he hadn't forgotten the dressing-down she'd given him when he'd complimented her before, and decided silence was the better choice. He picked up his fork and gave his omelet an appreciative sniff.

"This smells as good as it looks," Carter said.

Charlie shrugged. "I have basic kitchen skills. I'm better at grilling. I used to grill at least twice a week when Annie and I were still together, but I don't do it anymore. Apartment living and all that."

Carter took a bite, and nodded as he chewed. "It's delicious. Thank you."

"No problem," Charlie said.

Wyrick filled a coffee cup, then got to work.

For a few minutes, the only sound in the room was the rapid click of the keyboard, and the occasional clink of flatware against a plate.

Charlie finished his omelet and got up to refill their cups.

"Hey, Wyrick. Need a refill?" he asked.

"I'm good," she said shortly.

Charlie put the carafe back on the stand and was going to get their empty plates when his phone rang. He glanced at it.

"It's Jason," he said. "Carter, remember, no talking."

Carter gave him a thumbs-up as Charlie answered.

"Hello."

"Charlie, this is Jason Dunleavy. Do you have a moment? We've had something happen that adds to the situation with Uncle Carter."

"Wait, I'm going to put this on speaker so my assistant will be able to hear, as well."

Wyrick stopped typing to listen as he switched it over.

"Okay, we're ready. What happened?"

"Do you remember the staff you interviewed the day you first came to the house?"

"Yes, Ruth, your housekeeper, Peter the chef, and three maids, Louise, Arnetta and Wanda...no, Wilma," Charlie said.

"Right. We received a call this morning that Wilma was found dead in her apartment. The police believe it was meant to appear as a suicide, but something changed during the attack, so the evidence left behind no longer supported the message on the note."

Carter was stunned and it showed.

Again, Charlie reminded him to stay silent, and Carter nodded.

"What about the note?" Charlie asked.

"Basically, it's written as a confession, stating that Wilma was the one who'd been making all the attempts on Uncle Carter's life. There was some half-ass excuse about how Carter was always mean and mistreating her, and she'd finally had enough. We all knew immediately that was a lie, and there were other factors about the crime scene that must not have played into that story," Jason said.

"Sounds like whoever's behind it was unhappy that Carter got away alive and silenced the only person who could finger him," Charlie said.

"That's the theory the cops are working on, too. I need you to tell Uncle Carter about this update in the case. Now the cops have a new lead to work from. Wilma has an elderly mother in a nursing home. Her mother no longer knows anyone and requires around-the-clock care. It's my personal belief that if this scenario is true, then it was likely the cost of her mother's care that led Wilma to agree to this. Everyone is upset here, as you can imagine."

"Do you have personal information on Wilma, like a Social Security number and a birth date? I'll get my assistant right on this, and see what we can find out from this end."

"Yes, of course. I'll call my accountant now and have him text the info to you."

"Thanks," Charlie said.

The moment the phone call ended, Carter erupted. "I cannot fucking believe this!" Then he turned to Wyrick. "Forgive my language. It's a shock."

"Nothing to forgive," Wyrick said. "Do I continue the

search on Miranda, or do you want me to concentrate on the murder victim, instead?"

"On Wilma, for sure," Charlie said, and when the info came through, he gave it to her. She flexed her fingers, and began a whole new file on Wilma Short.

Miranda Deutsch was still cursing and screaming when she realized Jason hung up on her. Her anger turned to shock, then to disbelief, then to raging disappointment. She stared at herself in a mirror, wondering what it was about her that no man wanted. She knew she was pretty. Her strawberry blond hair and features were like her mother's, but she was taller. She had a fit and shapely body, and the intelligence to carry on in any social gathering.

She'd been reasonably happy until she'd found her mother's old journal up in the attic, and then got depressed reading about her mother's social life, the girlfriends she'd had, the daring escapades she'd pulled off without ever getting caught. She'd even been engaged once, then ended it.

A few months later, Johannes had proposed. Miranda sighed, wondering what it was about the quiet, raw-boned butcher that had attracted a vivacious woman like her mother. She'd died young, but hadn't wasted one day of her life. Miranda didn't have a close circle of women friends. She didn't have old boyfriends, and now she didn't even have the new one. She didn't belong to anyone except her father, and she wanted so much more.

In a fit of pique, she grabbed her purse and car keys and stormed out of the house without a word to anyone. She couldn't believe this had happened. Everything between her and Jason had been so perfect, or so she'd thought. It was a slap in the face to find out she was the only one in love.

Her cell rang. It was her father. She let it go to voicemail as she took an on-ramp onto the freeway. The urge to keep on driving was strong, but that would be running away, and Father didn't believe in running away, so neither did Miranda. He'd fought for what he wanted, and she was going to fight for what she wanted, too. Even though her plans and dreams were gone now... Feeling rebellious, she rolled down all the windows, scanned Sirius XM for an oldies playlist and floored the accelerator. "Highway to Hell" was blasting from the speakers as she hit a hundred miles an hour.

Rey Garza was in the kitchen of his apartment, eating Pop-Tarts with his morning coffee and watching a news program when his cell phone rang. He glanced down at the caller ID. His eyebrows rose, and then he answered.

"Hello?"

"What would you do for a hundred thousand dollars?"

He frowned. "Are you kidding me?"

"No."

"Oh. You mean you need someone," he said.

"Yes."

"Well, then, for a hundred thousand dollars, I'd probably shoot my own mother—except she's already dead. Is that what you want to know?"

"Yes. I want Jason Dunleavy dead. Get to the estate immediately. Catch him as he's leaving for work and follow. When you find an opportune time, take him out and get lost in the traffic. We meet at Cherry Creek Reservoir directly afterward and I pay you in cash."

"What does he drive?" Rey asked.

"A red Fiat."

"I always get my money up front," Rey said.

"There's no time. I'll make it two hundred thousand."

"Done," Rey said. "But if you don't pay up, I'll find you. Understand?"

The line went dead.

Rey took one last drink of coffee, ran into his bedroom to get his gun and took off out of the house with it tucked in the waistband of his jeans. He peeled out of the apartment complex, heading toward Greenwood Village. He'd driven past that castle more than once, so he knew where it was. Hell, everyone in Denver had probably driven past it just to look.

He reached the area in record time, but without knowing whether or not Jason had already left for work. However, all he could do was sit and wait, so he parked down the street, still giving himself a clear view of the driveway.

To his surprise, his wait was brief. Within a few minutes, a red Fiat came out of the drive and turned left.

Rey started his car and followed, staying far enough behind that he didn't call attention to himself. He followed him on the freeway, and then took the same exit toward downtown where the Dunleavy Building was located. Time was running out and traffic sucked. But now that Rey knew where he was going, he played a hunch and turned off a few blocks early, took a side street, then turned again, hoping to come out at the same light, but on the intersecting street.

After that, he would play it by ear.

Four hours later, Miranda walked back into the house. Her eyes were red rimmed and swollen from crying, and her hair was wild and windblown.

Johannes caught her in the hall and grabbed her by the arm.

"Where have you been? I was so worried. I called and called but you never answered. I thought something had happened to you."

"Something did happen to me, Father. Jason dumped me. Evidently I'm great in bed, but not good enough to marry."

Her father was horrified and then angry. No matter how rich he got, there was always someone richer who looked down on a man selling sausages.

Johannes wasn't good at showing his emotions—Johannes was obviously out of his element, hearing his daughter talking so casually about sex—but Miranda knew he was heartbroken over her grief. He took her in his arms, patting her on the back like he'd done when she was a baby. But back then a few pats, a burp, and she was all better. He didn't know what to do with a grown female's tears.

"Don't cry. If that's the kind of man he is, better you find out now."

Miranda sobbed.

Johannes handed her his handkerchief.

She blotted her tears, then wiped her nose and laid her head back on his chest.

"I loved him. I feel so betrayed. I don't know what's wrong with me, but I can't find a man to love me. I wish I'd never been born."

"Come, come, darling. Here's your Binni. Let her get you back to bed. I'm going to call the doctor."

Miranda turned to the housekeeper who'd become the stand-in for the mother she'd lost, and let the woman's soothing words be her guide as she went back to her room and got into bed.

Johannes hurried down to his office to phone their personal physician, and explained what was happening. The doctor agreed to call in a prescription for Miranda and said it would be delivered.

"Thank you." Johannes hung up.

He needed to think of something he could do for her. Something he could buy her that would get her out of this emotional state. He didn't leave his office for almost an hour, and even then he didn't go back to her. He didn't know what to say.

It wasn't long afterward that the pharmacy delivered the

prescription. Johannes opened the sack, saw that it was Valium and frowned, then sent for Binni.

"Yes, sir, what do you need?" Binni asked.

"This is a prescription for Miranda. Please take it to her, dole out the amount she is to have and watch her take it, then bring the bottle back to me."

"Yes, sir," Binni said and hurried away.

But what Johannes didn't know was that after the letdown, Miranda was thriving on being the center of attention. When the housekeeper came and handed her two pills, she happily downed the Valium and floated off to sleep.

This was not the outcome Johannes had expected when Miranda first told him she was dating Jason Dunleavy. Months later when she announced she was going to Europe to shop for a trousseau, he was even more pleased. This was the closest she'd come to getting married, and she was almost thirty. Finally, a wedding was on the horizon.

He had pictured his daughter marrying into one of the richest families in the US. And now this. After all the money he'd spent, it was not how he'd imagined things would be.

Jason was nearing the Dunleavy building when he got stuck at a red light. Being late for the board meeting was on his mind, so when the light turned green, he wasted no time accelerating. But as he did, he glimpsed movement to his right just as a car ran a red light and blew through the intersection.

"Asshole!" Jason yelled. He hit the brakes, then automatically leaned across the console to catch his briefcase from sliding to the floor.

At that moment his windshield exploded. He threw his arms up to shield his face and then slammed the car into Park. His heart was pounding from the shock, and he was already beginning to feel a stinging sensation on his face as he slowly sat up.

"What just happened?" he muttered and then looked at himself in the rearview mirror. There were tiny bleeding abrasions all over his face, obviously from the shattered glass.

Then he saw drivers getting out of their cars and running toward him. The first one to reach him was a woman in scrubs.

"I'm a nurse!" she said. "Are you all right? Were you hit anywhere?"

"What? Hit? No. I missed the car. I don't know what happened."

"Someone in that car fired two shots at you as he raced through the intersection. At least one bullet, maybe both, shattered your windshield. I saw it."

Jason's head was spinning. He clutched the steering wheel to steady himself as the nurse reached into the car and grabbed his arm.

"Ow!" he said and pulled back in pain.

"You've been shot," she told him.

And the moment she said it, he began to feel the burn.

Sirens were approaching as everything began going out of focus.

"Getting dizzy," he murmured.

The nurse had a hand on his shoulder. "I'm right here, sir. I'll stay with you until the ambulance arrives."

"My name is Jason Dunleavy. Tell the police to call Charlie Dodge. Number is in my phone," he said, then passed out.

Dina was a little put out with Kenneth. They were going to take a drive this morning in his new car, but he'd insisted on having his lesson with the tennis pro from the club first. So here she was, sitting on a single tier of bleachers out by their court, watching Kenneth play. His stroke was getting better. At least that was something, she was thinking when she heard someone call her name. She turned toward the house, then frowned. Ruth was running in her direction, shouting, "Miss Dina! Miss Dina!"

Dina heard the panic in Ruth's voice. She climbed down from her seat and started toward her.

Ruth was wide-eyed and out of breath by the time they met up.

"Miss Dina! The police just called. Mr. Jason's been shot. He's being taken to St. Joseph's."

Dina screamed.

Kenneth heard her, dropped his racquet and began running. Dina collapsed into his arms, sobbing hysterically.

"Ruth, my God! What the hell has happened now?"

"Mr. Jason has been shot. Detective Bruner just called again to tell us. They took him to St. Joseph's for surgery. I don't have any other information."

"Does Edward know?" Kenneth asked.

"No, sir."

"He won't want to be left behind," Kenneth said. "I'll bring the car around. Please help him get ready and bring him outside. Can you do that for us?"

"Yes," she said and took off running back to the castle, while Kenneth grabbed Dina by both shoulders and gave her a little shake.

"Darling. Get a hold of yourself. I need to change out of these shorts and get the car keys. Come with me."

Dina took his hand, and by the time they got back inside, she'd gone into mother mode and pulled herself together. He ran upstairs to change out of the tennis gear, while she went to help Ruth.

Ruth was assisting Edward out of his house slippers and into street shoes when Dina broke the news to him.

"I don't understand! I don't understand! Why is our family suddenly under attack? I wish Carter was here," Edward cried.

"I wish Carter was here, too, but we still have each other, right? And what one can do, more can do better," Ruth said.

After that, Edward seemed to pull himself together, too, and let himself be led out the door to the car Kenneth had waiting. Moments later, they were loaded up and gone, leaving Ruth in tears as she watched them go.

CHAPTER FOURTEEN

Charlie was determined to visit Annie and was at his apartment getting ready when his cell phone rang. Denver PD. He frowned.

"Hello, Charlie Dodge speaking."

"Mr. Dodge, this is Detective Bruner from the Denver Police Department. Jason Dunleavy was shot in his car on the way to work this morning. He asked that you be notified."

Charlie's heart skipped a beat as he turned around and bolted from his bedroom, looking for Carter. No success.

"Is Jason alive?" he asked, heading for Wyrick next.

"Yes, he's in surgery now."

"What happened?" Charlie asked and snapped his fingers at Wyrick to get her attention, and then pointed to his phone and mouthed, *Denver PD. Jason was shot.*

Wyrick flew out of her chair and ran to find Carter as Bruner continued to explain.

"He was stopped at an intersection. Light turned green, and as he started to accelerate, another car ran the red light. Jason slammed on the brakes, and if he hadn't leaned sideways to catch his briefcase, this would be a different story.

Whoever the driver was, it was a deliberate move. He fired two shots straight into Jason's car. The windshield shattered, and he was hit in the shoulder. We don't know yet if it was the same bullet, but according to a witness, two were fired."

"Tell the family I'll get there as soon as I can," Charlie said.

"Where are you?" Bruner asked.

"I'm in Dallas."

"You're the PI who found Carter Dunleavy, right?"

"Yes. Listen, I need to notify Carter myself because he's still in hiding. Thank you for calling. We'll talk more after I get there."

Carter walked in as Charlie ended the call.

"What's going on? Wyrick said it was an emergency."

Charlie hated like hell to have to say this, but he couldn't possibly sugarcoat the truth.

"Jason was shot on his way to work this morning. He's in surgery."

Carter groaned. "I've got to get home. How fast can we be in Denver?"

"I'll call Benny," Wyrick said.

"Just get packed, Carter. I'll take you home, but I'm not leaving you there. I'm going to assume you have an extra bed somewhere in that castle of yours."

"Make that two beds," Wyrick said. "Flying back and forth is a waste of time when you need information ASAP. I'm staying with you. As long as you're there, I'll work from your place."

Wyrick ran over to her desk to call her mechanic. As soon as she had everything she'd been working on downloaded onto a flash drive, she dropped it in her bag, put her jacket back on and ran down the hall, yelling.

"Charlie!"

He came out of the bedroom. "What?"

"Benny was on-site, so he's fueling up now. My place is on the way. I'll stop there long enough to pack a few things. You two meet me at the hangar."

"Will do," Charlie said and then stopped her. "Whatever there is about me that ticks you off, can we put that aside while we're working from their home?"

"Yes."

And then she was gone, slamming the front door behind her. She ran without her usual caution, and came flying out of the building into the parking garage—only to find Mack Doolin hunkered down beside the front fender of her car.

"You bastard!" she screamed, dropped her things and leaped on him before he could stand up.

The impact was so sudden, Mack's chin hit concrete as he went down and then he rolled, taking her with him and took a swing at her before scrambling to his feet. She deflected the blow with her forearm, and then both of them were up.

He came at her again, only to get the toe of her boot between his legs.

"Bitch!" he screamed as he grabbed at his crotch, then sprang at her.

His momentum slammed her hard enough against a van that she lost her breath, but when he started to turn and run, she tackled him from behind and took him down hard.

And that was what Charlie saw as he and Carter came through the door into the garage.

"What the hell?" he shouted as he dropped his gear and ran.

Wyrick didn't know Charlie was there until his arm was around her waist, pulling her up and off Doolin. Then Charlie grabbed Doolin by the back of the shirt and yanked him up so fast his neck popped.

It wasn't until Doolin was on his feet, that Charlie realized he knew him as another private investigator.

"Mack! What the hell?"

But Mack wasn't talking.

Wyrick's eyes narrowed. "You know him?"

"He's a PI for hire, like me," Charlie said.

Wyrick snapped, "No! He's not like you. He's a stalker. And you don't hit women, damn it!"

Charlie's grip tightened on Mack's arm. "You hit her?"

Mack shrugged. "I swung at her, but it was reflex, I swear."

Charlie slammed Mack against the nearest car and pinned him there, then looked at Wyrick.

"Talk to me. What the hell's been going on?"

"Oh, I'll talk," Wyrick said. "He's been stalking me for weeks. He bugged my car. I watched him do it, and I caught him doing it again just now."

Then she jabbed Doolin in the chest. "You're working for them, aren't you?" she snapped.

Doolin was angry, but she could tell he was also scared, and right now, he probably didn't know which one of these two people scared him the most.

"Nothin' personal," he said. "It's just a job."

"Working for who?" Charlie asked, but again, Wyrick answered for him.

"A company I used to work for. And just so you know, Doolin, I got your tag number when you bugged my car the first time. I ran a search to get your stats. I know about you all the way from elementary school to getting kicked out of college, to the money you've been hiding in a bank in the Caymans. You have two choices. You can keep tailing me to collect your fee or you can tell them you quit. But if you choose to continue this chase, I will make that money disappear with one click on my keyboard and it'll happen so fast not even God will know where it went."

"You can't do that!"

"I can and I will, and you won't be able to say a word to

the authorities without giving away the fact that you've been hiding money from the IRS," she said.

"Before you bother to answer," Charlie told him. "One son of a bitch already hurt her this week, and you just gave her another bruise and her knuckles are bleeding." Then Charlie yanked Doolin so close they were barely an inch apart. "If I ever see your sorry-ass face again in the city of Dallas, I will beat you to within an inch of your life."

Mack groaned. "I'll quit. I choose the money, and I'll be out of here by sundown. Is that good enough?"

"You know the way out. Take it before I call the cops and get your license revoked," Charlie said.

Doolin ran.

Wyrick hated to admit she was shaking and blamed it on adrenaline, but when Charlie tilted her chin so he could see the abrasion on her face, the urge to lean into his strength was so strong it scared her. She pushed him away.

"I'm fine. He was a pain in the ass, but nothing I haven't dealt with before. I've been dodging people like him off and on for the past ten years."

"Why?" Charlie asked. "Who is this company, and why do they want you?"

And because she was so rattled, she finally dropped her guard.

"Universal Theorem. UT for short. I used to work there. When I got cancer, they thought I was dying, so they no longer considered me of value and dropped me. When I survived, they wanted me back. That's all."

Charlie had never heard of them—but then he'd never heard of Carter Dunleavy until he was hired to find him. He needed to get out in the world more.

Carter had been quiet through all of this until he heard her mention UT.

"Are you that good?" Carter asked.

Wyrick froze. Charlie didn't know squat about UT, but Carter obviously did as he revealed by asking that question.

She shrugged it off. "Obviously. However, we need to save this for another time."

She gathered up what she'd dropped and put it inside her car, then got down on her knees. She found the tracking device he'd put under the front wheel well, another beneath the rear wheel well and one under her front bumper. She dropped them on the concrete and stomped them until they shattered.

"I'll meet you at the hangar," she said, then jumped in her Mercedes and peeled out.

Charlie watched until she disappeared. He went back to get their luggage, loaded it into his Jeep. He said nothing until they were out of the garage and back on city streets.

"Hey, Carter."

"Yes?"

"What is Universal Theorem?"

"Their public face is a think tank of some of the most brilliant minds in the world," he said.

Charlie thought about the abilities he'd witnessed over her time in his office, and wondered what other marvels she was hiding.

"So what's behind the public face?" Charlie asked, as he negotiated moving into another lane to take the next on-ramp to the freeway.

"Oh, there are always rumors, but no one knows for sure, although I'm certain Wyrick does."

"What kind of rumors?" Charlie asked.

Carter was silent for a moment. "Rumors about medical experiments. About gene-splicing and manipulating DNA, most of which is still illegal. But as you know, when you have enough money and power, you can rise above legalities. There was talk some years back that they'd sidestepped using lab rats and the like, and were experimenting on human embryos."

Charlie was silent, wondering how Wyrick fit into all of that, and was beginning to understand why she wanted nothing to do with them again. They'd left her to die and when she didn't, they wanted her genius back.

"That's cold," Charlie finally said. "And all kinds of wrong."

Carter shrugged. "But that's all speculation and rumors."

Charlie nodded.

Carter shoved his fingers through his hair. "I don't have the words to express how much I appreciate all the effort you two are making on my behalf. I know I'm paying you, but I've paid thousands of people over the years to do jobs for me, and none of them have gone to the extent you have, Charlie Dodge. I won't forget it."

Miranda had cried for what felt like hours, until she was disgusted with herself for being this hurt. She wasn't ugly. She wasn't stupid. She could find someone else.

She rolled off the bed and went into her bathroom to wash her face, grimacing at what she saw. Her eyes were red, swollen and streaked with black from the mascara she'd cried away. Her cheeks were tear streaked and puffy, so she began to clean herself up. Except that now, without makeup, she felt she looked like some long-ago European peasant woman with pink cheeks and a ruddy complexion. She made a face at herself and went back to her sitting room. She needed to eat something or she'd just fall asleep again. She called down to the cook, asked for soup and a sandwich, and then turned on the TV for something to do while she waited for her food.

She channel surfed for shows to watch, but she never watched daytime television and had no idea what the programming was like. So she chose one of the local stations to see what was going on in Denver.

As fate would have it, the first thing she saw was a picture of Jason's face covering most of the screen and then some kind of update.

Pissed off as she was, she still wanted to know what had happened, but when she heard "shot and taken to surgery," she leaped up from the sofa, screaming as she ran.

Her father was outside in the greenhouse, working on one of his bonsai trees. He'd taken up the hobby years ago, and now the greenhouse was full of them.

He had just taken a final snip from a lower branch of a miniature spruce when his cell phone rang.

"Hello?" Then he heard his personal assistant's voice.

"Sir, I'm sorry to disturb you, but your daughter is in the office with me, very upset and calling for you."

Johannes could hear screaming in the background, and thought *upset* didn't begin to describe what he was hearing.

"I'll be right there," he said, giving the calm and beauty of his work a regretful glance before hurrying inside.

Miranda was sobbing as she met him in the hall, and threw herself into his arms.

"Father! Father! It was just on the news. Jason was shot! Gunned down in his car! He was taken to surgery. I have to go to him."

Johannes tore her arms from around his neck and then clutched her shoulders and shook her.

"No! He discarded you. He used you and then dumped you. He treated you like garbage and threw you away, and he does not deserve one more minute of your life. No daughter of mine goes crawling back to a man who does this! No daughter of mine begs. Ever! Do you understand me?"

Miranda was so startled that she sucked up her tears, hic-cupped once and then stared at him.

"What if he dies?" she whispered.

"So what if he does?" Johannes snapped.

"But, Father—"

Johannes shook her again. "No *buts*. For once, you will act with dignity. We are not paupers. We do not need the Dun-leavy name to matter in this world. I am the King of Sau-sages. I am enough. You are my daughter. You are enough. Go, and do not mention that name in our house again! Do you understand me?"

Miranda nodded.

"Make yourself presentable! Tonight I am taking you out to dinner. We will dress in our finest clothing and eat the best of fine dining. And other men will see you and want you. You do not chase after anyone. They come to you, Miranda! They come to you."

Miranda's shoulders were smarting from his grip as she re-turned to her room. She was in shock. Her father had never spoken to her in such a way. He had never mentioned any-thing about her lifestyle, but it was obvious he had not ap-proved. This was such a sobering moment that she gave up envisioning a mad rush into Jason's hospital room and being the angel who pulled him back from the brink of death.

Her food was likely in her room by now. She would have her soup, and then take a nice long bubble bath and relax. Later, she would go to dinner with her father. She still be-lieved in miracles. Maybe one would happen tonight.

Wyrick drove like a bat out of hell all the way back to her apartment, and once inside, changed to tennis shoes instead of three-inch heels, jeans instead of turquoise pants, and changed the bolero jacket for a brown leather bomber jacket and her white blouse for a white t-shirt. Then she began throwing clothes, shoes and makeup into a suitcase.

She gathered up two laptops, some flash drives, along with an iPad, another phone and the charging cords for all of them, then packed it all in a separate suitcase. Without knowing how long they'd be gone, she checked her fridge to see what was going to spoil. She put butter in the freezer and poured a small container of cream down the sink. The rest would keep, which said something for eating takeout most of the time. She loaded her car, sent a text to Merlin telling him she'd be out of town for a few days and then she was back on the street, heading for the hangar.

Charlie reached the private airport and drove straight to the hangar where Wyrick kept the Ranger. Benny came out to meet them as Charlie pulled up.

"Hello, Mr. Dodge. Would you like to park your Jeep inside the hangar? It's locked up when Miss Jade isn't using her chopper. She always parks in there. It'll be okay."

Shit. He calls her Jade. I'm not even allowed to admit I know that's her name. "The owner won't mind?" Charlie asked.

"She owns it. It's her private hangar. I've already pulled the chopper out. You can load your things behind the backseats. The boss lady will do her preflight checks, but the luggage won't interfere with that."

Charlie was still trying to wrap his head around the fact that the hangar was hers as he drove to the chopper.

"Sit tight, Carter. I'll unload."

Carter simply nodded, and Charlie knew he was so shaken about Jason he couldn't focus.

Charlie off-loaded their bags, then drove inside the hangar and parked.

Benny came out of the office, talking. "If you want something cold to drink, the refrigerator in the office has bottled water and some candy bars. She likes sweets when she flies."

"How long have you worked for her?" Charlie asked.

Benny shrugged. "Maybe three years. One day she landed here in that fine jet chopper, asking if she could rent space. It's a Bell 206 Long Ranger, you know. So she rented until she had her own hangar built."

Carter was watching Charlie's face. The longer he knew these two, the more they intrigued him. They were lightning in a bottle when it came to working together. Then he remembered Charlie's wife, and not for the first time, was glad he'd never fallen in love like that, and glad he'd never married. The pain of Charlie's loss had to be hard to bear.

"Hey, Carter, do you want a bottle of water?" Charlie asked.

"Sure," Carter said and then saw a door marked Bathroom and stepped inside to wash up before boarding the flight.

Charlie handed him the bottle as he came out, and before he had the lid unscrewed, Wyrick arrived. She pulled up to the chopper to unload her gear, then drove into the hangar and parked beside his Jeep.

"As always, thanks, Benny," she said.

"You're welcome, Miss Jade."

Wyrick glared at Charlie, warning him without words that he did not have permission to call her that.

Charlie handed her a bottle of water, too.

She took it and walked off without comment. They followed.

Charlie escorted Carter all the way to the chopper and then into the rear seating. Again, Carter chose the seat by the window, but this time, he leaned back and closed his eyes.

Charlie got into the copilot's seat and, like Carter, leaned back and closed his eyes.

Sorry, Annie. I meant to go see you. I tried to go see you. It wasn't meant to be.

A few minutes later, Wyrick slid into the pilot's seat and shut the door. Both men appeared to be asleep as she started the engine. The rotors began to turn in a slow, steady swoosh, then faster and faster. She put on her headset, wincing as it brushed across the wound from being hit in the head with the beer bottle. She tapped Charlie's arm.

He roused, then sat up and shook Carter awake. "Buckle up," he said.

Carter reached for the seat belt to comply.

Charlie buckled up and reached for his headset. As soon as he had it on, Wyrick started talking.

"I rented an SUV on my way here. It's being delivered to a small airport outside Denver, which is where we're going to land. I'll store the Ranger there until we're ready to go home. The car will be waiting when we arrive."

"Do you pay attention to driving while you're conducting all this business?"

"Hands-free calling, all kinds of neat apps on my iPad," she said, then looked over her shoulder. Carter had his headset on, too, and when he saw her, he smiled and gave her a thumbs-up.

Wyrick resisted the urge to smile back. It wouldn't take long for Carter Dunleavy to work his way into her good graces.

After liftoff, she made a half circle above the airport, then headed due north.

The Dunleavys were on their second hour in the waiting room. The longer they waited, the more tension mounted. For Dina, time had slowed down to heartbeats.

"Who is doing all of this to us?" she wailed.

Kenneth hugged her. It wasn't the first time she'd asked that.

"The police don't know yet, but they will, I'm sure."

"They couldn't find Carter," Dina said. "It took that investigator to make it happen."

She laid her head against Kenneth's shoulder and closed her eyes. Edward sat beside her, nervously tapping his cane on the floor. They were still sitting in silence when a man in surgical scrubs walked into the waiting room.

"Are you the Dunleavy family?" he asked.

Dina stood abruptly. "Jason is my son."

"I'm Dr. Wagner, his surgeon. Jason is doing great. The bullet broke his collarbone and lodged near his rotator cuff. There were bone fragments, as well. But he's young, and he's healthy. Barring any complications, I expect a full recovery."

"Thank God! When can we see him?" Dina asked.

"He's still in Post-op. A nurse will come let you know when he's moved to a room."

Edward stood and held out his hand. "Thank you, sir, for taking care of my nephew."

The doctor saw that he was blind and grasped Edward's hand firmly. "You are most welcome. I'll check on him again tonight before I leave the hospital," he said and left the waiting area.

Edward felt for his chair, then sat back down. "What a relief not to be sitting here wondering about worst-case scenarios."

Dina kissed her brother's cheek. "Yes, dear, it is a relief." Then she walked to the window overlooking a parking lot, bowed her head and wept quiet tears of gratitude.

Kenneth came up behind her and gave her a hug.

"It won't be long now before you see him," he said.

"I love my son so much, and you are such a dear. It hurts me that the two people I care for most don't get along," Dina whispered.

Kenneth sighed. "I'm sorry. I sensed his dislike early on and

I could have been more understanding, rather than responding to his remarks. I promise to do better. Okay?"

Dina leaned back against him.

The waiting wasn't over yet.

Carter fell back asleep within fifteen minutes of being in the air. Wyrick was visibly intent but silent, which left Charlie with too much time to think.

Before all this began, he'd never let Wyrick irritate him for long, because they went their separate ways at the end of a day. But right now she was in his home from early morning till late afternoon, and the vibe that lingered after she was gone messed him up.

Today changed things between them even more. Coming out of the building into the parking garage and seeing her take that bastard down in a flying tackle had rattled him. There'd been a moment of sheer panic before he got to her and pulled her off. Maybe it was just responsibility that he was feeling.

He didn't know what to think about the bits and pieces of her past she'd revealed, but he'd learned more about her this morning than he had in the years she'd worked for him. At least now he understood why she kept moving.

He was itching to Google UT and see what kind of organization would stalk an ex-employee. It was harassment, pure and simple, but he guessed Wyrick would never call them on it. He glanced at her once. She looked like she'd been in a bar fight. He turned away. Damn Mack Doolin. It was one thing to trail someone. That was part of being a private investigator. But he'd damn sure never stalked or attacked anyone.

He was back to thinking about possible areas to consider for new office space when Wyrick touched his shoulder.

"We're coming up on the airport," she said, then radioed the tower.

Charlie reached behind Wyrick's seat and tapped Carter on the knee.

"What? Are we there?" he asked, blinking in confusion.

Charlie nodded, then pointed down.

Carter glanced out the window, saw the mountains in the distance and sighed. He wasn't there yet, but it already felt like home. Now all he needed was for Jason to recover. He felt guilty as hell for leaving, and no matter what happened next, he wasn't running again.

When the chopper went into landing mode, Carter looked away from the window. Watching the ground come up to meet him that fast was unnerving, but down they went. The skids touched lightly as they settled.

"We're going straight to St. Joseph's, right?" Carter asked.

"Yes. We have a car rented," Wyrick said. "We'll be there soon. I just need to get the Ranger in a hangar before we leave."

The rental car was waiting for them in the parking lot, and as soon as Charlie and Carter were out, they carried their luggage past the fenced-in area, found the man waiting with the car Wyrick had rented, and loaded their gear.

Charlie looked back once to check on Wyrick's progress and saw her overseeing the Ranger being pulled into a hangar. She followed it in, and a couple of minutes later, came out carrying her bags.

Charlie went to meet her at the gate, eyeing her long stride in the neon-green tennis shoes, her straight-legged blue jeans and brown bomber jacket. She still had that unconscious swagger, and when she walked through the exit, he reached for her bags.

"I can carry them," she insisted.

"I know you *can*," Charlie said. "But I haven't gotten past watching you hit Doolin in the back with a flying tackle. You should be sore all over after what you've gone through, so I'm carrying your damn bags to the car, and I'm driving us to the hospital."

Wyrick gave up without an argument. She *was* sore, and knew she would get worse before she got better. She climbed into the passenger side of the car, fastened her seat belt, then sank back against the cool leather and turned the air vent toward her face.

Carter touched her shoulder, then handed her a bottle of cold water.

"They were in the car. Nice touch."

Wyrick took a long, satisfying drink, then set it in one of the cup holders in the console.

Charlie got into the car, scooted the seat back as far as it would go and buckled himself in.

"I Googled the address of the hospital. It's in the GPS on my phone."

"I can drive if you want," Carter said. "I know the way."

"You just stay where you are, and if you see me take the wrong direction, speak up. Even though the windows are tinted, the less you call attention to yourself, the better."

"Okay, yes, you're right," Carter said. Charlie put the car in gear and drove out of the parking lot, following the GPS directions to St. Joseph's.

Not one to sit idly by, Wyrick was on her phone, calling the hospital to find out the number of Jason Dunleavy's room.

As soon as Charlie had parked, they got out. They'd been sitting so long it felt good to stand up and stretch. Then Charlie dug his Texas Ranger ball cap out of an outer pocket in his duffel bag and handed it to Carter.

"Put this on and don't look at anyone," he said.

Carter's expression was grim as he settled it on his head and pulled down the brim. He knew he was on home territory again, but just now, it wasn't safe territory.

"Walk between us," Charlie added. "My partner and I know how to look mean."

Wyrick was taken aback by being referred to as his partner. She was fine with assistant, but *partner* seemed personal, and she didn't do personal with anyone. Still, she'd promised not to argue with him here, so she made no comment.

CHAPTER FIFTEEN

The lobby was full of people coming and going as the trio entered the building. Carter led the way to the elevators, and then they waited. Once the first car to reach the lobby had emptied, Wyrick walked in first. Carter followed, and Charlie brought up the rear.

"What floor?" he asked.

"Fourth floor," Wyrick said. "Room 424."

Carter leaned against the back of the elevator as it began to rise, eyeing Charlie's assistant with unmistakable envy.

"Wyrick, you are a true marvel of organization. What I wouldn't give to have someone like you on my team."

"Except she's on mine," Charlie said. "So no poaching."

Wyrick stood between them, listening to their banter and hoping the lighthearted moment would hold true after they learned Jason's condition. Then the doors opened and there was no longer any need for supposition. They were about to find out.

They went down the hall and paused at the door of Room 424.

"You ready to do this?" Charlie asked, and when Carter nodded, Charlie knocked once, then opened the door.

★ ★ ★

Dina was on her feet and leaning over Jason's bed, smoothing the wisps of red hair away from his forehead.

Kenneth was sitting beside Edward and was the first to look up and smile when he saw who walked in.

Dina heard footsteps and turned to look, too. She saw Charlie Dodge first, but when the man behind him suddenly took off his cap, she gasped.

"Carter! Thank God!" She burst into tears and walked into his open arms.

Kenneth patted Edward's arm. "Charlie Dodge is here, Edward. He brought Carter home!"

The relief on Edward's face said it all.

Jason wasn't conscious, but Carter went straight to his bedside. "How's he doing?" he asked.

"The doctor said he should make a full recovery. The bullet broke his collarbone and lodged near the rotator cuff. They had to remove quite a bit of bone fragment, too," Dina said.

Carter smiled. "This news is wonderful. Kenneth, it's good to see you," he said, then went straight to Edward, sat down beside him. "Hey, Eddie, how's it going, buddy?"

Edward grinned. Carter was the only person in the family who still called him by his childhood name, Eddie, and he loved it.

"I'm glad you're home," he said.

"Me, too," Carter told him. "And I'm not running again. Mr. Dodge and his assistant are both staying here with me until this mess is over. Between them and my security team, I'll be fine."

The mention of an assistant shifted Dina's focus. It was then that she saw another person leaning against the wall near the door.

Charlie had been waiting for it, and when Dina's eyes widened and her mouth opened, he spoke before she could utter a word.

"Everyone, this is Wyrick. She's my assistant as well as the pilot who flew us here. You have her to thank that we arrived as soon as we did."

Kenneth was stunned when Charlie said "she." He'd seen the person who'd walked in behind Charlie, certain it was a man, especially with all the bruises on his face and head.

Wyrick said nothing. She'd already taken the woman's measure and knew she was going to disapprove, but Wyrick didn't give a damn.

Then they heard a moan. Jason was waking up.

Carter hurried to Jason's bedside. "Hey, Jason. Hey, buddy."

Jason moaned again, but now his eyelids were fluttering. "Uncle...?"

Carter smiled. "Yes, it's me. I'm here."

Jason opened his eyes and reached for Carter's hand. "You came home."

Carter nodded. "Yes, to stay. Don't worry about a thing. Just rest and heal."

Jason managed a half smile, then was out again.

Charlie tapped Carter on the shoulder. "Are you planning to stay at the hospital?"

Carter shook his head. "Until I make an official announcement that I'm back, my presence here would only cause chaos. Especially if the media finds out I'm back, and Jason doesn't need that. However, I am concerned that there's no security here. Someone just tried to kill him, and at this moment, anyone could walk in and finish the job."

Dina moaned, "I didn't think of that!"

"I'll get some people from our security division. They'll be here 24/7 until Jason is released."

Dina hugged him again. "Thank you, and thank God you're home."

"Charlie, since I'm no longer going to be secluded, it's okay to use my own phone, right?" Carter asked.

Charlie nodded.

Carter moved toward the window to make the call. Within minutes, he had security notified, and men on the way.

"They'll be here shortly," Carter said. "I'll wait until they arrive, and then I think we should leave."

"Okay," Charlie agreed, but he was watching Wyrick. Not only had she made her way to where Edward was sitting, but he'd watched her introducing herself, and now they were talking. From the expression on Edward's face, she was charming him. Charlie wondered where the hell all that personality came from, and then it hit him. She was free to be herself with Edward because he couldn't see her to judge.

Ten minutes later, two men from Carter's security team were knocking at the door. Carter stepped out into the hall to speak with them, and Charlie went with him.

"Good to see you, sir," the men were saying.

"It's good to be home, too," Carter said. "You do understand the seriousness of this?"

They both nodded. "Of course. We're here for the first shift. The shifts will change every eight hours, through a twenty-four-hour day, as you requested."

"Yes, perfect," Carter said. "And you know if any incident occurs, however small, you're to notify the Denver PD."

"Yes, sir. We were given all the particulars. We won't let you down."

Carter shook each man's hand, and then went back inside.

"Dina, we're going to leave now. If you want an around-the-clock nurse on the job, all you have to do is notify the doctor and request it."

"Thank you," Dina said. "I'll see you at dinner this evening."

Carter glanced at Edward. "Eddie, if you're tired, you can ride home with us."

Dina looked relieved. "Yes, Edward, do that. Now that you know Jason is recovering, you should go."

"I would like to go home now," he said.

Wyrick touched his hand. "Take my arm, sir, if you'd like."

Charlie handed his baseball cap back to Carter as they left. They exited the hospital without incident, and when they reached the car, Carter and Edward got in the back together. Charlie slid into the driver's seat, while Wyrick buckled up on the passenger side.

"Do you know where you're going?" Wyrick asked.

"I've been there before. Do *you* know where we're going?" he asked.

"Of course I do. The directions are on my phone. You may proceed," Wyrick said.

Charlie drove out of the parking lot, once again on his way to Greenwood Village.

Carter had one ear on Edward's conversation, but he was also watching the byplay between the pair in the front seat. The energy between them was so strong it was almost visible, and he could also tell that Wyrick knew it, and Charlie didn't.

It was 6:15 p.m. when Detective Bruner stopped by the hospital, hoping Jason Dunleavy was cognizant enough to talk about the shooting. But when he got to Jason's room, there were two men standing guard outside the door. Before he could enter, they stopped him.

"We need to see some ID."

Bruner flashed his badge. "Detective Bruner. Denver PD. I'm investigating the shooting and I'd like to speak with him."

"Oh, sorry, Detective. Some of his family just left. Maybe he's still awake."

"I won't be long," Bruner said and went in.

The head of Jason's bed was raised a little. His eyes were closed, but he opened them when Bruner approached.

Bruner immediately displayed his badge.

"Good evening, Jason. I'm Detective Bruner. Finally we

meet, but I'm sorry it's this way. As you know, I caught the Wilma Short case, which is connected to your family. And when someone tried to kill you today, we're thinking it might be connected. Are you up to answering a few questions?"

"I'm still a little groggy from pain meds, so I don't know how much help I'll be," Jason said.

"First question—did you see who shot you?" Bruner asked.

"No. All I know is when the light turned green, I started to cross the intersection. I saw movement from the corner of my eye and the flash of a car running a red light. I slammed on my brakes, and as I did, my briefcase, which was in the passenger seat, began sliding to the floor. I reached across the console to grab it, and the next thing I know, I'm covered in glass. I had no idea what the hell had happened until a woman was at my window asking if I was okay. She said she was a nurse. I still didn't know I'd been shot."

"So she saw the shooter?" Bruner asked.

"I guess she saw something," Jason said. "She said a man took two shots at me. She reached for my shoulder. I remember intense pain, and her saying, 'You've been shot.' I think the last thing I said was to tell the police to call Charlie Dodge, that the number was in my phone. Then I passed out."

"Did the woman tell you her name?" Bruner asked.

"No, only that she was a nurse. But she must have passed on the message to someone, because Charlie Dodge showed up here today, just after I came out of surgery."

"I won't bother you further, Jason. Get some rest."

Bruner left the hospital no closer to an answer than before he arrived, but as soon as he got back to the office, he checked the incident report for the woman's name and testimony—and noticed another interesting thing or two about the shooter. His left arm was out the window as he was shooting, so he was left-handed. And that the arm had a complete sleeve of tattoos.

★ ★ ★

Rey Garza took country roads to get to Cherry Creek Reservoir, which had added to his driving time. Once he reached the meeting place to collect his money, no one was there. He reminded himself it wasn't like this customer could stiff him, so he settled in to wait. But for Rey, patience was hard to come by, and after two cars had driven past without stopping, he was getting antsy.

Finally, he saw another car approaching, and this one slowed and then pulled up right beside him. When the driver rolled down the window, he breathed a sigh of relief and lowered his window, as well.

"Hey!" he said, then leaned across his console and smiled. "Just toss it in."

"You missed," the driver said and shot Rey between the eyes. Blood spattered the driver's-side window, along with brain matter.

The shot, muffled by a silencer, was hardly more than a pop, and then the driver was gone.

A couple hiking the area a few hours later found the body and called the police.

As Charlie drove through the gates toward the residence, Carter directed him to follow a bricked road that went behind the house.

"Just park in any of the empty spaces," he said, pointing to a long multicar garage.

Charlie did, and as soon as he stopped, they got out to unload the luggage. Edward stumbled. Wyrick caught him, but Charlie could tell he was exhausted.

"Carter, you go ahead and take Edward inside. I'll bring your bags. After someone tried to pick off your nephew this morning, I'd just as soon you were inside, too," Charlie said.

"Yes, all right," Carter said and pointed toward the mansion. "We go in through the kitchen."

"We'll be right behind you," Charlie said.

Carter slipped his hand beneath Edward's elbow. "We're on the brick pavers, Eddie, and walking straight into the kitchen."

"Okay, Carter, thank you. It sure is good to have you home."

"It's good to be home," he said, not for the first time, as they started for the residence, with Charlie and Wyrick a few steps behind them.

Wyrick was not fond of meeting new people, and the closer they got to the entrance, the tenser she became. Strangers always made her feel less than she was, and the looks on their faces were either shock or confusion. Like they'd just walked into a freak show and saw the bearded lady—for free.

And now, as if she wasn't noticeable enough, she had new scrapes and bruises to add to it.

Ruth was in the kitchen shelling peas for dinner. She glanced up as the door opened, then a look of delight spread across her face. She dropped the peas back in the bowl and stood up, wiping her hands on her apron.

"Mr. Carter! How wonderful to have you back home!"

"Thank you, Ruth. I feel the same way, although Wilma's absence is noticed and regretted."

"Yes, sir," Ruth said.

"Now I'm going to see Eddie to his room. He's had quite a day," Carter said.

"I can do that," Ruth offered.

Before Carter could answer, the door opened again, and Charlie and Wyrick walked in.

"Thank you, Ruth, but I need you to show Charlie and his assistant, Miss Wyrick, to our guest rooms. I think the green suites, please," Carter said.

Ruth smiled. "Yes, sir, and, Mr. Dodge, it's a pleasure to see you again." Then she saw Wyrick behind him and smiled. "Welcome to Dunleavy Castle, ma'am."

"Thank you," Wyrick said.

"If you two will follow me…"

Charlie set down the bags he was carrying. "These aren't mine, they're Carter's."

"Where are yours?" Ruth asked.

"They're still in the car. I'll go back and get them later."

"No, we'll wait for you. Staff can take Mr. Carter's bags to his room. Just set them over there."

"If you're sure," Charlie said.

Ruth grinned. "I'm sure. Making people's lives easier is part of what we do here."

"I won't be long," Charlie said and ran back to the garage, leaving Wyrick alone with the housekeeper.

Ruth sent a text message, and less than a minute later, two women came hurrying into the kitchen, then did a double take when they saw Wyrick.

"Girls, this is Miss Wyrick. She and Charlie Dodge will be staying with us for a few days. Miss Wyrick, Louise is on your right, and Arnetta on your left. Anytime you need something, all you have to do is ask. The phones in your rooms are connected to our in-house communications. Pick up the receiver and press the star button, or nine for the kitchen, and someone will answer."

"Nice to meet you, ma'am," they said in unison.

Ruth pointed at the suitcases. "Those bags belong to Mr. Carter. Take them to his room."

"Yes, ma'am," they said, and began rolling them out of the kitchen as Charlie came back with his luggage and Wyrick's.

"This is all of it," Charlie announced.

"Then off we go," Ruth said.

Wyrick was somewhat in awe of the size and decor of the

place, and quite taken with an old suit of armor in the hall. The ornately framed family crest was an elegant reminder of the Dunleavy family's lineage.

There would be no family crest, no matching DNA, no bloodline to anyone for Jade Wyrick. There was no one like her, and never had been. Not anywhere on the planet.

They reached the grand staircase, but instead of climbing the steps, Ruth took the two of them behind the stairs to an elevator. She pressed the button and the doors opened instantly.

Wyrick and Charlie walked in with their bags, and Ruth followed, explaining the layout of the castle as she pressed a button to the second floor.

"This is more convenient when there are things to be carried. Feel free to use it rather than the stairs, if you wish. As you can see from the panel, there's a level down below, which is mostly for storage and where power units for heat and cooling are located. But it also houses the Dunleavy wine cellar, which is quite large. The second story is all family bedrooms, with a wing for guests. There are quite a few rooms not in use at this time. The Grand Ballroom is on the third floor. It's quite magnificent. Anytime you want a tour of the property, just let me know."

The elevator stopped and opened into the hall above.

"These two suites are adjoining," Ruth said, as she led them down the hall and then into the rooms. "This one is yours," she told Wyrick.

"This room is amazing," Wyrick said, looking up.

The ceilings had to be at least thirty feet high, and the dark green draperies over the tall arched windows were velvet. The living area had a massive stone fireplace, a long sectional sofa covered in some kind of dark leather, with dozens of colorful throws and pillows scattered along the length of it. The armchairs were leather, too, in an oxblood red, while a huge wrought iron chandelier hung from the ceiling, lit with bulbs made to look like candles. A long table with six chairs stood at the other end of the room.

Ruth showed them down a short hall and into the bedroom, where a massive four-poster bed with a gold-and-green velvet canopy dominated the room.

Ruth beamed, as if she was solely responsible for the elegance. "Your en suite bath is through those doors, and the dresser and wardrobe are empty, so feel free to use them as needed."

"It's like a fairy-tale room for a princess," Wyrick said.

Charlie hid a smile as Wyrick put down her bags and wandered off to inspect the bathroom, and then he heard what almost sounded like a squeal before she hurried back.

"Biggest claw-foot bathtub I ever saw," she said.

"Yes, ma'am." Ruth nodded. "It's French, and an antique. Bathtubs in medieval Ireland weren't what one would call comfortably functional. The family chose beauty and elegance over authenticity there. All the bath salts and bubble baths are there to enjoy, as well."

Charlie arched an eyebrow at Wyrick's delight, and when she saw it, she glowered, only to have Charlie mouth, *You promised.* She had a feeling she was going to regret that.

"Mr. Dodge, your suite is right through this door," Ruth said and led them into an identical room, with the same decor as the one Wyrick had been given. "As you'll notice, your adjoining door has different dead bolts, so neither occupant can go into the other room without both parties unlocking it from their side. Privacy first," Ruth said.

"Part of me feels like I just stepped back in time," Charlie said. "It's really impressive."

Ruth smiled again. "If you need anything, pick up the phone. As I mentioned, the star button or the number nine will reach the staff," Ruth told them and then left.

"I'm going to unpack now," Wyrick said.

She'd been in the midst of new research on Miranda Deutsch and then Wilma Short, and wanted to get back to it, but first things first.

She hung up her clothes, then took the bag with her equipment to the sitting area and began setting it up on the long table.

As soon as she was up and running, she retrieved the files she needed, and was about to begin when her phone signaled a text. She frowned when she saw it was from Merlin.

Two men came to my door this evening asking for you. I told them you had been here for a brief visit, but that you were already gone. I have security footage of them talking to me if you're interested.

"Son of a bitch!" She slapped the phone down on the desk, then leaned back in her chair and shut down her thoughts so she could be calm enough to shed the anger.

Within seconds she heard footsteps. Charlie must have heard her curse. Without turning around, she threw her arms up in the air and shouted, "I'm fine!"

The footsteps stopped. She was willing him to leave, and when he did, she picked up her phone and sent back a message.

I'm interested. Hang on to it until I get back. I'm sorry that happened. I should not have gone to your place. I will move out when I return.

About three minutes later he responded.

I'm going to pretend you didn't just say that. And they won't be back. I have searchlights mounted on top of the roof. I might even have turned them on to strobe function as they were driving out. It's quite the sight. Makes the place look like the yard of a penitentiary during an inmate escape. And I might have used the remote to shut the iron gates on the back end of their car as they were leaving.

Wyrick almost smiled at that, and the tension in her stomach was already fading.

She sent one last text back.

I owe you one.

She took a deep breath, then got up. When she turned around, there was an ice bucket and a drinking glass on the counter that hadn't been there before, and an unopened can of Pepsi beside it.

Charlie.

She filled the glass half-full of ice, poured in some Pepsi, then carried it to the window and pushed back the drapes. She took her first sip looking out at the front of the estate and wondered what it must be like to be so grounded in your ethnicity that you'd chosen to replicate an Irish castle, reminiscent of your Celtic roots.

She tried to imagine what kind of house she would build that fit who she was and where she'd come from, and then realized there was nothing but a laboratory. The rest of her memories were so far removed from her reality they might as well have been holograms.

I am a freak. An experiment. I don't have family. I don't belong to anyone. I don't belong anywhere.

Charlie's voice was right behind her. She turned abruptly, startled that he'd been able to sneak up on her, then she saw he was in his sock feet.

"Am I in danger here or am I allowed to speak?" he asked.

She narrowed her eyes. "You took off your shoes."

"Yes. No shoes is one of my small passions. Stop changing the subject. What happened?"

"I got a text from my landlord. They found me again."

Charlie frowned. "Does that mean you have to move?"

"I need to get back to the Wilma Short file," she said instead of answering.

Charlie didn't bother with a second question. Good. She was through sharing.

She took her Pepsi, sat down at the computer and was soon deep into background checks.

Charlie watched her long enough that it bothered him how invested he was becoming in her personal life, and then went back to his laptop and began pulling up everything he could find on Jason Dunleavy. Neither the family nor the police knew if the incidents involving Jason and Carter were connected. The odds were strong that they were, but not necessarily a given.

CHAPTER SIXTEEN

Miranda Deutsch dressed in black for the dinner with her father, as an homage to the grief of her breakup. But this wasn't just any little black dress. It was a purchase from the now-defunct trousseau. She'd pictured Jason being the first one to see her in it, but now it seemed fitting it was her father, instead.

Johannes was her constant, her touchstone. He'd fought her battles with her, and sometimes for her, and without judgment. He was always there for her, and she'd taken that for granted. But no more. His words had shaken her out of being the aggressor in relationships. From now on, men came to her, or not at all.

She took one last look in the mirror, blew herself a kiss, then dropped a tube of lipstick into a Judith Leiber evening bag—a bejeweled replica of a Yorkie—that her father had given her last Christmas.

Johannes was standing at the windows overlooking the gardens, and for a moment, she thought he looked sad.

"I'm ready," she announced, but his delighted smile as he turned around proved her wrong.

"Miranda! You look beautiful! If only your mother had lived to see you grow up. She would have been so proud."

She loved the mention of her mother because they were rare.

"Thank you, Father."

Johannes slipped his hand beneath her elbow. "The car is waiting. We are going to have a wonderful evening together and I hope you are hungry."

"I'm starving," she said.

He smiled. "Then we'll have to do something about that!"

The sun was less than an hour away from sunset when they exited the house. The chauffeur was standing outside the car.

"We're taking the limo?" Miranda asked.

"Only the biggest and best for my girl," Johannes said.

Their chauffeur opened the door for them.

"Good evening, sir. Good evening, Miss Miranda."

"Good evening, Perkins. We'll be going to Morton's tonight," Johannes said.

Miranda stepped into the limo, then settled in the middle of the backseat.

Johannes slid in beside her as Perkins shut the door.

"I trust the steakhouse suits you," Johannes said, as the chauffeur got into the car.

"Father! It's Morton's! Five-star service and steak to die for! Of course it suits me," she said.

"I want nothing but the best for you, and if you're happy, then I'm happy."

Miranda leaned against his shoulder as they drove away. The houses became a blur as the limo went faster, and she imagined herself throwing the remnants of her broken dreams out the window and watching them blow away.

Carter was happy to be home, even though his situation had not improved. He still didn't know who was after him, and now Jason had been targeted, too.

He was in his room getting ready for dinner when it occurred to him that he should have given Charlie and Wyrick a heads-up about meals, and quickly rang Charlie's suite.

Charlie was doing background checks on the gardening and maintenance staff when the house phone rang. He reached across his laptop to answer.

"Hello."

"Charlie, my apologies, but I completely forgot to tell you about mealtimes. We eat breakfast at 8:00 a.m., lunch at noon and dinner at 7:00 p.m."

Charlie glanced at the time. "That's in twenty minutes."

"I know. Would you please tell Wyrick for me, and apologize for the late notice?"

"Sure, but this place is huge. Where's the dining room?"

Carter laughed. "There are actually three. I'll meet you at the foot of the stairs at seven, and escort you there."

"Okay. See you shortly," Charlie said, then shut down his laptop.

The door between their suites was still open, so Charlie walked to the threshold and looked across the room. Wyrick was at the computer. He'd seen that focused expression before; instead of barging in and startling her, he knocked.

"Come on in," she said without looking up.

"Carter just called. Dinner is at seven. We're supposed to meet him at the foot of the stairs. He'll escort us to the dining room, and he sends his apologies for the short notice."

She finally raised her head. "We can't find a dining room by ourselves?"

Charlie shrugged. "He said there are three of them."

She hit Save, closed the laptop on which she'd been working and stood.

"I have to change. Close the door on your way out."

"Yes, ma'am," he said and pulled it shut.

Wyrick went straight to the bedroom, chose an outfit from

the closet, then went to the bathroom to put on makeup. Normally, it took her twenty minutes just to do her eyes, but tonight she was on speed dial. Not a problem.

Twenty minutes later, Charlie knocked on their adjoining door and when she opened it, for a moment he forgot to breathe.

She was stunning. The gold and green eye shadows she'd blended together made her dark eyes look huge, and the gold sparkles on her eyelashes caught the light every time she blinked. He'd never seen her in a dress, but it was no less daring than the other outfits she wore to work. The fabric, at least what there was of it, was gold lamé, and clung to her body like a second skin. The hem of the dress stopped a good four inches above her knees, leaving her long legs bare all the way to her gold three-inch heels.

The deep V would have called attention to her missing breasts, except for the fact that the entire head of a fire-breathing dragon was framed within that space.

"Way to show me up," he murmured as they left the room.

"I don't know what you're talking about," she said, but she'd already given Charlie Dodge a mental thumbs-up on style, and tonight was no exception.

He'd gone for dressy casual in gray slacks, a pale blue shirt he wore open at the collar and a gray-and-blue-plaid sport coat. Despite her three-inch heels, he still towered above her.

As promised, Carter was waiting. He saw them appear, and then watched them descending the stairs in silent awe. Wyrick was stunning.

"Good evening, Miss Wyrick, Charlie. My apologies again for the short notice. I hope you're hungry. Chef Peter was all excited to be cooking for guests, and from the wonderful aromas, I think we're in for a treat."

Everyone else was already seated as they entered the room.

"Good evening, family. Charlie and Miss Wyrick are with me, and will be dining with us until their work here is done."

"Hello again," Edward said, smiling.

She smiled back. "Just call me Wyrick."

"Welcome to our table," Dina said, but her gaze was locked on that dragon head, and for once, Kenneth was speechless.

Carter hid a grin as he seated Wyrick, then Charlie in the next chair down. He'd never seen his sister at a loss for words, and it didn't last long.

Dina said, "Miss… I mean Wyrick, your tattoo is—"

"Striking!" Kenneth interjected.

"Um…yes, striking," Dina agreed. "Um…was it painful… having it done, I mean?"

"Not as much as when they removed my breasts," Wyrick said and then smiled.

Dina flushed. "Oh, my God. I am sorry. That was appallingly thoughtless of me. I think I was so struck by the power of it that I forgot my manners. You're a beautiful woman. That's all I mean."

And because Wyrick knew that was a big deal coming from this woman, she accepted the compliment graciously.

Charlie was still in a bit of shock. He'd never seen Wyrick in a social setting of any kind, and not only was she comfortable, she was nailing it.

And to everyone's relief, as the meal service began, her friendliness lightened the mood.

After dinner, the Dunleavys moved to the library, following their tradition of nightcaps. Wyrick was sitting beside Edward again, revealing a side of her that Charlie had never seen. She was holding the cold soda she'd requested without taking a sip, letting it go warm in her hands as they talked.

Charlie was still nursing his single shot of bourbon, while Carter had opted for a beer. He wasn't much of a beer man,

but it was a safe choice because he'd also been the one to remove the cap.

After a few minutes, Wyrick caught Charlie's attention.
He read the look. She was ready to quit the party, so he set
his drink aside.

"Wyrick and I want to thank you for a great meal and
wonderful company. We'll see you in the morning. Carter,
if it's okay with you, I need to talk to Jason after breakfast."

"Of course," Carter said. "Rest well."

Wyrick touched Edward's shoulder. "Good night."

"And a good night to you," he said.

"Oh, I forgot to tell you Mack Doolin left Dallas," Charlie said as they walked back to their rooms.

"How do you know that?" she asked.

"Don't trust the bastard, so I had him followed."

"Why?" she asked, pausing outside her door.

"Because he pissed me off. If you need anything, knock.
Otherwise I'll be in bed." Then he went into his suite and
closed the door.

Wyrick locked herself in her own suite, then locked Charlie out at their adjoining door. Showering off her makeup
every night was like shedding the skin of her public self. By
the time she got into bed, she was Jade again. She thought
about what she wanted to release, then consciously saw all of
it in her mind, like pages in a book. One by one, she mentally threw them away. The last page in her memory was of
Charlie, pulling her off Mack Doolin in unapologetic anger.
That one she was going to keep. She brought the covers up
beneath her chin, and within seconds, was in a deep and
healing sleep.

While Wyrick was sleeping, Charlie was reading an email.
When he opened the one from Annie's doctor, he frowned.

Charlie,

We did an evaluation on Annie today because the staff had been reporting changes in her behavior. I wanted you to know that her cognizant level is on a lower scale than it was before. She's not as responsive to stimuli, and we're having a staff member sit with her when she eats, to make sure she gets enough sustenance.

Yes, you and I have discussed this on several previous occasions, so I know this will not be a surprise. But it is happening faster than I estimated, and understand this will not be a message well received. I am so sorry.

In the meantime, Annie is being well cared for, and if you have any questions at all, don't hesitate to call me.

Ted

Charlie stared at the words. Annie was disappearing far faster than had been predicted. He'd been so certain he'd have more time with her. They still had pieces to add to her puzzle, but he was torn. He didn't want to lose her, but when he thought about their relationship, he had to admit it was already gone. Wanting the physical presence of her body, without the bright, shining woman within it, was selfish as hell. Just because she was still breathing, that didn't hide the fact that the fucking disease had already buried her.

He sent a reply to Ted. Part of him felt guilty for not being there with her, but she wasn't there, either. The message was a shock, and hard to accept as he logged off, then went to shower.

He came out a short while later, his hair still damp when he pulled back the covers and got into bed. But when he closed his eyes, all he saw were images of Annie—the way she threw her head back when she laughed. Seeing her waiting at the gate when he returned from Afghanistan for the last time.

Their holidays together. The day they learned she'd miscarried their only child. The look on her face when the doctor gave her the Alzheimer's diagnosis.

"Worse than cancer," Annie had said, and she'd been silent all the way home.

Their beautiful life had died that day.

This email was news of another milestone on her journey, and he had to accept it.

He fell asleep, dreaming of the missing pieces of Annie, and believing if he found them all, he could put her back together again.

Miranda had been awake since daybreak. She wasn't normally a morning person, but since she was turning over a new leaf, so to speak, she thought it prudent not to sleep away half the day.

The night out with her father had been fun. It was exactly the lift she'd needed. Her heart was still broken. Her feelings were still hurt. But it wasn't the end of her world, and last night proved it.

Jason might have quit her, but as long as she had batteries, Rubber Dicky wouldn't. And now that she thought about it, Rubber Dicky stayed hard no matter how long she played. Jason's best was twice and then he was done.

She headed downstairs with coffee on her mind, wondering what her breakfast choices were this morning, and met her father coming out of his office.

"Good morning, dear. Did you sleep well?"

Miranda thought of Rubber Dicky again and smiled.

"Yes, I did."

He put his arm around her shoulders as they walked toward the breakfast room.

"I just want you to know how very sorry I am for your

disappointments. If there's anything else I can do to help, you will tell me, yes?"

Miranda nodded. "I know you were disappointed, too. You were looking forward to grandchildren. It will still happen. I promise you will have your grandchildren one day. And I expect you to spoil them as much as you've spoiled me."

Johannes frowned as they entered the breakfast room. "I did not spoil you. I only gave you what any father would give his daughter."

"And what's that?" Miranda asked.

"The world. I wanted to give you the world. What good is money if you cannot spend it on the people you love? Now we sit, and we eat the most important meal of the day. Breakfast!"

Miranda grinned. "And that meal wouldn't be complete without some fine Deutsch sausages. That's what I want this morning. Sausages and eggs."

Because she was planning to work, Wyrick dressed as if she was going to the office before they went down to breakfast.

This morning it was a neon-yellow leather jacket and pencil-leg pants, a turquoise silk camisole beneath the jacket and ankle-high boots the shade of overripe plums.

Her makeup was purple eye shadow with yellow eyeliner, and two swipes of deep purple for her lips.

She unlocked the door between their suites and knocked once, then heard Charlie tell her to come in. When she opened the door, he was nowhere in sight. She raised her voice. "It's three minutes to eight."

"I'm ready," Charlie said as he came around the corner. Then he took one look at her, made a U-turn in the hall and disappeared again.

Wyrick frowned, but he wasn't gone more than a few seconds before he reappeared, wearing sunglasses.

"We're going to breakfast first," she said.

"I know, but you're glowing, so I thought—"

"Take them off now," she said.

He put them in his jacket pocket as she turned around and marched to the door. Even though he was grinning as he followed her out, he had a feeling she'd get even with him before the day was over.

Carter was already at the table and laughing with Edward when his very own Batman and Robin walked in.

Dina was seated, too, and waiting for Kenneth to fix her plate. Her eyes widened when she saw Wyrick, but she said nothing.

"Good morning! Did you both rest well?" Carter asked.

Wyrick nodded. "Yes. Good morning, Edward," she said.

Edward beamed. "Good morning, dear lady."

"The accommodations are superb," Charlie said.

"Breakfast is serve yourself, buffet-style, but if there's something else you'd rather have, Ruth will tell Chef," Carter said.

Charlie eyed the brimming sideboard. "Considering the bowl of cold cereal that usually passes for my breakfast, there'll be no need for requests. That is a feast." Then he stepped back for Wyrick. "After you," he said.

Wyrick's eyes narrowed warningly as she passed him on the way to the buffet—then she saw waffles.

"I love waffles," she said to no one in particular and picked up a warm plate. She started with bacon, then a full-size Belgian waffle, added butter and slathered the waffle with heated syrup. She poured herself a cup of coffee and returned to her seat.

Charlie took scrambled eggs and bacon, two pieces of buttered toast and his coffee, before sitting down beside her.

Within a couple of minutes, everyone had food and began eating. Conversation was light for a bit, and then Carter got down to business.

"Charlie, do you still want to speak to Jason this morning?"

"Yes, if he's up to it."

"I've spoken to the floor nurse," Dina said. "He had a good night, and they had him up once this morning."

"Great news!" Carter said. "After we've finished, I'll notify Security that we'll be needing an escort to and from the hospital."

"Thanks," Charlie said.

Wyrick got up and went back to the buffet for more bacon and a refill of coffee.

Charlie looked up as she came back to the table. "Good bacon, isn't it?"

"Shut up," Wyrick said and then obviously remembered they were supposed to have a truce.

Carter burst out laughing. "I love to see a woman enjoying her food."

"I envy you," Dina said. "You're so tall and thin. You must have good genes."

"Oh, I'm chock-full of all kinds of genes," Wyrick said and popped the last bite of bacon into her mouth.

It was the tone of her voice that wiped the smile off Charlie's face. He knew what bitter sounded like, and he knew what anger sounded like, and there was an underlying hint of both. It made him wonder what had happened to her when she worked for Universal Theorem.

CHAPTER SEVENTEEN

After breakfast, Wyrick returned to her suite to work on the Wilma Short file, hoping to find a connection to whomever had paid her to go after Carter Dunleavy.

Charlie and Carter left the estate in one of the company cars driven by his chauffeur, with one security escort behind them, and one in front.

Once they reached the hospital, a two-man security team accompanied them inside and up to Jason's room, where two more members of Carter's security team were on guard just outside.

"Everything going okay?" Carter asked.

One of them nodded. "Yes, sir."

Carter knocked, then opened the door and walked in.

The television was on. Jason was obviously drifting in and out of sleep, but when he heard the door open, he saw his uncle and smiled.

"Uncle Carter. So good to see you. Did you come to break me out of here?"

Carter laughed. "Not yet, son. Are you up to talking a bit? Charlie has some more questions."

"Sure thing," Jason said. "Ask away."

"I'll keep this brief," Charlie said. "We'd be careless to assume that the attempt on your life is not connected to Carter, and I need to ask a few questions."

"Okay, I'm ready," Jason said.

"Do you have any personal or business enemies?"

"Nothing remotely like the ones Uncle Carter has. I have a couple of people who hated my guts in college, but that was at Yale and years ago."

"I know you're seeing Miranda Deutsch now. Are there any women from your past who hold grudges against you?"

"No. I've never had a serious relationship with anyone. Never been close to an engagement. Never brought any of them home to meet my family. They were just casual partners for social events. Oh…and I'm not seeing Miranda anymore, either."

"When did that end?" Charlie asked.

"Yesterday morning."

"Was it an amicable parting of the ways?"

"Not really."

"What exactly do you mean by 'not really'? Did you two have a fight?"

"I wasn't fighting. I just told her I thought we needed to take a break from each other. She cursed at me like a sailor, then started screaming at me. I disconnected."

Charlie frowned. "Okay, for the sake of clarity, how long between the time you two had this conversation, and the time you were shot?"

"I guess…two hours more or less."

Carter had been quiet until then. "Charlie, what are you getting at?"

"Bear with me, Carter. Just a couple more questions, and then I'll let Jason rest," Charlie said.

"I'm okay," Jason said.

"So, if I'm remembering correctly, everyone in the family would gain the same amount of shares if your uncle had been killed, right? I mean…no one profits more than another if it happens."

"That's right," Jason said.

"And you are the person who's been groomed to take his place, so it's not like you had any new expectations, either, right?"

"Correct," Carter replied.

"Yes, that's been a given in the family for years," Jason said.

"Okay, last question. Do people outside the family know this?"

"The people on the board know, of course," Jason said. "Even though it's not a secret, I have no idea if anyone else does."

"Carter, what about you?" Charlie asked. "Is it common knowledge among the people you do business with?"

"Anyone who's ever done business with us knows Jason will be the heir to this position, and he proved himself fully capable when I went into hiding. But as far as the inheritance angle goes, I doubt it," he said.

"What about your girlfriends? Was Miranda Deutsch aware of that?" Charlie asked.

Jason's brow knitted slightly. "I doubt it. We never discussed work or families when we were together."

"Okay, that covers everything I need to know. I'll fill Wyrick in on this, and see what she can do with it. Sometimes all she needs is that one tiny bit of info to break a case wide-open for me."

"That's quite an assistant you have," Jason said.

Carter smiled. "You have no idea how freaking amazing she is."

"And some days, aggravating as hell," Charlie added.

The conversation ended with laughter.

But even after they'd said their goodbyes and were on their

way back to the estate, Charlie's thoughts were all over the place. He could see the puzzle pieces now, but none of them were fitting together. In most of the cases he worked, there was that one piece they had yet to find. Once they got it, everything else always fell into place.

That hadn't happened here, not yet.

The Denver PD was in something of a pressure cooker. Two members of the Dunleavy family were under attack, and they couldn't find a single lead as to who was doing it or why.

What they did know was that Wilma Short had been murdered. The autopsy had revealed a huge bruise on the back of her head, and DNA beneath her fingernails that wasn't hers, nor did it match anything in the database.

All they knew about the attacks on Carter was what he'd told them, plus the lab test from the hospital stating traces of arsenic had been found in his system. As well, there was a report from the inspection on his vehicle when he'd lost his brakes coming down a mountain—and they'd found a small cut in the brake line.

Chief Forsythe had personally cleared Rom Delgado of any wrongdoing in helping Carter hide, and Carter had already recompensed the Denver PD for the costs they'd incurred during the two weeks they'd been searching for him. But there were still no answers as to who was behind this.

Every precinct in the Denver area had received a BOLO from the central division regarding Jason Dunleavy's shooting. Thanks to traffic cams, they had a make and model on the car, but no tag number because it had been smeared with mud.

The police knew the kind of gun the shooter had used from the bullet they took out of Jason's shoulder, and they had a description of the tattoo sleeve on the shooter's arm from an eyewitness account.

Like Charlie Dodge, all they needed was one break.

★ ★ ★

Dr. Wooten, the pathologist who'd done the initial autopsy two days ago on Buddy Boy Pierce, also wound up with the body of Rey Garza on his slab yesterday. After the autopsy, Wooten measured the distance between the eyebrows where the bullet went in, he realized it was the same measurement on Buddy Pierce's body. The fact that they'd both been shot between the eyes within a millimeter of the same location was unusual. It made him curious, and so the next morning he checked the striations on the two bullets, and determined that the same gun had been used to kill both men.

At that point, Wooten made a call to the detectives working each case, and asked them to come down to the morgue.

Neither knew the other had been called until they both showed up and were taken into the morgue together.

"Detective Reed, Detective Spick, I'm Dr. Wooten, and thank you for coming. This may mean nothing, and then again, these bodies might connect to other similar cases you're working that are still open."

"What's going on, Doc?" Detective Reed asked.

"Just let me show you first, and then we'll talk," Wooten said and led them to the lockers and opened two different drawers.

"That's Buddy Pierce. He's mine," Detective Reed said.

"This is Rey Garza. He's mine," Detective Spick said, and then Reed and Spick looked at each other and shrugged.

"Same perfectly clean bullet hole between the eyes in the exact same place. Same caliber bullet," Dr. Wooten said. "I have a bullet from Pierce and a bullet from Garza. Seems to me that they have the same striations. Find the gun, and you'll likely find the killer of both men."

They left the morgue more confused than they'd been before they got there. Now they were going to have to work up backgrounds on the two men to see what they had in common. It had to be *something*, considering the same gun was used to kill them.

When Detective Spick got to the precinct, he had reports to add to working files, his usual handful of messages and a few BOLOs sitting on his desk.

One of the reports concerned the preliminary autopsy report Dr. Wooten had done on Garza. Spick casually reviewed it, noting the mention of the sleeve of tattoos and the accompanying photos.

He put the copies in the case file and then went through the BOLOs. As he was reading them, he found one regarding the Jason Dunleavy case. The shooter they were looking for had a whole sleeve of tattoos on his left arm…and she'd described them as gang related in appearance.

He pulled the autopsy he'd just filed on Rey Garza and studied the photos again. They looked gang related to him. It was a long shot, but worth letting the detective know. Spick reached for the phone.

Bruner was writing up a report when his phone rang. He hit Save on his computer, then picked up the receiver.

"Detective Bruner, Homicide."

"Detective Bruner, this is Detective Spick. I'm working a homicide on a man who was found murdered in his car out by Cherry Creek Reservoir. I was reading your BOLO regarding the Jason Dunleavy shooter, and my murder victim has a sleeve of tattoos on his left arm that look like gang images. He's also left-handed, which would match the info on the BOLO. The name is Rey Garza, and that's spelled *R-E-Y*."

Bruner's pulse kicked up as he reached for a pen and paper.

"Do you have photos of the tattoos?" Bruner asked.

"Yes. They're in the file. We also recovered a gun from Garza's car that's the same make as the one you're looking for in the Dunleavy shooting. I can't prove that any of this is a match, but it looks good on the surface," Spick said.

Bruner tapped his pen against the paper. "I would need a ballistics test on that gun, and pictures of the tattoos to show my witness."

"I can ask the medical examiner's office to send you the pictures, and get a ballistics test run for you," Spick said.

"Chief Forsythe is breathing down all our necks to solve this," Bruner said. "So thank you for the info, and let me know as soon as you get the ballistics test back."

"No problem," Spick said. "And there's one more thing. The coroner called me and a Detective Reed from another precinct into the morgue at the same time because he found an unusual common denominator between my vic and another body he'd worked. While they'd both been killed with the same make of handgun, which isn't all that surprising, it was the bullet holes between their eyes that caught his attention. He said the single shots that killed both vics was in the same exact place on their faces. Not even a millimeter of difference. Right between the eyes, with equal margins between the shots and the eyebrows. After that, he checked the striation on the bullets he pulled out of the vics, and they were a match to the same gun."

"Wait! What was the name of Reed's victim?" Bruner asked.

"Buddy Pierce, but he lived in a different part of the city from Rey Garza."

"Okay, I'll make a note and check it out," Bruner said.

When the digital pictures Spick had requested arrived. Bruner took one look at them, then reached for the phone to call Megan Simmons, the witness who saw Jason's shooter.

She answered quickly.

"This is Detective Bruner, Denver PD. May I speak to Megan Simmons?"

"This is Megan."

"Would you be willing to come in and view a photo lineup of tattoos? We may have a lead to the Jason Dunleavy shooting."

"I can be there within the hour."

"Great," Bruner said. "I'll leave word at the front desk to have you escorted to an interview room."

"All right. See you in a little while," Megan said.

As soon as he hung up, he began picking out more photos. Now all he needed was for her to ID the tattoo that belonged to Rey Garza, and he might just have found his shooter.

Once he had the lineup and an interview room reserved, he glanced at the time. Megan Simmons would be here soon. He needed to let the front desk know where to bring his witness.

A few minutes later, there was a knock at the door, and an officer walked in with Megan Simmons.

"Detective Bruner, your witness is here."

Bruner stood and quickly shook her hand. "Megan, thank you for coming at such short notice. Just have a seat here," he said. "I want you to look through these photos and see if any of them fit the description of what you saw."

Megan set her purse aside and calmly stepped up to examine them. Bruner was impressed by how she immediately removed three.

"None of these," Megan said. "They're too ornate, and I didn't see any color on the shooter." Then she reached for the one Detective Spick had just sent. "This looks like what I saw."

"You're sure?" Bruner asked.

She didn't hesitate. "I'm sure. I'm a nurse. We're trained to observe. Sometimes the smallest things will be the only warning we get before a patient starts to crash. And while I was watching the whole thing unfold, from Mr. Dunleavy slamming on the brakes to the other car flying through the intersection like the stoplight wasn't even there, everything seemed to happen in slow motion. I wish I'd seen his face, but when I saw that arm come out of the open window, and then the gun in his hand, that's where my focus stopped and stayed."

"You've been a great help, more than you can imagine. Wait a moment and I'll walk you out."

Bruner gathered up the photos, slipped them into a manila envelope and escorted her to the front door.

"Thank you, and have a safe trip home," Bruner said.

"You're welcome," Megan said.

As soon as Charlie and Carter got back to the estate, Carter went to his office, and Charlie went upstairs with the new information. But when he found Wyrick in deep concentration, he hated to interrupt.

"I know you're there," Wyrick said. "I'm listening."

"I'll wait until—"

"I can do two things at once. Talk," she said, her fingers flying over the keyboard.

"Jason Dunleavy broke up with Miranda Deutsch about two hours before he was shot. She didn't take it well. She was screaming at him and cursing when he hung up. Just to tie up loose ends, when you run a background check on her, see if there's any way to connect her to the cases on Carter and Jason."

"Why would she want Carter gone if she's dating Jason?" Wyrick asked, still typing.

Charlie was fascinated watching how fast her fingers moved, and almost forgot to answer.

"Oh…uh…it was a thought I had."

"To the point of killing one rich man to marry another rich man in the same family? That's mental illness, if you ask me, but duly noted," Wyrick muttered. "With regard to Wilma Short. I found something."

Charlie pulled up a chair and sat down at the table. "What did you find?" he asked.

"A large lump sum of money deposited into her mother's bank account four months ago. Before the deposit, the only money that came in was the mother's Social Security money, but it was used to pay part of her monthly care. After that deposit, Wilma began using it to pay for all her mother's care."

"How much was deposited?" Charlie asked.

"Half a million dollars," Wyrick said. "But there's no way to trace it. It was deposited as cash, and I haven't been able to match up a withdrawal of that size to anyone we know."

"Good job," Charlie said. "That pretty much proves she was the inside person here at the estate. But there has to be at least one more person who was responsible for trying to wreck Carter on the freeways and who could have known how to cut the brake line."

"I'll see what I can find out about Miranda," she said. "Now, go away. I need to think."

"You said you could do two things at once," Charlie said as he got up.

"I can, but you're slowing down the process."

Charlie eyed the slight frown between her eyebrows, and the neon-yellow leather she was wearing and wondered why she bothered to get this dressed up in Carter's home.

"Why are you still here?" Wyrick asked without looking up.

"You're not the only one who can think of two things at once," Charlie muttered, then got up and walked out of the room.

He took off his shoes, helped himself to a cold drink from

the wet bar and started going through emails and paying bills online. He might be away, but that didn't stop what was happening back home.

Detective Bruner kept staring at the names Buddy Pierce and Rey Garza. He had a positive ID from Megan Simmons as to Garza being the shooter. He'd already pulled up rap sheets on both men, and they were lengthy, with a multitude of charges between them. Now he wanted to find out if Carter or Jason Dunleavy knew these men. He had a number for Jason's room at the hospital. He called him, then counted the rings until Jason answered.

"Hello."

"Jason, this is Detective Bruner. I have new information. Would it be possible to visit you for a few minutes?"

"Yes. No problem," Jason said.

"I want to talk to your uncle, as well. Do you have a number where he can be reached?"

"Call his cell phone. That way you won't have to go through the housekeeper, who usually answers the house phone."

"Thanks," Bruner said and quickly wrote down the number Jason gave him. "I'll see you shortly."

Bruner then called Carter to make sure he'd be available, too. The call rang twice and then Carter answered.

"Mr. Dunleavy?"

"Yes."

"This is Detective Bruner. Would you be able to see me today?"

"Yes. I'm home all day," Carter said.

"I'm on my way to see Jason now, and when I'm finished there, I'll let you know," Bruner said.

"I'll be expecting you," Carter said.

Bruner grabbed his file and left the precinct. A short while later, he was at the hospital again, exiting the elevator. Once he reached Jason's room, he encountered two guards and immediately flashed his badge.

"Jason is expecting me," he said. "Just a minute, sir. Mr. Jason has been having a rough morning. Let me check," the guard said. He opened the door and stepped into the room. "Mr. Dunleavy, Detective Bruner is here. Are you ready for visitors?"

"I'm fine, Danny. The pain meds are kicking in," Jason said and raised his bed up to a sitting position as Bruner entered.

"I'm sorry. I didn't know you weren't up to visitors today. You should have said something when I called," Bruner said.

Jason shook his head. "Just pain. But the meds they gave me are beginning to work. Tell me about this new lead!" he said.

Bruner took a picture out of the file he'd brought with him.

"Your witness, Megan Simmons, just identified this tattoo as the one she saw on the shooter's arm. Unfortunately, it was taken before the coroner began an autopsy on his body."

"You mean this man is dead?" Jason asked.

"Yes. His name was Rey Garza. Do you know anyone by that name?"

"It isn't familiar, but there are thousands of people who work at our different facilities. Do you have a picture?" Jason asked.

"I have the one on his rap sheet." Bruner took it out of the file and handed it over."

Jason looked at the face intently, then shook his head. "No, sorry. He isn't the least bit familiar to me."

Bruner pulled Buddy Pierce's rap sheet out next. "What about his man? His name is Buddy Pierce."

Jason looked at that one as well, and shook his head again. "No, don't know him, either. What's the connection between these two men?"

"The coroner thinks there's a strong possibility that both

men were killed by the same gun. We're trying to find a link between the two, in the hope that it leads us to the person behind all this," Bruner said.

"What does Uncle Carter think?"

"He doesn't know yet, but I'm going there next. If something does occur to you, call me. I'll leave my card."

"Will do," Jason said, laying the card aside.

"Thank you for your time. Hope you have a better day," Bruner said and left the room.

His next stop was the castle.

Charlie was answering emails and running background checks for a couple of new clients when someone knocked at his door.

"Come in," he said.

It was Carter. "Charlie, do you have a minute?"

He closed his laptop. "Yes, sure. What's up?"

"Detective Bruner is coming over shortly with some new information. Would you and Wyrick sit in on it?"

"Absolutely. Do you have any idea what it's about?" Charlie asked.

Carter shook his head. "No, but maybe he has a new lead."

"Just so you know, we have some new information ourselves, and since Bruner is working Wilma Short's murder, I'll share it with him, too. Wyrick found a half-million-dollar cash deposit in the bank account belonging to Wilma's mother. Wilma has been paying her mother's monthly care out of it for the past four months. But since it was a cash deposit, Wyrick hasn't been able to match it with anyone in your circle of family and employees."

Carter stared at him. "A half-million dollars to take me out? Who in the hell hates me that much?"

"We'll find out," Charlie said. "And maybe Bruner's info will be a good lead."

"For sure," Carter said, and then the phone in his pocket buzzed. He glanced down at the text. "Detective Bruner is waiting for us in the library."

"I'll get Wyrick," Charlie said and walked into Wyrick's suite, where she was working.

"Are you at a stopping point? Carter wants us downstairs. Detective Bruner is here with some new information."

Wyrick nodded, typed two more words and hit Save, then joined the men without comment as they headed down the stairs.

CHAPTER EIGHTEEN

Bruner was sitting in a wingback chair and texting on his phone when they entered. He immediately put it away as he stood.

"Here we are, Detective, as requested," Carter said. "I don't believe you've met Miss Wyrick. She's Mr. Dodge's assistant. Wyrick, this is Detective Bruner."

Bruner didn't even blink at the Amazon in yellow leather. "Ma'am," he said and then shifted his focus to Carter Dunleavy. "We found the man who shot Jason. His name is Rey Garza—but before you celebrate that news, he was dead when we found him. The witness who saw Jason's shooting has already identified him. And the gun in Garza's car matches the kind Jason was shot with. We're running a ballistics test on Garza's gun to see if the striations match the bullet that was removed from Jason during surgery."

Carter frowned. "Is this connected to Wilma's murder?"

"We're working that as a possibility," Bruner said.

"What was his name?" Charlie asked.

"Rey Garza, and that's spelled *R-E-Y*."

Charlie knew Wyrick was mentally filing that name for further review.

"That's not all," Bruner said. "The coroner caught an odd similarity between Garza's body, and another one that he autopsied—a man named Buddy Pierce. Both men had been shot, and the coroner said that both shots were right between the eyes, with the same distance above the nose and centered perfectly between each man's eyebrows. And the bullets he pulled from their bodies were shot from the same gun."

"Wait… Are you saying this Buddy Pierce might also be connected to both Dunleavy cases?" Charlie asked.

Bruner shrugged. "It's a theory we're working on."

"After I found Carter and learned about all the different attacks he'd been under, he mentioned the possibility that there might be more than one person involved," Charlie said.

"How so?" Bruner asked.

"Other than the chef, who doesn't live on the premises, there are only women staffed inside the residence on a daily basis, so that would explain some of the incidents. But he also had a brake line tampered with and nearly wrecked twice on the freeway by a car suddenly cutting him off."

Detective Bruner turned to Carter. "Was it the same vehicle that cut you off both times?" he asked.

"Yes. It was a dark red late-model Ford Escape," Carter said.

Bruner made a note. "I'll check to see what kinds of cars both vics had."

"If Pierce was driving a car that matched that description, then it would link his murder to Wilma Short and to Rey Garza," Charlie said.

Wyrick turned around and walked out of the library.

Bruner looked a little startled.

Charlie quickly explained. "It's nothing personal. She's a woman of few words, but she's damn good at her job. She'll

know the answer in about five minutes, give or take, counting the time it takes her to get upstairs."

Charlie noticed that Bruner didn't comment, which meant
he didn't believe what he'd just said. Charlie also knew Wyrick
was about to change Bruner's mind. He watched as Bruner
pulled the pictures of both victims and handed them to Carter.

"These are the two men's rap sheets. Have you ever seen
either one of them before?" he asked.

Carter looked carefully at both, then handed them back.

"No. I've never seen those faces before, but there are so
many people who work for the Dunleavy Corporation and
all the subsidiaries that I can't swear they aren't any of our
employees."

Bruner shrugged. "That's pretty much what Jason said."

Charlie's phone signaled a text. "It's from Wyrick," he said
and read it aloud. "'Buddy Pierce owned a 2016 Ford Escape.
The color is Canyon Red.'"

"I'll be damned," Bruner said. "Okay, Dodge, you might be
right about Pierce being part of the attacks on Carter, which
means that not only is there someone trying to kill Carter
and Jason, but he's taking out the people who failed him."

"Does that make him a serial killer?" Carter asked.

"No, because he just has one goal, and that's to get to you
and Jason," Charlie said. "All he's doing now is taking out
the people he hired so they won't talk."

"That's right, and it makes him one very dangerous man,"
Bruner added.

"Or woman," Charlie added.

"What made you say that?" Bruner asked.

Charlie shrugged. "Jason broke up with a woman he'd
been seeing and that happened about two hours before he
was shot. I asked him how she took the breakup, and he said
she was screaming and cursing him when he disconnected."

"But that wouldn't tie her to Carter, because all his attacks happened way before the breakup."

"I have a theory," Charlie said. "If it pans out, I'll let you know."

"Oh…what was her name?"

"Miranda Deutsch."

Bruner looked up from his notepad. "As in Johannes Deutsch's daughter?"

"Yes," Charlie said.

Detective Bruner sighed. "Let's both hope your theory falls flat. The chief is already on us to catch whoever's been after Carter, and no way do I want to tell him that a member of the second-richest family in Denver has become our main suspect."

Charlie's phone signaled another text. "It's from Wyrick. She says Rey Garza and Miranda Deutsch went to the same high school, same graduating class."

Bruner stared. "I am officially in awe of your assistant."

Charlie's phone dinged again. "She also says Buddy Pierce and Wilma Short were once married, but Wilma's mother had the marriage annulled because Wilma was underage."

Bruner shook his head.

"What's wrong?" Carter asked.

"I'm just waiting for your assistant to divulge the name of the killer," he said.

Charlie grinned. "That might take a bit longer. However, as I mentioned, she did uncover a half-million-dollar cash deposit into the account of Wilma Short's mother, who's in a memory care facility. It was made four months ago, which was right before all the incidents with Carter began. Wilma has been using it to pay for her mother's care."

Bruner stood up again. "I am *really* impressed. How did she even think to look in that direction so quickly?"

"I already had her researching both Wilma Short and Miranda Deutsch for some time, but there's no explanation for how her mind works."

"I've covered everything I came to ask," Bruner said. "I thank you for the added information. I'm assuming you'll stay in touch?"

"Absolutely," Charlie replied.

"I'll see you out," Carter said and walked the detective to the lobby as Charlie went upstairs to where Wyrick was working.

"You rocked Detective Bruner's world, and I'm not even going to ask what made you check high school records. Oh, and remind me to give you a raise."

Wyrick ignored him. "The new info really points a finger at the Deutsch woman."

"Yes. Now see if you can find payoffs between her and the three murder victims. If you can, it links her to the cases on both Carter and Jason."

Wyrick nodded. "I'll get started on the money trail."

Miranda Deutsch was in her private office, going through a drawer she kept locked, shredding invoices and paid receipts, wondering why the hell she'd kept them in the first place. After all the breakup stuff with Jason, it felt good to rid herself of the last connections she had to him.

She stopped once, thinking she heard footsteps in the hall, but then they were gone, so she continued shredding documents, one by one. If only it was this easy to get rid of memories, but what was done was done.

She'd just fed the last paper through the shredder when someone knocked at the door. Then she heard her father's voice.

"Miranda, it's me."

She jumped up and ran out of the office into the sitting area. "Come in!"

Johannes opened the door but didn't enter. "I'm leaving for a meeting and won't be back for dinner. I wanted to tell you in person. Will you be okay on your own?"

"Of course. And may I say, you look very handsome."

Johannes smiled. "Thank you, my dear. Remember, if you have an emergency, I will always take your calls."

She crossed the carpet in her bare feet and stretched up to give him a kiss on the cheek.

"I know that. You are the best father ever. Now, go do your thing. I have no plans for this evening and am looking forward to a night in. Popcorn in bed and one of my favorite movies. You know how I love to do that."

"Just like your mama," Johannes said. "I'll probably be late, so I'll see you in the morning," he said.

"See you then," Miranda said and walked out into the hall, knowing he'd look back. When he did, she waved at him once more, and then he was gone.

She went back to her room, thinking about her father's life and how hard he'd worked to get where they were today. She'd grown up in the back of his butcher shop, but by the time she was twelve, Deutsch Sausages had gained national recognition. She was no longer the butcher's daughter. She was the daughter of Johannes Deutsch, the Sausage King.

She went to the windows overlooking the front of the estate to watch her father leaving in the limo. Then she smiled, her pulse already racing as she ran across the carpet to lock the door.

She looked in her office to make sure she hadn't missed anything, then hurried to her bedroom and locked herself in there as well, then stripped and headed for the nightstand by her bed.

"Rubber Dicky, Rubber Dicky, come out, come out, wherever you are."

To hell with popcorn and a movie.

★ ★ ★

Lunch was long since over and Wyrick had changed out of her yellow leather and spike heels into jeans and a lightweight long-sleeved shirt that hung almost to her knees. She was back at work in her bare feet, and with a glass of Pepsi at hand.

Charlie was at the same table fielding calls and emails. He'd just received a phone call from Detective Bruner, confirming the ballistics test they'd run on the weapon from Rey Garza's car. It was the one used to shoot Jason Dunleavy.

And the fact that Wilma intimately knew Buddy Pierce, who drove a car like the one that had cut Carter off on the freeway, tied the two of them together in the attacks on Carter.

There were still reasons to suspect that Miranda Deutsch was behind Jason's shooting, but there was a big gap in the theory. According to both Jason and Carter, Miranda had never been inside the Dunleavy home or met the family, so they lacked a motive to connect her to Carter. What was the missing link between the cases? Who had reason to want both of them dead?

Charlie was still typing when he realized Wyrick wasn't. The silence was startling. He looked up. She was sitting in front of her laptop, staring at the screen.

"What?" Charlie asked.

"Miranda Deutsch did a DNA test on one of those ancestor sites."

"What made you go there?"

"Just double-checking her expenditures. It was the only purchase that stood out as different from everything else, so I got curious."

"And?"

"And I'm not going to tell you how I found this, but Johannes Deutsch is not her biological father, and if she didn't know it before she got the test results, she knew it afterward."

Charlie pushed his laptop aside and leaned forward. "Okay... That's a big deal, for sure, but how does this play out with the cases we're working on?"

"Less than a month after she got the test results, she had an abortion."

"Whoa! Didn't see that coming," Charlie muttered, but he felt the pieces were beginning to fall into place.

"Was she dating Jason Dunleavy at that time?"

"Yes." Wyrick looked over her laptop at Charlie. "Why would a woman who wants to marry a specific man and professes to love him suddenly need to get rid of his child?"

"If it wasn't his child," Charlie said.

"But what other reason is there for aborting a fetus, other than a life-saving procedure or just not wanting to have children?" Wyrick asked.

Charlie narrowed his eyes. "You already know the answer. You're trying to lead me to it so I'll think I figured it out myself. This isn't what I pay you the big bucks for. Spit it out."

"What if the mother and the father of a baby were blood relatives? What then?" she asked.

Charlie slapped his hand on the table so hard it rattled the ice in her glass of Pepsi.

"Are you shitting me? But who? Wait. Jason's deceased father was also her father? Half brother and half sister?"

"No. Not the Reed side. The Dunleavy side. Because of that DNA test, she found a connection on the ancestor site to a Dunleavy in Ireland. And that Irish woman, who would've been a great-great-aunt to Miranda, was already linked to Dillon Dunleavy, who was father to Edward, Dina, Carter, and Ted. So Miranda had to know she was somehow related to them, but she obviously wanted to learn more. I began searching in her credit card records and found she'd paid a private lab to perform two more DNA tests. Another one for her and one for Jason," Wyrick said.

"She could easily have collected a sample for Jason while they were still dating. Did you find out the results there?" Charlie asked.

"They're first cousins."

"Carter? Carter Dunleavy is her biological father?"

She shrugged. "One of them is. Carter, Edward or Ted."

"I don't say this often, but I feel like throwing up," Charlie muttered. "What's her mother's name? How old was she when Miranda was born? Find a link to her with one of those three and we're closer to a motive."

Wyrick nodded. "Her mother's name was Vivian Morrow, and I'll dig deeper into her life, but I need candy."

"Candy?"

"Yes. The stuff with sugar, and chocolate would be an added bonus," she said, then went back to work.

Charlie picked up the house phone and buzzed the kitchen.

"Good afternoon, Mr. Dodge. How can we serve you?" Ruth asked.

"Wyrick is in need of something sweet. Preferably with chocolate. Would you have anything remotely like that available?"

"Of course. Would you prefer a slice of Sacher torte, a wonderful chocolate mousse or possibly some fine Belgian chocolates?"

"So nothing like a Hershey's bar?" he asked.

Ruth giggled. "I'll have one of the girls bring up a tray for both of you. Would you care for coffee, as well?"

Charlie sighed. "Coffee would be great."

"We'll have it right up," Ruth said.

Charlie replaced the receiver. "Chocolate is on the way."

Apparently unaware he'd even been on the phone, she paused. "Really?"

"I'm a PI, remember? I can find stuff, too. I need a good old-fashioned stakeout. Or a standoff somewhere. This sitting around looking at computer screens is likely to affect my sanity," he muttered.

"Well, Mr. Cranky Pants, I hope they bring enough chocolate for both of us. Sounds like you're running low on sugar, too."

He glared. "You sound like that candy bar commercial."

"What candy bar commercial?"

"The one where… Oh, never mind. And I'm not cranky."

Wyrick stood. "Excuse me. I'm going to wash up. Get the door for me when they bring up the chocolate, will you?"

Charlie watched that oversize shirt billowing out around her as she walked out and shook his head. It made her look like she'd had to set sail before leaving the room.

Damn woman.

A few minutes later there was a knock at her door.

"I'm getting the door!" he yelled, knowing it would tick her off.

Louise was there with a small tea trolley and promptly pushed it inside. "Don't worry about the trolley when you've finished. Just push it into the hall and give us a ring. We'll remove it for you."

"Thank you, Louise. It all looks very good. Pass on my thanks to the chef."

She smiled. "I will."

Charlie shut the door, studied the assortment of sweets and then stuck his finger in one before pouring himself a cup of coffee.

Wyrick sailed back into the room. "I smell fresh coffee."

"And an assortment of chocolate desserts."

She leaned over the trolley, admiring the array, and then saw a hole punched right in the middle of a serving of chocolate mousse. She looked at the hole, then at him.

"Did you just put your finger in that mousse?"

"Back when we were kids, that's how my brothers and I staked our claims. So yes, I claimed the mousse."

He watched her eyes widen, and then she threw back her head and laughed. Still grinning, she leaned over the trolley and stuck her finger in the slice of Sacher torte, then poured a cup of coffee, picked up the torte and a fork to eat with, and carried it all back to the living room.

"Well! Don't just stand there looming," she said. "Get your mousse and a spoon and come sit. You loom when you're standing."

Charlie stuck a spoon in the mousse and went to join her, but he couldn't look at her without revealing what her laughter had done to him. He didn't want to see her that way. He needed her to be prickly and short-tempered.

"How old is Miranda?" Charlie asked, then put a spoonful of mousse in his mouth.

"Twenty-nine," Wyrick said as she licked the chocolate from her fork.

Charlie looked up just as she licked the fork, then immediately looked away. "I need to know details about her mother. What do we have?"

Wyrick cut herself another bite of cake. "*We* don't. But *I* do. As I said earlier, she was Vivian Morrow before she married Johannes Deutsch. She was twenty. If she'd lived, she would be fifty now. And, in case you're about to ask this next, she had to have been pregnant when she and Johannes married, because Miranda was born eight and a half months after the ceremony."

"How old would the Dunleavy brothers have been thirty years ago?"

"Hang on a sec." Wyrick got up. She returned with her notes and a pen. "Let's see, Carter is fifty-five now, so he would've been twenty-five. Edward is sixty, so he would have been thirty, and Ted's forty-six, so he would only have been sixteen. One of those three is her father."

"Even if she knows—or believes—that Carter is her father, why want him dead?" Charlie asked.

Wyrick took another bite, chewed and swallowed before she answered. "Maybe she freaked out because of the cousin aspect of being pregnant. Or maybe she thinks her birth father rejected her mother because of the pregnancy, which would also be a rejection of Miranda." Wyrick sighed, then waved her fork in the air. "We're doing too much guessing. I need to check out her mother's background to see if I can link her to any of the brothers. Eat your pudding."

"It's mousse, not pudding, and it's good," Charlie said. "And we still need to connect Miranda to Rey Garza in some way other than graduating together."

"Why?" Wyrick asked.

Charlie was surprised by the question. "When there are hundreds of people in your grade level, it's entirely possible to go all through high school together and never meet."

"Really?" Wyrick said.

Charlie frowned. "Why don't you know that?"

"Because I never went to school," she said.

"Ah…homeschooled," Charlie said.

"After the age of five, I did not have a home, and was not homeschooled. I grew up at UT, cared for by technicians."

Now Charlie was past curious. "Then how in the hell did you learn how to do all that you do?"

Wyrick looked away for a moment, then back at Charlie, locking straight into his gaze.

"I didn't have to learn anything. I was born knowing how. I need to take a break. I'll be in the back gardens."

Charlie was speechless as she made her exit. He got up, put his empty dessert dish on the trolley, then went back to his suite.

Sometimes Wyrick almost scared him, and sometimes he thought she was a genius, but he damn sure didn't understand her or how her life worked.

He did, however, know how *his* life worked, and he needed to reconnect with it, so the first thing he did was call Morning Light to check on Annie.

"Morning Light. This is Pinky."

"This is Charlie Dodge. Is Dr. Dunleavy there by any chance?"

"No, sir, not at the moment. Would you like to speak to one of the nurses?"

"Yes, please."

"I'll connect you," Pinky said.

The call went straight to music, which Charlie detested, but then everything about that place got on his nerves. Everything except Annie. He was still deep in thought when the call was finally answered.

"Matty speaking."

He got an instant picture of the short middle-aged blonde with the big smile.

"Matty, this is Charlie Dodge. I'm out of state on business and just wanted to check on Annie. Dr. Dunleavy has already informed me of her decrease in cognizance. Can you give me an update on how she is?"

"She's doing okay, Mr. Dodge. She's eating when we feed her. Not a lot, but enough. And she'll walk around for exercise if someone walks with her and holds her hand."

Charlie was trying to imagine this and couldn't. His Annie laughed and ran.

"The puzzles. Does she still try to put a puzzle together?" he asked.

"Not lately," Matty said. "I'm sorry I don't have better news."

"She's not in any pain, is she?"

"Oh, no! Not at all. She's not fretting in any way."

"Okay, thank you," Charlie said and disconnected. He put the phone back in his pocket, then got up and went downstairs to the library and stood at the windows until he caught a glimpse of Wyrick walking along one of the garden paths. When no one was looking, her whole body appeared to be at rest. She paused near a topiary that had been clipped into the shape of a dragon. He watched as she put both hands onto the topiary, as if she was greeting someone. After a few seconds, she moved up a path bordered by purple heather.

Satisfied she was where she said she'd be and that she was safe, he went upstairs, picked up his laptop and went back to his suite to go through his email. Work was another way of filing away the heartache of Annie's unstoppable descent. All he knew was that he felt off-kilter. This case needed to be over. It was already so convoluted, but it had to come to an end. He needed to go home and put his world back in order.

Wyrick walked until the truth of her existence was neatly put away again, then came back inside and went upstairs.

The door was still open between their suites, but Charlie was absent. Good, she thought and started pulling up everything she could find on Vivian Morrow Deutsch.

CHAPTER NINETEEN

It was nearing dinnertime when Wyrick logged off and went to change. She switched from the jeans and the big shirt to a black long-sleeved jumpsuit. The neckline mimicked a priest's collar, including the little white tab below her chin. The back of the jumpsuit was bare to her waist.

Her heels were red spiked Louboutins. They matched the bloodred color on her mouth, making her lips rather than her lack of hair the focus.

She was leaving her bedroom when someone knocked on her outer door.

"It's open," she said.

Charlie walked in and stopped. *Damn!*

She looked up long enough to indulge in one of her many fantasies about him, then frowned because he was still staring.

"What?"

Charlie blinked. "Trying to decide if I should confess my sins now or later."

"I'm ignoring you. Are you going down to dinner?"

He nodded, then as she sauntered toward him, he caught a glimpse of red shoes. A priest collar, and hell-bent red on her feet. And then she passed him on the way out, giving him more than a good view of her bare back, and another piece of that dragon tattoo—this time a foot climbing up her body.

The dichotomy of piety and temptation was too much to ignore. He said nothing, but when he slammed the door behind him, Wyrick had one moment of satisfaction that, once again, she'd rattled his cage.

They went downstairs in silence and entered the dining room the same way, but once they crossed that threshold, Wyrick dialed herself down and she and Charlie cordially greeted the family.

"Good evening!" Carter echoed.

Dina was wearing a summer gown, a pale butter yellow, blinged out with an embarrassing amount of Swarovski crystals and something else—an engagement ring, finally—on her hand.

Wyrick immediately spotted it and smiled. "It appears congratulations are in order tonight. Best wishes to both of you," she said.

"What did I miss?" Charlie asked.

Edward piped up from the far end of the table. "What's going on?"

Carter heard Edward's question as he entered the room.

"Dina and Kenneth are officially engaged," he said. "Kenneth asked for my blessing, which was unnecessary but very thoughtful, and of course I gave it on behalf of the family."

"Wonderful!" Edward said, and clapped. "We should drink a toast to this. Congratulations, Dina and Kenneth. I am very happy for both of you."

Dina gave Wyrick a teary smile for noticing while Kenneth beamed.

"I also asked Jason for his blessing, and he gave it," Kenneth said. "We both want the same thing for Dina, which is to see her happy."

Carter sat down just as Ruth stepped into the room.

"Ruth, we'll be needing a bottle of one of our best champagnes for a toast."

"Yes, sir," she said and left to fulfill the request.

A few minutes later, she came back with a bottle of Dom Pérignon on ice. Carter eyed the label and nodded.

"A 2004 vintage! Excellent choice, Ruth."

"Thank you," she said, then skillfully opened the bottle as Arnetta came hurrying in with a tray of champagne flutes and placed one at each seating.

Ruth looked concerned. "If I'd known there was something special to celebrate, I would have had your sommelier come in."

"No need," Carter said. "This is a family event. We'll save him for our large gatherings."

Ruth filled the glasses and slipped out of the room as Carter stood and raised his glass.

"To Dina and Kenneth, and the ties that bind. We wish you both a long and loving union."

"Hear, hear!" Edward said.

Dina was beaming.

Wyrick had one brief pang of longing for what she'd never had, and then it was gone as she lifted the champagne flute to her lips and took a slow sip, savoring the taste and the sparkle as she swallowed.

Charlie smiled in all the right places, and laughed at someone's joke, and tried not to think of how this family would fare when the truth about the attacks was made known.

Once the celebration was finished, the meal began.

They went through the first course and then the second, and were waiting on the entrée to be served when the conversation rolled around to young love.

Carter was the first to mention his, and it was obvious the family knew the story well, because every time he tried to talk about the incident, Dina interrupted and corrected his version of the tale. Finally, Carter held up his hand.

"Dina! This was my girlfriend, not yours."

"But I knew her," Dina muttered.

"So did I, but you weren't in the backseat with her, and I was!" Carter said, which made everyone laugh, even Dina. "Since Dina and Kenneth just got officially engaged, I don't think we need revelations about past loves from them." He looked straight at Charlie. "What about you, cowboy?"

The reference to Texas made everyone smile, including Charlie.

"My life is an open book. My wife was my first love, and she still is," he said.

When Carter glanced at Wyrick, she stared back without comment. Carter quickly moved to Edward.

"Eddie, fess up! You're five years older than me, so there's bound to be someone from your past that we know nothing about."

Edward smiled. "I did a little socializing when I was younger, but the only girl who stayed in my memory came along after I went blind." At that moment, the room went silent, with everyone listening as Edward's tale unwound. "It was New Year's Eve and my friends had talked me into going to a party with them. I was hesitant, but they swore the guests would be people I already knew, so I gave in. I was having an okay time drinking spiked punch and listening to the sounds of a party without being an actual part of it. And then a woman's voice was in my ear, asking me if I'd dance with her to ring in the New Year."

"Oh, Edward, that sounds so romantic," Dina said.

Edward managed a wry grin, but it was obvious he was moved by the memory.

"I told her I would be honored, but since I couldn't see, it was very likely that I'd stomp on everyone's toes. She said we'd go into the library across the hall so we couldn't bump into anything but the furniture. She said we'd still hear the music from in there, and she promised to watch out for her own feet. She made me laugh, and so I went."

He paused, silent for a moment, remembering. Then he sighed. "It was the first time I'd touched a girl since I went blind, and it was my last dance with one, as well. The night was… It was… She was… She was special, and that's my best memory."

Wyrick leaned forward. The move was barely noticeable, except to Charlie, because her hand was locked onto his forearm and he didn't think she even knew it.

"What was her name, Edward?" Wyrick asked.

"Vivie. She called herself Vivie. I didn't get a last name, and it didn't matter."

Charlie grieved at the revelation and what it was going to do to Edward. Wyrick wouldn't look at him, but he felt her squeeze his arm.

"That's a beautiful story," Wyrick said. "Thank you for sharing it."

"I never knew a bit of this, Eddie. You're a heck of a guy and my favorite brother, but don't tell Ted," Carter said.

Everyone laughed, and the mood became even more cheerful when the entrée was served.

The meal finally came to an end, and when everyone began moving to the library for nightcaps, the back of Wyrick's jumpsuit, or the lack thereof, triggered a whole new drama of its own.

"Wyrick, at the risk of getting my feet cut out from under me again, may I say the bits and pieces of your badass tattoo are intriguing. We have a dragon topiary in the heather gardens," Carter said.

"We've met." Wyrick followed Charlie to the bar.

"What'll it be, pardner?" Charlie asked as he moved behind it.

"Sparkling water with a twist of lime," Wyrick told him.

A couple of minutes later, he handed it to her, then poured brandy for Carter. Edward passed on any more alcohol, and not long afterward, it was his decision to go to bed that ended the evening.

Charlie and Wyrick ascended the stairs in silence and said nothing until they reached her room. The moment the door shut behind them, they looked at each other in disbelief, and then Charlie started talking.

"Can you believe what just happened? A random conversation at dinner, and all of a sudden another piece of the puzzle falls in our laps."

Wyrick's face was emotionless, but her voice was not. "Neither Vivian nor Edward could have dreamed what the consequences of that night would be. Edward was blind, and so much older than Vivian, that I think Miranda automatically excluded him. And she took a wild guess that Ted would've been too young, which left Carter, but she was wrong," Wyrick said.

Charlie nodded. "We can't be sure why she wanted him dead, but it now seems likely that she's behind it all."

"If I can find a trail of payments going out to three different people, we've got her," Wyrick said.

"In the morning," Charlie said. "We'll search more in the morning."

"Agreed. I'm ready to turn off my thoughts," Wyrick said.

Charlie grimaced. "If only that was possible."

"Right, if only," Wyrick said.

She wasn't about to tell him she knew how to turn off all thought and just be. She'd already revealed more about herself than she'd meant to. It was not good for her peace of mind to be living next door to the boss. It made her careless.

"See you in the morning, and great job," Charlie said, then went into his room and pulled the adjoining door shut.

Wyrick locked herself in and spent the next few minutes getting ready for bed. Finally, she crawled between the sheets and logged out of her thoughts, just like she logged out of her computer.

Even without a motive to tie her to Carter and Jason Dunleavy's case, Detective Bruner was coming to believe Miranda Deutsch was their best lead, but he had to be damn careful about how he proved it without some snitch in the department alerting the media. Blaming someone like her for criminal activities without the backup to prove it got people fired and police departments sued.

What he needed was motive and a money trail from Miranda to Wilma, Rey and Buddy. He'd put one of their best guys on the research, and now all they could do was wait to see what turned up. There was no one left to interview.

It was late, and he was tired of dealing with murder and deceit for today. The sun was setting as he left the precinct, and as he headed west, a beautiful sunset led him home.

Wyrick was already at work, looking for a money trail, when Charlie showed up to walk her to breakfast. He realized, as he approached the table where she was working, that the cut on her head had healed and the bruises were so faint now that he'd forgotten they'd been there.

"I'm not going to get dressed and sit through a whole hour or more of conversation when we need to figure this out before someone else winds up dead," she said.

"If I had someone to tail, I wouldn't be going, either," Charlie said. "Okay if I ask Ruth to bring you up some coffee and a Danish?"

"Yes."

Charlie rolled his eyes. "You're welcome," he said before shutting the door without so much as a click.

Wyrick ignored him. She was already into Miranda Deutsch's business.

But when Charlie showed up alone, everyone assumed she was ill.

"Is Wyrick okay?" Carter asked. "If she's not feeling well, I can call our doctor to stop by."

"She's fine," Charlie said. "She's busy working and didn't want to leave what she's doing."

"We can send her some food," Dina said. "Sometimes I have breakfast in the suite, especially if I'm not feeling up to par."

Ruth overheard the remark as she came in with a basket of hot biscuits and set them on the sideboard.

"I'll see to getting a tray to her," Ruth said. "What does she want?"

"Coffee and a Danish...or any kind of sweet roll," Charlie said.

Ruth smiled. "I'll get it sent right up."

"Thank you," Charlie said and went to the sideboard to serve himself. Those hot biscuits were calling his name.

As the meal progressed, Charlie became quieter. He couldn't help thinking about what they knew and the Dunleavys didn't. It wasn't as if any of them had betrayed the others, but it was going to impact Edward and Jason the most. One had a daughter he never knew existed, and the other had fathered a child who'd been aborted without his knowledge.

Carter noticed his silence, and when Charlie glanced up and caught him staring, Carter reacted.

"What's wrong, Charlie Dodge?"

Charlie shifted into his poker face. "Nothing's wrong. I was just thinking through everything we've learned so far, and trying to make sense of it. As you know from Detective

Bruner's visit, it's more complicated than we first thought. I'm afraid my social manners are still in mothballs, which is where I put them when Annie had to leave our home."

"No apologies necessary. But ask if you ever need anything," Carter said.

"I will. If you'll all excuse me, it's time I got to work, too. If anything breaks, you'll be the first to know."

Wyrick was licking sugar off her finger and watching one of her search apps sort through data, knowing if there was any data anywhere that had to do with money and Miranda Deutsch, this app would find it for her. She'd written the program she was using, and while it was very effective, it also broke a good number of privacy laws.

She wiped her finger on her jeans and was reaching for her coffee when a digital voice from the computer program suddenly cried out, "Hallelujah!"

Wyrick grinned as a new screen opened on the monitor. It was a financial readout of a trust fund belonging to Miranda Deutsch, and up until four months ago, no withdrawals had ever been made. The first withdrawal was for half a million dollars. Within a week, another one for fifty thousand, and yet another for two hundred thousand, withdrawn the same day Jason Dunleavy was shot. And there was a matching deposit the next day.

Just then, Charlie walked in.

She jumped up, pointing at the screen.

Charlie knew from the gleam in her eyes that she'd found something.

Wyrick started rattling off her latest revelations. "First off, I found registration for a handgun in Miranda Deutsch's name, and it's the same make as the one used to kill Buddy Pierce and Rey Garza. And then this!"

Charlie leaned over to look at the screen.

"This resembles a bank statement, but it's not. What am I looking at?"

"A readout of cash withdrawals from a trust fund belonging to Miranda Deutsch. There's the half-million-dollar amount we were looking for. And here's another withdrawal for fifty thousand soon afterward, maybe for Buddy Pierce. And here's the third withdrawal on the day Jason was shot, but it went back in the next day. So why—"

Charlie grinned. "You did it! Hot damn, girl, you did it! Don't you see? The breakup between Jason and Miranda was unexpected and he'd never been a target of hers before, so she didn't have a chance to pay anyone ahead of time. This was going to be a payment on completion of the job. And when Garza didn't kill Jason, she killed him and put it back."

"That's it!" Wyrick said, then shook her head. "I know how to do all kinds of things, and I can make money hand over fist, but I still don't understand human emotions."

Charlie frowned. "Why not?"

"Oh, I meant because of how isolated I was from interaction with normal people."

"Oh. Yes, I can see that," he said. "For a minute I thought you were going to try and make me believe you were an alien life-form, and I was gonna call bullshit on the whole story."

Wyrick laughed. "I've had plenty of people think I was an alien, but I'm an Earth hatchling. Now, how do we do this? I can't tell your detective how I found this. But can we tell him it's there, and he'll go through the proper channels to get the same info?"

"Yes, absolutely," Charlie said.

"So what are you waiting for?" she asked. "What I want to know—and we'll only find out if Miranda talks—is why she wanted to kill off her birth father, or rather the man she *believes* is her birth father—and the baby of the man she supposedly loved."

"Bruner's going to need motive, so it's time to give up the DNA and abortion info, too. Are there any records of her paying for the abortion that we can access legally?" Charlie asked.

Wyrick grinned. "Actually, she paid for it with a credit card, and I'm guessing they have an accountant who just pays the bills without questioning the expenditures. I guess she thought if it wasn't filed through insurance, no one would know. Let me start printing hard copies of what we have."

"This is getting too complicated to do over a phone. Are you up for a trip downtown to the police department?" Charlie asked.

"Yes."

He hesitated. "This isn't going to get you into any trouble, is it? Because if it is, we'll find another way to—"

"I don't leave tracks."

Charlie grinned. "Then get some shoes on while I call Bruner."

Detective Bruner was on his way to Chief Forsythe's office. He'd been summoned, which made him nervous. The chief was going to want to know where they were in the investigations, and learning about the addition of three murders connected to the attacks on Carter and Jason weren't going to make him happy.

He was pulling up into the parking lot when his cell phone rang. He started to let it go to voicemail, then saw it was from Charlie Dodge.

"Lord, please let this be a good call," Bruner muttered, then answered. "Detective Bruner."

"This is Charlie. We've got news. It's convoluted as hell, but we have all the proof you need to arrest Miranda Deutsch. Your problem is going to be finding it again through proper channels to keep it legal."

Bruner groaned. "Sweet Mother of God, you did not just say that. This is my worst nightmare coming true."

"Is there somewhere private we can talk to lay out what we know for sure? After that, it'll be up to you as to how you go about verifying the same information."

"Yes, I can do that," he said. "I'm about to go in to see Chief Forsythe. Let me get that over with. I doubt it'll take long. It's just our weekly ass chewing for not having all the answers. By the time you guys make it to the precinct, I'll be back in the office."

"I'm bringing Wyrick."

"Works for me."

"Then we'll see you later," Charlie said and disconnected.

Wyrick had made a quick change into pants and a blue-and-white-striped tank top and white knee-high boots.

Charlie was on the phone with Carter when she returned.

"Wyrick and I have an appointment with Detective Bruner. We're leaving now, but we'll fill you in after we get back."

"New info?" Carter asked.

"Yes."

"By the way," Carter said. "Dina and Kenneth left a short while ago. Jason is being released from the hospital. It'll be good to have all the family together again."

"Glad to hear it," Charlie said. "Then we can fill everyone in at the same time. Do you still have security on the grounds?"

"Yes, they're here."

"Stay close to the house," Charlie said and ended the call.

CHAPTER TWENTY

As soon as Bruner got back to his office, he went to see if they had an open conference room. If what Dodge and his assistant were going to give him was this controversial, he needed to hear it in total privacy first. As soon as he had one reserved, he went down to the lobby to wait for them.

He wasn't there long before they arrived. Even from this distance, there was no mistaking Charlie Dodge. He moved like a man on a mission, and the woman beside him was just as compelling.

Bruner went to meet them, greeting each of them with a handshake.

"I have a conference room reserved." They rode the elevator in silence, and then walked to the room the same way. Once they were inside, Bruner relaxed, but Wyrick obviously did not.

She walked the room from corner to corner, looking for cameras.

"Is it possible for people to listen in?" she asked.

"No," Bruner said. "And believe me, I don't want this information out, either, until we have a lock on everything we need to get an arrest warrant."

Charlie sat down. "I'm going to let Wyrick explain most of what we've learned, because she broke the case. Neither of us saw this coming, so trust me when I say we know how you feel."

"Have a seat," Wyrick said.

"It's that bad?" Bruner asked.

Charlie shrugged. "It's that crazy."

Bruner sat as Wyrick began pulling pages from a manila envelope.

"This is what we know for sure," she said and started ticking off the various points, laying papers in front of him to corroborate each one she made.

"Miranda owns a handgun that's the same make as the one that killed Buddy Pierce and Rey Garza. While she was using these guys, she paid them out of a trust fund. There are withdrawals that coincide with paying off three different people. Charlie will explain the last withdrawal."

Charlie picked up the story. "There was a third withdrawal on the day Jason Dunleavy was shot, which was redeposited the next day because Jason survived, which is why she shot Garza. He failed her, like all the others had."

"Why did she go after Carter?" Bruner asked.

Wyrick pulled out another page and laid it in front of him.

"The answer begins here. I found an odd expenditure for a DNA kit. Curiosity got the better of me and I followed up on it. To make a long story short, Johannes Deutsch is not her birth father. On the ancestor site, she found a distant relative in Ireland who had already linked herself to a man in America named Dillon Dunleavy, who turned out to be the father of Edward, Dina, Carter and Ted.

"At that point Miranda bought two more DNA kits, collected a sample from Jason and one from herself, which she sent to a private laboratory. It verified Jason was her first cousin. After that discovery she had an abortion, but she still didn't know which of the three Dunleavy brothers was her birth father."

Bruner held up a hand. "Stop! Wait! What am I missing here? She's related to a family she's trying to kill, and she aborted a baby she was having with the man she wanted to marry? I don't get it."

"There's more," Charlie said. "We think she made an assumption as to which brother would be her natural father because of her mother's age at the time. Edward was thirty. Carter was twenty-five, and Ted was sixteen. Her mother was twenty, so she picked Carter as the logical one, but she was wrong. We found out through an innocent conversation at dinner the other night that it was Edward. He was already blind, and it was a one-night stand at a New Year's Eve party. He only knew her name as Vivie, and shortly thereafter, Vivie aka Vivian Morrow, married Johannes Deutsch. Eight and a half months later, Miranda was born. And just so you know, we haven't said a word to any of the Dunleavy family about what we learned. We waited until we could turn it all over to the police. It's going to be hard for them to hear."

Bruner wiped his hands across his face. "Hard for *them* to hear? I'm having a struggle of my own. My personal opinion? Miranda Deutsch is a psychopath."

Wyrick pointed to the file. "You have a hard copy of everything to back up what I said, and as dumb as it sounds, she paid for her abortion with a credit card. I'm also willing to bet that she wrote Wilma's suicide note in her own handwriting. Whatever else she is, she's a stupid criminal."

Charlie leaned across the table. "It's in your court now, and I expect total anonymity for Wyrick."

Wyrick frowned at Charlie. "I already told you I don't leave tracks."

Bruner stood. "Thank you, ma'am. You're a wonder. And thank you, Charlie Dodge, for picking up the slack when we dropped the ball on Carter's disappearance. I'll get my guys on the paperwork, and I'll let you know when we arrest her."

"Make it snappy," Charlie said. "I'm here until Carter is safe. That was our deal, but we're both ready to go back to Dallas."

Bruner nodded. "Understood. Now, let me gather all this up and I'll walk you out."

A few minutes later, Charlie and Wyrick were in the car, waiting for it to cool off.

"So do we go to lunch on our own or go back to the house?" Charlie asked.

"Lunch on our own," Wyrick said. "The food at the estate is impeccable in looks and taste, but I want a burger and fries."

Charlie grinned. "You read my mind." Then he paused, frowning. "You can't really do that, can you? Read minds, I mean."

"I'm going to pretend you did not ask me such an asinine question. Just drive."

Charlie pulled out of the parking lot and back into street traffic.

Wyrick sat in silence beside him, but it was a comfortable silence, and when he spotted a Red Robin Restaurant, turned in and parked, she smiled.

"Best burgers ever!" she said. "In my opinion, anyway."

"Agreed."

They got out, but as they were walking inside, Wyrick began to tense. Public places were not her friend, but she wanted the food badly enough to deal with the stares.

Charlie was immediately aware of the diners' reactions to seeing her. Some laughed. Some just stared. He saw the tension on her face and felt so indignant on her behalf, it was all he could do not to react. But he was determined that this meal would not be more of the same for her, so when they were seated, he leaned across the table and lowered his voice.

"Yes, people were watching every step we took, and I can't help it. No matter where I go, people stare. I can't decide if it's because of how good-looking I am or the way I dress, but when a guy has it going on, it's hard to ignore."

Damn. He's being thoughtful again. "You are so full of shit, and I'm fine. I'm ten years into this life."

"You doubt me? I never saw that coming." Then he reached for the menus and handed one to her.

As Wyrick took the menu, she saw him glare at a man sitting at the nearest table and wanted to cry. She didn't know how to feel about someone who had her back, but he deserved an acknowledgment.

"I'm going to deny I ever said this, but you are a good man, Charlie Dodge."

"I'm better than good. I am stupendous," he muttered.

She grinned.

Moments later, a waiter showed up to take their drink orders. When he brought them over, he asked if they were ready to order.

"I am," Wyrick said. "I want the Chophouse Burger with fries, and some mayo on the side."

"I'll have the Burnin' Love Burger with onion rings," Charlie said.

The waiter left. Wyrick had a slight smirk on her face.

There was a moment of silence between them.

"When do you tell the Dunleavys?" she asked.

"When we get back, I guess. Carter is going to want to know what we were doing at the PD, and Jason is going to be there, too," Charlie said. "We accomplished what we came here to do. They'll have some tough adjustments to make, but on the plus side, they're all still alive."

"No one could've seen this coming."

Charlie nodded, and they went silent again. A few minutes later their food arrived. He reached for an onion ring and took a big bite, while Wyrick took her burger apart, spread mayo on both sides of the bread, then put it back together again. After that, they ate in mutual silence and passed on dessert.

Wyrick went to wash up while Charlie was paying, and when she returned, they drove back to the estate. Their meal was the most normal thing they'd ever done together and neither quite knew how to handle the quiet aftermath during the ride.

Jason was so glad to be out of the hospital that he couldn't stop talking. The ride home had been a little harder than expected, but he breathed easier as they wheeled him in the front door.

Because the residence was so large, Jason's doctor had insisted he go home in a wheelchair. Walking was good for healing, but not in hallways so long that walking up and down them amounted to miles every day. And since they had the elevator, there'd be no problem getting him up and down the stairs to his room.

Charlie and Wyrick's absence was duly noted at lunch, and when they learned Charlie was meeting with Detective Bruner because he had information to share, they were even more excited. They were still at the table having coffee together when Charlie and Wyrick returned.

"Hey, Jason! Good to see you!" Charlie said.

Jason smiled. "It's good to be home. I hear you have news. We can't wait to hear it."

Charlie glanced at Wyrick. Her face was expressionless again, but there was a faint tic at the corner of her left eye. He knew she was anxious, and so was he. Jason's health was a concern.

"Jason, are you up to this now? If you need to rest for a while, I'll hold off, because when I tell this, you all need to be together."

"I'm not exerting myself at all," Jason said. "As soon as you've finished, I'll go up to my room and rest."

"Then how about we go to the library? It's a little quieter there, and we won't be disturbed," Charlie suggested.

The Dunleavys filed out of the dining room, chattering among themselves and talking about Jason getting well so he could walk his mother down the aisle.

Wyrick dreaded the revelations, especially for Edward, whom she'd come to adore. "I hate what's about to happen," she whispered.

"It's okay. I've got this," he said.

She tensed as they entered the library, and Charlie could relate to what she was feeling. They were about to drop a bomb on this family that would change them forever.

Carter seated Edward on the sofa and then sat down beside him.

Kenneth pushed Jason's wheelchair between the two wing-back chairs in which he and Dina had chosen to sit, and now they were all looking at Charlie, who was standing in front of them.

The time of questioning was over. Charlie felt like a judge delivering a bad verdict to people he knew were innocent.

"I'm going to ask you to hear me out without a lot of questions right now. Wyrick will back me up with details if I forget any. And I need to tell you one last thing before I start. You're not to take on any guilt whatsoever after you've heard me out, because not one of you carries any blame."

"You're scaring me," Dina said.

"Yes, ma'am, and I'm sorry. I hardly know where to start, but I guess the best place is to let you know the police have everything we collected and are working toward getting it documented in their own way so it won't be thrown out in court. Right now, what I'm going to tell you is not to be discussed anywhere, with anyone, because there's been no arrest.

But the person behind the attacks on both Carter and Jason is Miranda Deutsch."

"What the hell?" Jason shouted as everyone began talking at once.

"You're sure?" Carter asked.

"As a heart attack," Charlie said. "We're just not sure why she did it, but here's what we do know. Some months back, Miranda bought a DNA kit from one of those ancestor sites. I already had Wyrick running background on her once I found out she was Jason's girlfriend, but when he was shot, the timing of that, directly after their breakup, was too odd to ignore. So I had Wyrick dig deeper. She initially thought the kit was an odd expenditure for Miranda and followed up, but this is where it's going to get hairy. Miranda found out Johannes is not her birth father. She followed the DNA trail on the ancestor site and linked up to an older woman in Ireland who was distant kin. Then she discovered who the old woman was linked to and found herself a much closer relative named Dillon Dunleavy."

"Oh, my God! That's Dad!" Carter cried.

Charlie nodded. "At that point, she bought two more DNA kits, which she sent to a private facility for results. One was for her and one kit was Jason's."

Dina gasped. "Why would—"

"The tests revealed that she and Jason are first cousins," Charlie said.

Jason moaned, "I'm gonna be sick," and covered his face.

Charlie went on a moment later. "And once she discovered that—I'm so sorry to say this, Jason—she aborted the baby she was carrying."

Jason's voice broke. "She killed a baby we made? Before we broke up?"

"Months before," Charlie said. "And the reason you were targeted, Carter, was just a stab in the dark. She didn't know which one of Dillon's sons was her father, but since you were closest to her mother in age, you got tagged."

Carter frowned. "I don't even know who her mother was."

Jason was shaking, but he pulled himself together enough to answer. "Her name was Vivian Morrow."

Carter shrugged. "I still don't know who—"

Charlie shook his head. "It's not you, Carter. It's Edward. He told us himself at dinner last night. About Vivie—Vivian. That's when Wyrick and I knew Edward was the father."

Edward was ashen and still, so still.

Carter reached for his brother's hand. "It's not your fault, Eddie. None of this madness is our fault."

Tears were rolling down Edward's face, but he couldn't speak.

"I'm so sorry," Charlie said. "This has been the worst case we've ever worked, and it's our first brush with a psychopath. There's no explaining how they think, no point in trying to rationalize their actions. But once we knew all that, Wyrick began looking for a way to connect her to the people she'd taken out, the ones who'd failed to deliver. We found Jason's shooter when his body was recovered. His name was Rey Garza. His car, and the gun inside it, matched up with witness testimony and the evidence they already had.

"When Garza's body showed up for autopsy, the coroner caught something else. He linked Garza's body with another murder victim named Buddy Pierce. Their wounds were identical, and the bullets he removed from each body were from the same gun.

"Buddy Pierce and Wilma Short had been married when they were young. Buddy was the one who kept trying to wreck Carter on the freeway, and Miranda went to high school with Garza. Miranda was paying for the hits with money taken from her trust fund. Bottom line, Carter, once she's arrested, the danger to your life is over.

Carter was too emotional to speak. All he could manage was a quiet "Thank you."

"Again, I caution all of you. *Tell no one.* You wouldn't want her to get out of the country before she's arrested," Charlie said.

Carter wrapped his arms around Eddie and hugged him.

Jason was obviously gutted and too weak to process this new reality.

"I'd suggest Jason be taken to his room now, and if they sent him home with pain meds, use them," Wyrick said.

Dina and Kenneth quickly wheeled him away, commiserating as they went.

"I'm going to take Eddie up and stay with him until he falls asleep," Carter said.

"I'm sorry," Charlie murmured.

Carter shook his head. "No! Never be sorry for finding the truth. None of this was easy to hear, but thanks to the both of you, we'll all live to see another day. If none of this had come to light, and she kept picking us off one by one, according to how our family estate is set up, she could have come forward as the only surviving member and inherited it all—if she'd escaped being a suspect."

"That's it! That's what we couldn't figure out!" Wyrick said. "But she's already rich. Why would any of this matter?"

"She's almost thirty years old and has never been married or even engaged. She grew up as a butcher's daughter—granted, a butcher who became a wealthy entrepreneur—but it's a whole other thing to be the heiress to the Dunleavy fortune and live in a castle," Charlie said.

"There's one other victim in this mess," Carter said in a quiet voice. "This is going to destroy Johannes."

Two days later, the Denver PD arrived at the Deutsch residence with a search warrant for everything on the property, and an arrest warrant for Miranda Deutsch. A half-dozen police cars with lights flashing immediately blocked off the drive and both ends of the street. Someone had tipped off the media, because they were right behind them all the way. They were stopped a block back, where police were already setting up barricades. Once they could go no closer, they piled out of the vans with cameras aimed at the residence, while journalists began getting ready to broadcast live.

Detective Bruner finished the text he was sending, and then dropped his phone in his pocket and picked up his warrants as he got out of the car. He and a half-dozen officers moved toward the door, while two search teams stood at the ready. He glanced back once to make sure everyone was in place, then turned around and rang the bell.

A moment later, a woman answered the door, then gasped at the sight of all the police.

Detective Bruner and his men pushed their way into the foyer.

"Ma'am, we have a search warrant for the property, and an arrest warrant for Miranda Deutsch. Where is she?"

The woman stared at him. "I'm sorry, but there must be some mis—"

Detective Bruner raised his voice. "Ma'am, where is Miranda Deutsch?"

The woman pointed behind her. "She and her father are in the breakfast room."

"Lead the way," Bruner said.

She led them directly into the room.

"I'm sorry, sir. I'm so sorry. They made me," she said, then threw her apron over her face and ran away.

Johannes stood abruptly. "What is the meaning of this? How dare you storm into my house without—"

"I'm Detective Bruner from the homicide division. We have a search warrant for this property, and an arrest warrant for Miranda Deutsch," he announced and put them both in Johannes's hand.

Miranda leaped up from her chair with the obvious intent to run, but was quickly subdued and cuffed.

"Stop, stop. You've made a mistake!" she said, then started weeping. "Father, do something!"

But Johannes was still standing there, staring at the warrants in his hand, so she turned the tears on for the detective. "Please, sir! Let me go, please let me go. I didn't do anything wrong. You have to believe me."

When Bruner didn't even bother to answer her, she screamed, "Father, for the love of God, *do* something!"

Johannes was in shock. "Miranda, I don't understand. It says you killed three people. What is happening? Why are they saying these things?"

"She's being arrested for the murders of Wilma Short, Buddy Pierce and Rey Garza," Bruner said and began to read Miranda her rights.

"Who are they?" Johannes asked. "We don't even know these people. Why would you say she did this?"

"Miranda knows them. She hired them to kill Carter Dunleavy and then Jason Dunleavy. When they failed, she killed them to keep them silent."

Miranda's heart skipped. *They knew all that? But how?* Panic was setting in. This couldn't be happening. "I didn't do it!" Miranda screamed. "You've got the wrong person."

"Then why did you try to run?" Bruner asked.

Miranda let out a scream of such rage it took all of them aback.

"Is this the father who raised me? Where is your anger? Where is the love you profess you have for me? Is talk all you've got, Sausage King? Now, in my time of greatest need, you let me down? To hell with you! It doesn't matter! You're not even my father. My father is Carter Dunleavy."

"No, Carter isn't your father. Edward is. You guessed wrong."

Tears dried up within seconds. "The blind one? It was the blind one? Why the hell would she fuck a blind man?"

Johannes gasped, suddenly seeing the monster she was behind the mask she'd presented to the world.

"Take her out," Bruner said.

Miranda walked with her head down, her shoulders slumped, completely ignoring the fact that her father was behind her, still in shock, still begging for answers.

Charlie was getting out of the shower when his cell signaled a text. He grabbed a towel, wrapped it around himself like a sarong and dashed to answer. It was Bruner.

We're serving the arrest warrant. Media got wind so it's probably going to be on TV. Chief Forsythe asked me to personally thank both of you for closing this case.

Charlie ran toward their adjoining door and knocked.

"Turn on the TV. The arrest is going down!" he yelled and then called Carter as he ran back to turn on his TV.

"Good morning, Charlie, what's up?" Carter asked.

"Just got a text from Bruner. They're serving the arrest warrant now. He said to turn on the TV."

Charlie was scanning for local news stations as Carter hung up. He was adjusting the sound when Wyrick opened the door.

"What were you—" she began, then took a deep breath. "Look!" Charlie said. "They're making the arrest as we speak. Ah, damn it. Her father just collapsed!"

Wyrick stepped up beside him. "Look at her. She saw him fall and just kept walking. That's one cold bitch, and I'm going to pack." She hurried out of the room.

It took a couple of seconds for that to register, and then Charlie realized she was leaving.

"Pack. Right. This is over. We get to go home."

At the same time, he noticed that the towel was all he had on. He was as close to naked as the law would allow, and she'd been standing right beside him.

"Well, hell," he muttered. "The flight back to Dallas should be interesting."

The entire Dunleavy family was waiting for them when they exited the elevator with their gear.

Jason was in his wheelchair, and as Charlie and Wyrick stopped for their goodbyes, he reached out to shake Charlie's hand.

"Charlie Dodge, it took an act of God and the mention of my uncle's name to make you call me back, but I am forever grateful that you did. You found Uncle Carter when no one else could, and you and Wyrick saved us all. Now I'm going to owe Ted a favor, and he's a total ass about collecting."

Charlie laughed. "You also owe Wyrick some thanks. I'd never heard of your family or the business. She's the one who read me the riot act for being so uninformed. And she's the one who told me to call you back. If it hadn't been for her, it would never have happened."

"However you got here, we're grateful to you," Carter said. "And we couldn't let you leave without a proper Irish send-off. Ruth packed a lunch, including chocolate goodies for you, Wyrick, and a bottle of our finest Irish whiskey for Charlie." Then he took an envelope from his pocket. "And this, Charlie Dodge, is a printout of the money transfer from my bank to yours for a well-earned fee. What I want both of you to know is that you've become friends, and friends are always welcome in this house." He hugged Charlie, then in a grand gesture, kissed the back of Wyrick's hand. "I'd hug you, too, but I'm afraid you'd take the hide off me for doing it."

Wyrick hid her delight with sarcasm. "Is this where I'm supposed to say 'I'll never wash my hand again'?"

Everyone laughed, including Charlie, but it was the laughter that prompted Edward to lift his own hand as if asking for permission to speak.

"Laughter. Such a beautiful sound, and I was feeling we'd never hear it in this house again. Thank you, dear Wyrick, for your wit. It is a thing highly revered by the Irish. I also thank you for your kindness, and I will miss our little talks."

Wyrick was suddenly fighting back tears, and in a move she never saw coming, she pushed past all of them and wrapped her arms around Edward's neck.

"I didn't want your last hug from a woman you didn't know to have been a sad one." Then she lifted his hands to her head, and then to her face, and let him "see her" in the only way he could.

A sudden hush moved through them as Edward "looked," beginning with the shape of her head, cupping the smooth, silky dome and then the shape of her face. Moving the sensitive tips of his fingers along the curve of her brow to the length of her nose. Then her mouth to the jut of her chin, until finally, he sighed.

"Ahh, Wyrick, you are a beauty."

Charlie couldn't look away. The thought flashed through his mind that he'd never been that close to her in all the years he'd known her. And if he knew what was good for him, he never would.

The family led them down the hall and then through a smaller hallway into the kitchen.

"Friends come and go through the kitchen, which is the heart of the home," Dina said. "On behalf of all of us, thank you for caring, and for sharing our life and our world without judgment. Kenneth will carry the food basket to the car for you."

Peter, the chef, and Ruth, Arnetta and Louise were standing beside the table where Charlie had sat with them, sharing coffee and tarts when he'd first arrived.

"Safe journey," Ruth said.

"Safe journey!" the maids echoed.

"Godspeed," Peter said.

Charlie stopped, scanning the faces of family and staff with purposeful recognition.

"You have something special going on here. You are far richer in family than any amount of money you can claim. My daddy always said a thing is stronger when it's held together by many smaller parts, rather than just one of a matching size. That it's because when one falters, the others are always there to shore it up. That's how I see all of you."

Wyrick groaned. "Somebody open the door. I don't like tears or goodbyes."

Laughter followed their exit as they took the bricked path to the garage and loaded up. A few minutes later, they were on their way back to the chopper.

"Are we still on truce time?" Charlie asked as they left the castle behind.

"I don't see the need," Wyrick said.

Charlie paused, accepting the disappointment and then letting it fall away.

"If you can't see a need, I guess it's over," he muttered and thought about seeing Annie.

Wyrick heard what sounded like regret, but ignored it. They still had a flight back to Dallas together. She opted for the old rule of thumb that "silence is golden," and Charlie didn't seem inclined to interrupt it. On the way to the airport, they learned Johannes Deutsch had suffered a heart attack, and that Miranda was behind bars on suicide watch.

"The higher you are, the farther you fall," Charlie said.

Wyrick was noncommittal as they loaded the chopper. She went through the usual flight checks, then powered up and headed south, back to Texas.

Only twice did Charlie even acknowledge her presence. Once to offer her a bottle of water, and once to give her half of the Hershey's bar he'd found in the basket Ruth had packed.

When they landed at the hangar outside Dallas, Benny was there, waiting to help her. They transferred the luggage to their respective vehicles, and then Charlie followed her to her car and handed her the food basket.

"Take it. I've got all I want," he said, holding up the bottle of Irish whiskey. Then he left her standing there.

He was tired to the bone and tired of dealing with her and an anger he hadn't caused.

He drove out of the hangar without looking back, and when he got home, he ignored the "office" still present on his dining room table.

There was only one thing on his mind, and that was having dinner with Annie. Morning Light had private rooms for family visits, and he called them to set it up.

To pass the time, he began searching online for new office spaces and bookmarked five before he quit to get ready for his date.

After a quick shower and shave, he chose dark blue slacks, with a blue-and-gray sports coat and a white dress shirt sans tie. He stopped on the way to get flowers, then drove to the center with one hand, steadying the vase with the other.

His gut was already in a knot as he walked in with them, mentally preparing himself for the crying woman, the man looking for his lost son, Marty, and his first sight of Annie. It was always a jolt to see the absence in her eyes, but he told himself that there was a part of her somewhere that might still register his existence.

Pinky, the receptionist, was getting ready to leave. The doors would soon be locked to visitors, but she'd been notified that he'd be dining in and was waiting for his arrival.

"Good evening, Mr. Dodge. I'll let them know you're here."

"Thank you," Charlie said as he signed in.

He waited at the door for an escort, who arrived almost immediately. He didn't know her name, but he recognized her face.

"Oh, the flowers are lovely, Charlie. We have your dining room all set up, and they've gone to get Annie," she said as she led him into their private room. "Do you want someone to be here with you?"

"No. Why?" Charlie asked.

"She doesn't feed herself anymore."

"I'll feed her," Charlie said.

"As you wish. There's a call button on the wall. If you need help, or whenever you've finished, just press it. Someone will come."

"Okay, thanks," Charlie said and had a moment of actual fear when she walked out, thinking of being alone with Annie, which was stupid as hell, but that was how he felt.

A crisp white tablecloth covered a small dining table, with flatware, napkins and drinking glasses already in place. As he placed the flowers on the table, he noticed how close the chairs and place settings were, like an intimate dinner for lovers.

A few minutes later, he heard footsteps, and then an orderly arrived, pushing Annie in a wheelchair. They'd dressed her in beige slacks and a ruffled yellow blouse, even done her hair and painted her nails. She was beautiful—and she looked right through him.

"Good evening, Mr. Dodge. Let me get Annie settled in the dining chair before I leave."

"Can I help?" Charlie asked, wanting to put his arms around her just to feel the shape of her body again.

"I've got it," the orderly said.

Charlie stood back, watching as the orderly grasped both her hands, gently coaxing her to stand, then settled her in the dining chair and pushed it up to the table.

"Oh, here comes your food," the orderly said and stepped out as a couple of servers brought in a small food trolley, transferred the plates to their settings, filled the glasses and set the desserts in place before leaving.

Finally, they were alone.

Charlie sat down beside her, then laid his hand on her arm.

"Hello, sweetheart, you're so beautiful tonight. It's me, Charlie. I came to eat dinner with you. Everything looks good. I hope you're hungry."

He knew she heard him talking, because she turned her head toward the sound of his voice, but she didn't react, not even when he tucked her napkin into the neckline of her blouse, then unfolded his own napkin and put it on her lap.

Looking at the meal, he realized they were now feeding her foods that were easy to chew and easy to swallow—meat loaf, mashed potatoes with gravy and a serving of peas. The little dishes of fruit cobbler were dessert. The drinks were cold. No danger of burns from hot coffee.

He picked up a fork, then put it back and chose a spoon. Checking to make sure none of it was too hot to eat, he scooped up a bite of potatoes and gravy. But when he lifted it to her lips and she didn't open her mouth, he realized she needed a prompt.

"Annie, open your mouth," he said, and she did. When he put the spoon in her mouth, she ate what was on it.

He took a bite of meat loaf while he was waiting for her to swallow, then spooned up a small bite of meat loaf for her, which she ate. Then the peas, which she also ate, and he forgot about his own food. Everything he'd imagined, hoped, planned on, was out the window. It was all about the sustenance he was getting into her body. He was finally doing something for Annie, and the whole time he was feeding her, he was talking.

"I miss you, baby. Nothing is the same without you," he said as he gave her a drink. "I am so damn sorry this happened to you that it makes me ache. I'm a private investigator. I solve crimes, and find the lost for anyone who hires me, and yet I can't find you, the person I love most. I've registered a complaint with God, but it didn't change a thing."

And then, right in the middle of feeding her dessert, she quit. She wouldn't open her mouth again, and she wouldn't take a drink. He leaned over and kissed her cheek.

"Okay, I get the message. I just want you to know how special this was for me. I love you, Annie...so much."

Then he pressed the call button and stood behind her chair with his hand on her shoulder, waiting. He felt something brush his skin and looked down. She'd tilted her head so that her cheek was against his hand.

He quickly knelt in front of her, searching her eyes for even a flash of recognition, but her expression was blank and her eyes were closed.

"Oh, Annie...sweetheart... I know you're still in there. I love you, too."

And then staff was in the room and the moment was gone.

One woman wheeled Annie away, while another began cleaning the table.

"Mr. Dodge, what about your flowers?"

"She can't have them in her room, can she?"

"No, I'm sorry. Spilled water causes falls. Broken glass is dangerous, too."

Charlie nodded. "I thought not. Do whatever you want with them," he said, "and thank you for making this happen."

"Of course. Are you ready to leave?"

He nodded.

"I'll walk you to the door," she said.

"I've never been here when it was this quiet," Charlie told her as they walked back up a hall.

"Sundowning is hard for most of them. A lot of them are on meds for the agitation," she said and swiped an ID card through the lock to let him back into the lobby. Then she walked him to the front door, swiped another lock and let him out.

"Have a safe trip home," she said.

Charlie thanked her and walked back to his car.

It was dusk and night was quickly encroaching. Security lights in the parking lot were coming on, and he could already hear traffic and sirens and cars honking, and loud music from a passing car—the sounds of the city.

It was time to go home, but tonight he was taking a small piece of joy with him. In one brief flash of cognizance, he'd seen Annie again.

His Annie.

The one who remembered him.

It was enough, and now it was time to rest.

Wyrick had an agenda of her own as she headed back into Dallas, still watching the rearview mirror for tails. When she finally pulled into the drive at Merlin's, she breathed a sigh of relief. Merlin was sitting on the front porch with a cold drink and a set of headphones on. He liked to listen to audiobooks. She slowed down and honked to let him know she was home. He waved as she drove around to the back.

It took two trips to get all her things inside, then she locked herself in.

As always, the first item on her agenda was to secure the apartment, making sure there were no cameras or listening devices. Then she unpacked her clothes, laid one pile aside for the cleaners and started a load of laundry.

She thought of Charlie as she began sorting through the food basket and felt a measure of guilt. She'd been hateful to him from the moment they'd left the Dunleavy residence, but it was the only way she knew how to keep distance between them.

It wasn't the first time she'd been a bitch, and it wouldn't be the last, and Charlie had Annie. He didn't really care how she behaved as long as she did her job.

Once everything was in order, she went into her office and opened the first of twenty-five files. Each had a multitude of folders, all with different programs she'd written, all pertaining to Universal Theorem. She'd known for years that there'd come a time when she'd have to draw the line. The incident with Mack Doolin had been the last straw. She'd just had to wait until she was home to act.

She checked the time. It was an hour later at Universal Theorem. They'd be coming back from lunch, or were in meetings, or in labs trying to re-create versions of her.

She knew who they were. She'd sat in on those meetings. She'd seen their faces. She understood what they were really about. What they hadn't known at the time was the depth of what *she* knew and what she could do. Keeping her abilities a secret was the only way she had of protecting herself. While she worked at UT, she'd purposely slowed down her own projects, and time and time again, let them fail, completing only the assignments that were harmless to humanity.

But when UT failed her, she took it as her chance to escape. Either she would die from the cancer or she would survive it, and then she would run. And run she did,

But she wasn't running anymore.

They'd tracked and attacked her for the last time.

She opened the first program and without hesitation,

clicked Send. Then the next, and then the next. And for the following three hours, opened files and clicked Send.

It was a warm, sunny day in Richmond, but then most days were beautiful this time of year in Virginia. Cyrus Parks had just returned to the office from a business lunch, and was about to put a new tail on Jade. The last two men he'd sent after Doolin's disappearance had quit, which made Cyrus wonder what she'd done. Jade, being Jade, there was no telling, but he figured she was harmless enough, and he would have his way.

Before he could act, his computer went dark, and then the lights in the office went out. He picked up the phone to call maintenance, only to discover the phone lines were also dead.

He felt all over his desk until he found his cell, and sighed with relief. He could use it as a flashlight. But when it didn't work, either, he suddenly realized this wasn't a power outage. It was an attack. They'd been in conflict with a company in China over some patents, and he immediately laid the blame at their feet.

Because of security issues, there were few windows in the building, so the darkness was complete as he stumbled out of his office. The building was in an uproar. He could hear people shouting, a few screams and a lot of cursing, as they began trying to find their way about.

His secretary was shouting, "Mr. Parks! Mr. Parks!"

"Here! I'm here!" he said. "Find a wall and move toward the elevators."

"They don't work, sir. I just got off one when the power went out."

"Does your cell phone work?" he asked.

"No. I'm scared. Is this the attack where the world goes dark? My preacher talks about this in church all the time."

"I don't know what it is, but we need to find a stairwell and start feeling our way down."

"Oh, my Lord! We're on the fourteenth floor," she wailed.

"Well, we can't stay up here waiting, because this is obviously an attack on Universal Theorem. I need to get home. I can work from there."

They started feeling their way along the wall and ran into others, all moving carefully to a stairwell. But the building was huge, and the employees numbered in the thousands in this building alone. The stairwells were packed, the masses moving slowly as they felt their way down.

It took over an hour just to get down the stairs. People were leaving the parking lots by the dozens. When Cyrus finally walked into the fresh air, he was drenched with sweat and his legs were trembling. He staggered to his car, half fearing it wouldn't start, but it did. However, the phone in his car was also inoperable, and he was beginning to worry about what he'd find when he got home.

A short while later, he drove into his driveway, but when he tried to open the garage door with the remote, it didn't work, either. "What the hell?" he groaned. "Who's behind this?"

He used his door key to get inside his house, only to realize his computers here were as dead as the ones at UT. He turned on a television and was so relieved it was working that he dropped into the nearest chair and turned up the volume just to experience technology at work.

Within minutes, breaking news bulletins began to interrupt the programming, and they were all regarding the home office of Universal Theorem, where he worked, talking about a mass shutdown of the facility that was, as yet, unexplained. And then another bulletin popped up about a UT site in the Netherlands, and then a site in Osaka, Japan. They'd all gone dark like it just had here. He sat in stunned silence, learning that their labs in Alaska and a technology center in San Francisco were down, then more… One after another, every aspect of their purpose and accompanying research had been shut down.

He couldn't begin to imagine the scope and organization it had taken to make all this happen. He was seriously scared. Were there other countries beside China? Was there a consortium that had bonded to take them down?

The first day ended without a solution. The next day was a nightmare of trying to contact all their locations. The night of the second day passed, and Cyrus was on the third day of personal hell learning how many millions of dollars in experiments and resources they were losing by the hour, when his cell phone signaled a text message. He was so excited it was working again that he didn't even bother to see who it was from. He immediately opened it.

The last three days were just a warning. Leave me the fuck alone, or I will destroy you and everything you own.

Before he could react, the message disappeared, but his phone was still working. He ran into his office. The computers were on. He knew the message was from Jade—but she *couldn't* have done anything of this scope. She'd never shown herself capable of anything like this. It was impossible! She didn't have the—

And then it hit him. What if she'd been hiding what she could do? She'd been angry when she discovered some details about her life that they'd kept hidden. When she developed breast cancer and went from stage two to stage four within six weeks, she should have died. But she didn't. And there were all those drug cocktails and the chemo the doctors had given her. They already suspected it was the DNA they'd manipulated within her that helped her heal.

But what the hell else had it changed?

★ ★ ★ ★ ★

PRINCE ALBERT PUBLIC LIBRARY
31234900038157
The missing piece